POISON AND POOCHES

Also by Sandra Balzo

The Maggy Thorsen Mysteries
UNCOMMON GROUNDS
GROUNDS FOR MURDER *
BEAN THERE, DONE THAT *
BREWED, CRUDE AND TATTOOED *
FROM THE GROUNDS UP *
A CUP OF JO *
TRIPLE SHOT *
MURDER ON THE ORIENT ESPRESSO *
TO THE LAST DROP *
THE IMPORTANCE OF BEING URNEST *
MURDER A LA MOCHA *
DEATH OF A BEAN COUNTER *
FLAT WHITE *
THE BIG STEEP *
FRENCH ROAST *
ANY POT IN A STORM *
BREW UNTO OTHERS *

The Main Street Mysteries
RUNNING ON EMPTY *
DEAD ENDS *
HIT AND RUN *

* *available from Severn House*

POISON AND POOCHES

Sandra Balzo

SEVERN HOUSE

First world edition published in Great Britain and the USA in 2025
by Severn House, an imprint of Canongate Books Ltd,
14 High Street, Edinburgh EH1 1TE.

severnhouse.com

Copyright © Sandra Balzo, 2025

Cover and jacket design by Panagiotis Lampridis

Epigraph taken from 'The Old and New Pacific Capitals' by Robert Louis Stevenson in *The Project Gutenberg Ebook of The Works of Robert Louis Stevenson – Swanston Edition*, by Robert Louis Stevenson (https://www.gutenberg.org/files/30527/30527-h/30527-h.htm), paragraph 145.

All rights reserved including the right of reproduction in whole or in part in any form. The right of Sandra Balzo to be identified as the author of this work has been asserted in accordance with the Copyright, Designs & Patents Act 1988.

British Library Cataloguing-in-Publication Data
A CIP catalogue record for this title is available from the British Library.

ISBN-13: 978-1-4483-1438-6 (cased)
ISBN-13: 978-1-4483-1867-4 (paper)
ISBN-13: 978-1-4483-1684-7 (e-book)

This is a work of fiction. Names, characters, places and incidents are either the product of the author's imagination or are used fictitiously. Except where actual historical events and characters are being described for the storyline of this novel, all situations in this publication are fictitious and any resemblance to actual persons, living or dead, business establishments, events or locales is purely coincidental.

No part of this book may be used or reproduced in any manner for the purpose of training artificial intelligence technologies or systems. This work is reserved from text and data mining (Article 4(3) Directive (EU) 2019/790).

All Severn House titles are printed on acid-free paper.

Typeset by Palimpsest Book Production Ltd., Falkirk, Stirlingshire, Scotland.
Printed and bound in Great Britain by TJ Books, Padstow, Cornwall.

The manufacturer's authorised representative in the EU for product safety is Authorised Rep Compliance Ltd, 71 Lower Baggot Street, Dublin D02 P593 Ireland (arccompliance.com)

Praise for Sandra Balzo

"A story chock full of family secrets and plot twists"
Booklist on *Brew Unto Others*

"A challenging puzzle with an ingenious twist that'll keep you awake more effectively than a shot of espresso"
Kirkus Reviews on *Brew Unto Others*

"An inventive mashup of cozy subgenres"
Kirkus Reviews on *Any Pot in a Storm*

"Balzo's latest will keep readers on their toes . . . Solid cozy fare"
Booklist on *French Roast*

"Vividly drawn characters and dialogue crackling with wit"
Publishers Weekly on *French Roast*

"The body count rises quickly as Balzo's quirky cozy turns darker than a freshly brewed espresso"
Kirkus Reviews on *French Roast*

About the author

Sandra Balzo built an impressive career as a public relations consultant before authoring the successful Maggy Thorsen coffeehouse mysteries, the first of which, *Uncommon Grounds*, was published to stellar reviews and nominated for an Anthony and Macavity Award. She is also the author of the Main Street Murders mystery series published by Severn House. *Poison and Pooches* is the first title in the Dog-Sitting Mysteries featuring Arial Kingston.

www.sandrabalzo.com

One day—I shall never forget it—I had taken a trail that was new to me. After a while the woods began to open, the sea to sound nearer hand. I came upon a road, and, to my surprise, a stile. A step or two farther, and, without leaving the woods, I found myself among trim houses. I walked through street after street, parallel and at right angles, paved with sward and dotted with trees, but still undeniable streets, and each with its name posted at the corner, as in a real town [today's Pacific Grove]. Facing down the main thoroughfare—"Central Avenue," as it was ticketed—I saw an open-air temple, with benches and sounding-board, as though for an orchestra. The houses were all tightly shuttered; there was no smoke, no sound but of the waves, no moving thing. I have never been in any place that seemed so dream-like. Pompeii is all in a bustle with visitors, and its antiquity and strangeness deceive the imagination; but this town had plainly not been built above a year or two, and perhaps had been deserted overnight. Indeed, it was not so much like a deserted town as like a scene upon the stage by daylight, and with no one on the boards.

Robert Louis Stevenson on Pacific Grove,
California, circa 1879

ONE

A dog was barking somewhere, but the low fog that was blowing off Monterey Bay onto the peninsula had swallowed and dispersed the sound, making it impossible to locate.

Arial Kingston shivered and pulled the sleeves of her sweatshirt over her hands. It wasn't the dog that was unsettling her. In fact, just the opposite. It was good to hear other life out here in the dark.

She had set out anticipating sunrise but hadn't counted on the marine layer being so thick. July and August might be the foggiest months on the Monterey Peninsula, but her first month there—March—had provided an excellent preview. The fog likely would clear by noon, but for now, the bay was pitch-black, as though thick tar had swallowed the light and absorbed the sounds of everything but the muffled howling and barking, the waves hitting the rocks, and . . .

About to cross the two-lane Ocean View Boulevard to the coastal trail, Arial hesitated, squinting across to the bay where she could swear she'd heard voices. Nothing at first, but then, as the fog shifted and swirled, there was a light—no, more like a pool of light—hovering in the fog above the inky waters.

"Eerie," Arial muttered to herself. "ET, phone home. Or maybe paddle."

Because it had to be a boat, right? That was the only thing that made sense.

Another sound, and if Arial strained, she thought she could just make out the creaking of the hull. And was that the clang of lines? But what was a boat doing out on the bay in the fog and the dark? Whatever, it could be nothing good, she'd wager, at . . . she held up her phone to read: 5:46 a.m.

Even as the light of the phone illuminated her face, Arial flicked it off and stepped back. Being a "go where life takes me" kind of person throughout her twenty-five years, Arial's path had led through a few unsavory situations, one of them nearly landing her in jail. But jail was preferable to being a target because she'd witnessed something she hadn't been meant to. Not that she was prone to flights of fancy or anything.

Stepping behind a dark-colored parked car, she told herself not to be an idiot. Pacific Grove was a nice place, with nice people, who . . . she caught the reflection of movement in the car window and whirled, nearly bowling over a figure in a hoodie.

"Whoa," he said, putting out a hand to protect himself. "I didn't mean to scare you."

Arial backed up one, two, three steps out of his reach. "I didn't see a thing, honest. I'm just out for a walk."

"OK." The man cocked his head to study her. "But you should be careful out here alone. Coyotes, you know."

"Coyotes." Human traffickers, not drug smugglers. Regardless, she was right to be spooked. She took another step back, putting the back passenger-side fender between them.

"Yes," he said, his eyes narrowing. "Bold as anything, these days, though not looking to make trouble."

"I'm not either." Now she had both hands up. "Honest."

"You should carry a whistle anyway," he said, shifting what looked like an insulated bag from one shoulder to the other, to pull a key chain out of his pocket. "Even the mountain lions will back off."

"Mountain lions?"

"It's all the deer," he said, nodding toward the end of the peninsula. "They make easy prey."

Coyotes, mountain lions, deer. "You're talking about animals. I mean animal animals. With paws. And hooves. And such . . ." She let it drift off.

The man pushed back his hood and peered at her. He was younger than she'd first imagined. Maybe early twenties. "Are you OK? I mean, do you need some place to stay?"

To stay? "No, of course not. I have a house. Why—"

"Sorry," he said again. "I didn't mean to assume, but sometimes homeless—"

"I'm not homeless," she snapped, the assumption stinging all the more because she nearly had been. Not to mention her self-consciousness about the ratty yoga pants and faded gray Wisconsin sweatshirt she was wearing. "I was looking out at whoever that is on the water and you startled me."

"Them? That's just squids."

Squids, as in sailors, of course. The Coast Guard Pier was just down the way, not to mention the Naval Postgraduate School in Monterey. Arial glanced back out onto the bay, but the light on the water had disappeared. "Is it just maneuvers or some secret stuff . . ."

As Arial realized the man was staring at her blankly, she let the rest of the question drift away. Not for the first time since her move to Monterey, she felt like an outsider and wondered if he was re-evaluating his impulse to talk to a stranger—one who'd obviously caught him off-guard.

Clearing his throat, he adjusted the bag on his shoulder. "Well, listen, if you're sure you're OK, I have more deliveries."

"Food deliveries?" Arial asked. "Isn't it awfully early?"

"Ah, yeah, it is early." He had lowered his voice and chin-gestured toward the ostentatious white brick house behind them. "They like their bagels waiting for them when they wake up." A light came on in the house and the dog started to bark. "We should move away so they don't see us."

"Sounds like you do this regularly," Arial said, following him a few steps up the sidewalk. "And why don't you want them to see you? Do they think the bagels just magically appear?"

He snuck her a sideways grin, seeming intrigued rather than annoyed by her nosiness. "Maybe. But nobody wants to greet even a magical bagel elf in their jammies."

"Assuming they wear any," Arial said as a porch light went on and the door opened.

"Whoa," he said with an involuntary shiver. "That is a scary thought. You have no idea how scary."

Now she laughed. "Well, if I'd known this kind of service was available, I'd have had you bring me coffee and spare me this trip."

He stopped and regarded her. "You're out in in the dark

alone in search of coffee? I'm not an aficionado, but I hear you can make the stuff at home."

She ducked her head sheepishly. "I forgot to buy beans yesterday. This is something I didn't realize until I woke up at four a.m. with an awful caffeine-deprivation headache."

"Addict."

"Afraid so. I guess I'm still adjusting to the time difference between here and Wisconsin, where I moved from."

"When was that?" he asked.

Arial thought he seemed torn between getting as far away from the white brick house as he could and talking to her.

"A month ago." She waved her hand. "I know, plenty of time to adjust. But apparently, my caffeine clock is still off, and since the Starbucks on Cannery Row opened earliest, I—"

"You took off down the coastal trail on foot. You don't own a car?"

She grimaced. "It's a rental, until I decide what I want. I'm trying not to drive it much. Besides," she shivered as the wind shifted, blowing the marine layer further onto shore, "it sounded like fun. You know, a walk along the bay at sunrise?"

"*Before* sunrise and alone."

"You keep saying that, but you're alone, too."

"I am a—"

"If you say 'man,' I'll flatten you."

"I was going to say local."

"Which makes you impervious to everything you've warned me about?" She dipped her head. "But it is darker than I imagined. My flashlight app is already fading."

"Don't use your phone," he said, holding up his keychain again. "Take this."

"Your keys? I—"

He shook his head, unfastening the small blue cylinder that dangled from his keychain. "It's a whistle and also a flashlight if you push this." He flicked a small button on the side and held it out to her.

"Nice," she said, taking it. "But don't you need it?"

"Nope. I'm a—"

"Local, I know."

"I was going to say a man." He grinned. "My car is down here if you want a lift."

"That's very nice," she said, wary all of a sudden. "But I feel like a walk."

"Sure you do. But you're right to be cautious of strangers, even here." He paused for a moment before sticking out his hand. "I'm Aaron Henry. Shopper and rideshare driver, extraordinaire."

Arial hesitated, then shook the man's hand. It seemed rude not to introduce herself since he'd already done so. In another place, another time, she'd have given a fake name, but now she found herself saying, "I'm Arial Kingston. Dog-sitter."

"I've thought about adding that offering to my repertoire," Aaron said, stopping next to a gray car. "We have tons of animal lovers and they're happy to pay whatever they have to in order to go on vacation and not worry about their pets."

"I'm just starting out—well, here on the peninsula, at least."

"Now that is a tough gig," he said, pulling open his car door. "Moving here, from . . . Wisconsin, you said? Growing up on the peninsula we're used to the house prices, but for people coming in?" He shrugged. "It can be murder."

"But I inher . . ." Arial started and then let it drift off as he climbed into his car. She'd just met the man, for God's sake. Zip it, Arial.

He rolled down the window. "You sure I can't give you a lift?"

She shook her head. "No, thank you."

He tapped the rideshare sticker on his windshield. "When you do, just punch it up. Maybe I'll see you again."

"Maybe," Arial said, raising a hand as a siren started to wail in the distance.

Arial waited for Aaron's car to pass before finally crossing Ocean View Boulevard to get to the coastal trail. As he'd suggested, she was using the little flashlight to pick her way along the trail, but was relieved to see the sky brightening over Old Fisherman's Wharf. Golds and pink-tinged blues slanted through the marine layer onto the water. Dawn, at last.

The bay was empty now, with no sign of the boat she'd seen earlier. No voices either, or howling dogs, but she could hear the barks of sea lions—or maybe it was seals—as the coastal trail curved away from the shoreline at the Hopkins Marine Station—the marine laboratory of Stanford University. Just around the corner, she knew, was the sidewalk leading down to the Monterey Bay Aquarium on Cannery Row and, a few blocks down, blessed coffee.

As she approached the aquarium's main entrance, the historic facades of the Cannery Row that John Steinbeck had immortalized loomed larger. The buildings' weathered charm was steeped in the canning industry's past, despite the addition of signs hawking souvenirs and tasty treats to the visitors who would soon descend. This early, though, the street was quiet, except for workers preparing for the day. Employees and guides from the aquarium passed her in small clusters, chatting in low tones, while shop owners and restaurant staff swept sidewalks, set out trash for pickup, and hosed down the curbs.

And, yes. In the distance, the Starbucks sign glowed softly with the promise of caffeine. Arial crossed the street and almost broke into a run, pulling the door open to step into the coffee-scented space with a sigh. The line to order was short, and a few minutes later—with venti latte in hand—she glanced around at the tables and comfortable seating area.

Nah.

Even if Arial didn't have to be back at the house by seven, Monterey Bay was calling.

Retracing her steps past the aquarium entrance, Arial turned right at the facility's outside queuing area and onto the coastal trail. Just past the marine laboratory, Arial stepped off the trail to lace the fingers of her left hand in the chain-link fence. The beach laid out in front of her was reserved for seals and sea lions, the ones whose barks she'd only heard earlier. Now, in the dawn light, some were lazing on rocks, others chilling on the sand with their newly born pups or swimming in the relatively calm water of the inlet.

As Arial gazed through the fence sipping her latte, she felt herself relaxing. There was so much to do after the move, so many responsibilities that she'd never had to juggle before, but this made it all worth it. People wrote odes to the sea and now she understood why. It touched her soul—and she hadn't even realized she had one.

With a sigh, Arial drained the last of her latte and started up the trail to what awaited her at her new home.

TWO

In the end, Arial made it back from her coffee supply run in plenty of time for the main event of the day, which was . . . this. A giant, noxious circus tent being pitched in her yard.

And now, far from the calm she'd achieved earlier, her nose was wrinkled, her arms crossed over her chest, and she was barely able to stop her right foot from tapping.

Honest to God, becoming a homeowner had turned her from the carefree twenty-five-year-old she'd been just a month ago into some manic schoolmarm. "You are absolutely sure this is safe?"

"Absolutely, ma'am," a workman in white coveralls parroted, handing her a clipboard to sign. "Except for the termites, of course."

"And anything else that might call the walls or foundation home," snickered a second man—"Harold," the tag on his coverall said—as he pulled a hose past them toward the red and blue striped tent that now enveloped the snug white cottage that was her guest house. It was one of three structures that stood on her newly inherited property, along with the sage green main house and a garage.

"Anything else like what? Squirrels? Raccoons?" Or the adorable baby possums she'd seen crossing the yard as she left for her walk this morning. "And what about the deer? They seem to be everywhere. Could the fumes—"

"Not to worry, Ms. Kingston," the first man—Kenny, from his tag—said. "We check. And besides, any critters with half a brain would turn tail with all the racket we're making."

But what about the others? Didn't they deserve to live out their furry little brainless lives?

Arms still crossed, Arial tried to reclaim her zen, slowing her breathing as she gazed down the street to the water. The remaining fog had dissolved on her walk back, so much so that Arial could make out the Santa Cruz Mountains across the bay.

Arial stood in the picturesque coastal community of Pacific Grove on the western tip of the Monterey Peninsula. Dubbed Butterfly Town because of the thousands of monarch butterflies that wintered there every year, Pacific Grove was flanked by—and some would say overshadowed by—its better-known neighbors of Monterey, Carmel and Pebble Beach.

And PG residents seemed just fine with that. And Arial was just fine with PG.

Not that you could tell it at the moment. "I hate this," she muttered irritably to herself. "Killing doesn't belong in a place like this."

Kenny's chin lifted. "Folks have to live, too, and termites do a lot of damage to our homes. Did you have this place inspected when you bought it?" His expression said she was a fool if she hadn't.

"I inherited the property," Arial said.

"That explains it. Most times, inspection, extermination, and repairs of any damage are written right in the purchase offer. We do all three—full service."

"You inspect and then you also exterminate?" Seemed like a conflict of interest, somehow.

"And repair, as I said." He passed her a clipboard to sign. "We can give you an estimate if you like. Your living-room floor is pretty mushy. I'm betting there's structural damage."

"Mushy" didn't sound like a good thing for a floor. "From the termites? I mean they're little, right? How much can they eat?"

"You'd be surprised, especially if they've been working at it all these years." He nodded at the clipboard. "Now you sign that, and we'll have you back in the house to sleep on Thursday night, Friday latest."

"I live in the main house." She nodded at the sage green Victorian that stood on the corner not twenty feet away. "You're sure there's no problem being in there with the extermination so close? I assume the windows should be kept closed? And what about the neighbors? And their dog. Should they keep him in?"

"I wouldn't necessarily want him to come sniffing around the tent," Kenny said, turning to leave. "But otherwise, don't worry. It's perfectly safe."

"As was cigarette smoking," Arial muttered, "once upon a time."

"Not to mention asbestos insulation and lead paint."

Arial jumped and turned to see her neighbor, Shirley Cooper, in her usual outfit of leggings, hiking boots and an oversized sweatshirt. Despite the thirty-five-year gap in age between them, Arial had immediately taken to Shirley, who wore her white hair chin-length and always had a smile on her face and a smart remark ready to go.

Shirley, her husband Frank and their boxer/shepherd mix, Monty, lived next door, their white stucco cottage as close to the guest house on the one side as Arial's main house was on the other.

"Can this possibly be safe?" Arial asked her now. "And what about the environment? I know they vent the building afterwards, but where does the poison go? Does it just dissipate? It can't be—"

"Has anybody ever told you that you babble a stream of questions when you're nervous?" Shirley asked, taking Arial's arm to walk her away from the tenting to the curb.

"Yes, but it fails to shut me up."

"I respect that," Shirley said. "As for the tenting, I must admit that I'm not a fan. Which is why I thought I'd take Monty for a walk while they're actually pumping the stuff in. Do you want to join us?"

"I'd love to," Arial said, following Shirley down the sidewalk toward the Coopers' cottage. "Is Frank home? Would he want to come with us?"

"Fat chance." Shirley shook her head at the plaid café curtains covering their front kitchen window. "Give the man a mug of coffee and the *New York Times* Sunday crossword puzzle and he's good for hours."

Arial understood the coffee part. "Frank's an engineer, isn't he? Retired?"

"So he pretends," Shirley said, rolling her eyes. "But he still does speaking engagements—engineering conferences and such. Which is good, I guess. Gets him out of the house."

"He must be quite well-respected," Arial offered. "I mean, if he's being asked to speak to professional organizations."

"He is very good," Shirley admitted. "When we were younger, I would go with him to conferences. You know, record his speeches, meet the people he'd talk about the rest of the year."

"But you don't any longer?"

"It gets old after a while and, besides, we have Monty now." Shirley nodded toward the house.

Arial had a sneaking suspicion the boxer mix was more excuse than reason. "Well, you have me now to puppy-sit. So anytime you want . . ."

Shirley waved her off. "While I will take you up on that, it won't be for a conference. Monty is much better company than a roomful of engineers."

Suspicion confirmed. "You and Frank should go someplace fun. You know, take advantage of your—"

"Don't you dare say golden years." She glanced sideways at Arial and her tone softened. "I know I complain about Frank, but I just wish he'd apply his engineering talents to keeping up this place rather than monkeying around in his workshop."

She nodded to a wheelbarrow and lawn mower sitting off to one side of the garage door, nearly lost in the tall grass. "I'm just waiting for Karen to post about the yard on the online neighborhood board."

Karen's and Arial's yards backed up to one another across a small alley.

"Then I'm sure she won't be happy about this either," Arial said, nodding to her guest house. "She'll come to me first, though, won't she?" The last thing Arial wanted was trouble with the neighbors. And the neighbors' neighbors. "Before she posts anything online?"

"Now what fun would that be?" Shirley said with a grin and then relented. "But tenting is routine here when a house is sold, so even Karen has accepted it. There's no use worrying."

Worrying was Arial's life these days, it seemed, home

ownership not being exactly what she'd expected. "You mentioned lead paint and asbestos. Is that a problem? I mean, I know these are old houses, right?"

"And again with the questions," Shirley said, shaking her head. "Frank's advice: if you need to paint, just paint over what's there. Once you start scraping down to whatever they were using in the early 1900s, when these houses were built, you're asking for trouble."

"But it's all right to paint over more than a century of paint?" Arial asked.

"I'm just telling you what Frank said," Shirley said. "And while you're at it, don't go knocking down walls or pulling up things like asbestos floor tiles. Let the bad stuff stay safely encapsulated where it is, not in the air."

Which was going to be lethal enough, given the tenting. "The exterminators say the floor is—"

"Morning," a voice called.

"Oh, God," Shirley muttered, as a young woman with dark hair pulled tightly back in a ponytail wheeled a stroller with a fluffy white Pomeranian seated in it toward them. A small boy of about four toddled next to them, holding desperately onto the handle of the stroller.

"You don't like Karen?" Arial had said hello to the woman a few times in passing and found her a little judgy.

"She was born an old lady," Shirley said. "And by the way, her name is Emily. I just call her Karen because she is one."

Arial's jaw dropped. "But I've been calling her Karen. To her face." Probably explained why she hadn't been exactly friendly. "Why did you—"

"Excuse me," Emily interrupted, rolling up to them. "I need to have a word."

"I'm so sorry, Emily." Arial was trying to figure out a way to explain why she had called the woman Karen without throwing Shirley under the bus. "I thought—"

"Sorry for what? You didn't leave poop in my garbage bin, did you?" Her eyes were narrowed on either side of her freckled nose.

"Arial doesn't own a dog," Shirley said, "so I hope not. And if you're talking about me, I used your bin once because it was right there in the alley. And I put said poop in a poop bag—a biodegradable poop bag," she added before Emily could ask.

"Well, at least you picked it up, which is more than I can say about some people," Emily sniffed, lifting the Pomeranian out of the stroller so the toddler could climb in. "But even biodegradable poop bags can split and make my bin smell."

Shirley didn't bother to avert an eye roll, but just said, "Sorry."

"You don't use poop bags? What do you do with . . . what's his name?" Arial went to pet the Pom, but he growled.

"This is Casper," Emily said, smiling down at the ball of fluff. "Just like the ghost. And we compost his doo-doo, of course. The garden is flourishing."

That explained the odor wafting across the alley from Emily's backyard. Glad her trash bins were nice and fresh-smelling, though.

"You do know that's not safe," Shirley said, with her arms folded. "At least not on any plants that produce food for human consumption."

"I *know* that." Emily's eyebrows couldn't go up much higher in her indignation. "I'm not an idiot."

"Debatable," Arial thought she heard Shirley murmur as she turned away.

Usually a peacemaker, Arial decided to stay out of this particular skirmish. "Anyway, Emily, I wanted to apologize for the fumigation of my guest house. I know it's an annoyance, but I'm told the tenting will only be up two or three days."

"Oh, no worries about that," she said, waving her hand. "But I did want to talk to you about the light at the back of your main house, facing the back of ours."

"Yes?"

"It's white."

"I . . . well, yes, it is." Arial was trying to ignore Shirley, who was trying to catch her eye. "But aren't pretty much all lightbulbs white?"

"They had black lights in the sixties," Shirley said idly. "But that was when people were fun."

Emily shot her an irritated look. "I'm talking about color temperature, and you know it. We're more of a yellow, warm light neighborhood; that bright white light is simply jarring. Besides, it shines right into Dickie's bedroom."

"Don't you have curtains?" Shirley asked.

"We have plantation shutters, as you well know," the other woman said, her jaw tight. "But that white light just creeps in around all the slats."

"Not the only thing that creeps around at night," Shirley said darkly, again low enough not to be addressed directly to Emily, but loud enough to be understood.

Arial refused to be drawn in. "I'm so sorry," she told Emily again. "I didn't know there was some kind of neighborhood restriction. There was no bulb in the back porch light and that was the only replacement I could find in the house."

"Because the former tenant was kind enough to take it out, when I explained the restrictions, as you say, to him," Emily said.

Shirley, apparently having had enough, turned to Arial. "There is no restriction. Just people with too much time on their hands who stick their noses into other people's business."

Emily stuck out her chin. "I just care about the neighborhood. Is that a sin? Cool white is much too harsh for the historic houses we have here. And your front light, Shirley. It never fails to startle me going on at all hours. It's blinding."

"It's motion-activated," Shirley said. "Maybe you shouldn't walk by at all hours. It's not safe. Predators about."

To Arial's surprise, Emily just shivered. "You're right about that."

"You mean the mountain lions and coyotes?" Arial asked. "Somebody just warned me about them."

"They're nothing to worry about as long as you respect their space," Emily countered. "I'm talking about human predators—thieves. Didn't you hear the sirens this morning? Another robbery—this one in the Beach Tract. The big brick house on Ocean View Boulevard, someone said. I think it might be the Rowans'."

Arial frowned. She'd heard a siren start to wail as she'd left

Aaron Henry to walk toward Cannery Row for coffee. But there had to be plenty of big brick houses on Ocean View, other than the one where she and Aaron had stood discussing squids, mountain lions, and the gig economy. "You don't mean the big *white* brick house, do you?"

"Yes, that's the Rowans' house," Emily said, cocking her head. "Why? Do you know Simone and Charles?"

"No, but I've noticed the house," Arial said lamely. "Very nice." The last thing she needed was Emily spreading the word that she'd been in the vicinity of a house when it was robbed. Especially given Arial's dubious recent past.

". . . Lovely old house," Emily was saying. "When Simone and Charles bought the property, I was sure they were going to knock it down and build some modern monstrosity."

"No worries," Shirley said. "I'm sure a house of that size was considered a modern monstrosity when it was built in the day." She batted her eyes. "And don't you think it's *too* white?"

But the last comment was lost on Emily, who was shaking her head. "We didn't have all this crime when I was Dickie's age. I blame the newcomers moving in."

"The newcomers?" Arial asked, frowning. "My family has been here for generations and my grandmother Edna—"

"Oh, I'm not talking about an unfortunate traffic accident," Emily said with a dismissive wave of her hand.

It was only an accident if you didn't mean to do it, Arial thought. But if Emily didn't know the truth, it was probably best left that way.

"Besides," Emily was saying, "the Mayeses pre-date even my family. I'm thinking more of transplants like . . ." She head-gestured toward Shirley.

"Yeah," Shirley said, straightening, "Frank and I have only been here for thirty years. Virtual newcomers."

"I'm just saying that at one time, Pacific Grove was a small—"

"What are you, thirty years old?" Shirley burst out. "How are you qualified to give historical perspective?"

Emily stuck her nose in the air. "My mother told me—"

"Your mother—"

Arial jumped in. "Since both of you are such long-time residents—much longer than me—you can answer a question. I saw lights on the water very early this morning and somebody told me it was squids. I didn't get a chance to ask more, but are we talking about the Navy? Or the Coast Guard?"

The other two women just squinted at her, mouths open. Shirley tipped first. "You thought squids, like sailors? How very nautical of you."

"I don't know what else . . ." Arial got it. "Oh, you mean squids, the fish?"

"Mollusks," Emily corrected. "Cephalopods in particular."

"And calamari steaks on my plate," Shirley said. "Preferably with lemon and capers."

Emily made a "yum" noise, not having an argument with that, at least. "The boats fish at night, using bright lights to attract squid into the nets."

Didn't seem especially sporting. And if the mollusks weren't fish, then why were they "fished"? But Arial said neither of these things, since her two neighbors were finally in agreement. "It was magical seeing the boat out there like that. And a little eerie, I have to admit."

"The quiet, except for the clanging of the lines and the occasional word you can catch carried along the breeze." After this poetic summary, Emily returned to business. "So can I count on you, Arial? You'll replace that bulb?"

Arial crossed her heart. "Warm temperature. As soon as I get to the store."

"Perfect," Emily said, throwing Shirley a smug glance. "And are you a reader, Arial?"

Duh. She was named after a typeface. "Well, yes. When I have the time, of course."

"Then do join us for book club. We meet once a month, rotating hosts. We'll be at my house next Tuesday night. Seven p.m."

"I . . . well, thank you. I'll come if I can."

"Now don't be a Shirley." She smirked. "That's what we call somebody who says they'll come and never shows up."

"Karen," Shirley countered at the younger woman.

Arial held up her hands. "Enough. Can I tell you tomorrow, Emily?"

"Of course." She dug into the stroller and came up with a card. "My number is on here. Please do RSVP so I can have an accurate count. It is only common courtesy, after all."

"Of course," Arial repeated.

THREE

"You can't give in to her kind," Shirley muttered, as Emily, Dickie and Casper continued down the sidewalk.

"Well, you certainly don't," Arial said. "Emily obviously knows you call her Karen *and* she actually shuddered when she mentioned your front porch light."

"The woman is neurotic," Shirley said, shrugging. "She's worried about crime, yet she complains about my security light."

Shirley had a point. "True. And I have a giant poison circus tent in my yard, but she's worried about the color of my lightbulb? I suppose, though, if my back porch light is shining into her son's bedroom, it—"

"Don't do it," Shirley warned. "Give her an inch and she'll be telling you what color to paint your house and ratting you out to the city if you so much as trim a dead branch on one of your trees. But first, she'll post about you online in order to generate support. The woman loves to shame people publicly."

Oh boy. Arial hadn't realized how easy life was when she slept on friends' couches. "I can't trim tree branches?" Not that she'd ever felt the urge, you understand.

"Only limbs up to a certain size. Especially for native trees like that live oak of yours." She nodded to the fifty-foot tree whose wide-spreading branches filled the space between and above the main and guest houses. "If you want to trim that up at all, I'd suggest doing it in the dead of night with a hand saw so nobody will hear."

"And you'll unscrew your motion-detector bulb so they can't see?"

"Of course," Shirley said, giving her a friendly elbow-bump. "I'll even take Karen out, so she can't rat on you."

Arial looked sideways at her. "Out to dinner or out out?"

Shirley shrugged. "You pick. I know what I prefer."

Arial grinned. "You remind me of my aunt Sarah. You always know where you stand with her."

"Often wrong, but never in doubt, that's my motto," Shirley said, and then cupped her hands. "Frank," she called toward the house, "I want to take Monty for a walk. Can you bring him out?"

No answer except a twitch of the curtain, which could have been Frank getting up to do his wife's bidding, or the boxer mix himself, watching them from the window.

Most likely the latter.

Shirley sighed. "Frank's going deaf as a doornail. Not that he'll admit it."

"Maybe he's in the workshop," Arial said absently. She was watching the exterminators rev up some sort of generator.

Shirley twisted to look and then sighed. "You obviously hate the idea of tenting. Why are you doing it?"

"Apparently the damage is so widespread in the guest house that the exterminators think other methods wouldn't be effective," Arial said. "My tenant Chris swears he can't sleep over the munching in the walls."

"Christopher Buck," Shirley said, closing one eye to regard her. "He told me the other day that he's quasi-related to you. A pseudo-sibling, I think he said."

Quasi was right. Christopher Buck's half-sister Melinda was also Arial's half-sister. That meant that Chris and Melinda had the same mother, and Melinda and Arial the same father. It was all very messy and quite new.

To further confuse the matter, Chris had been renting the main PG house when Arial inherited it. It was a month-to-month lease, but Arial didn't feel right kicking him out. She did manage to shift him to the guest house so she could move into the main house. But a month in, the termites had raised their ugly heads, forcing the tenting and temporary co-habitation.

"Frank?" Shirley called again before starting for the house. "Fine, I'll do it myself, like everything else."

She swung open the door. "Monty? Walkie . . ." Before she could finish, the big dog had blasted past her and into the front yard.

Monty Cooper had been blessed with the big shoulders, large chest, and small waist of his boxer forebears, but the boxer's traditional short brindle coat was long and luxurious on Monty, likely a gift from his retriever ancestors along with his generous snout. A glorious plumed tail curled high over his back, completing the package. Suffice it to say he was pretty enough to stop traffic.

Just now, though, he was the one who stopped dead and glanced around, sniffing the air.

Shirley's sharp, "Monty, come!" brought him to her side as she ducked into the house to get his leash.

"I can't believe he listened for once," Shirley said, snapping the leash on the dog's collar before rejoining Arial. "Monty's a very good boy, but if he sees a squirrel or a deer, God forbid, he's gone."

"There was a family of deer in your front yard this morning as I was leaving," Arial said. "Just standing there looking like a postcard."

"They like to bed down in the brush or long grass," Shirley said. "Which means they love my yard, of course. Frank's second cousin wants to come out for a visit and I told Frank absolutely not, until we clean this place up a bit." She grinned. "Not that I want them to be too comfortable, of course. Shirt-tail relatives can be tough to get rid of."

"Hopefully not worse than termites." Arial was still watching the tenting. "Mine is sleeping on my couch for the time being."

"Who? Oh, you mean Christopher, your pseudo shirt-tail relative? You put that man on the couch?" Shirley adjusted Monty's collar. "He's cute and, from what he said, you're not related. In my day . . ." She shrugged.

"Believe me, the last thing I'm interested in right now is a relationship," Arial said, leaning down to give Monty a scratch behind one ear before they set off down the sidewalk toward the water. "I've got to figure out being a property owner and a landlord first. I thought I'd be set for life when my great-grandmother left me the house—with a guest house, no less—here. But the property needs work, and everything is way more expensive on the peninsula than I'm used to."

She glanced over at Shirley, aware she was whining. "I mean, I'll be fine. I just need to ramp up my dog-sitting business to supplement."

"Tell me about that," Shirley said. "You said you dog-sat back in Wisconsin?"

"Dog-sitting or really sitting for any kind of pet—cats, birds, whatever. But it's dogs that really need a human around to feel happy." Arial shrugged. "And I guess that makes me happy."

"To be needed?" Shirley asked, studying her new friend.

Arial cocked her head. "You trying to psychoanalyze me?

"Maybe." Shirley paused to untangle Monty's leash, which had wound itself around a paw. "My experience is that dogs are healing."

Foot freed, Monty gave a bark in agreement.

Arial grinned and gave him a quick butt rub. "Unconditional love, right, buddy?" She straightened up. "I didn't get much of it from my mother or grandmother growing up, but my mom brought home a puppy for me when I was five. A neighbor's beagle had gotten pregnant and had a litter."

"What was your puppy's name?" Shirley asked, smiling.

"Fido." She grinned back. "I think the other pups in the litter were equally original—you know, Snoopy, Rover, Spot. But my Fidey was . . ." Arial found her throat growing thick. "I loved that puppy," she managed to get out.

"Oh, no," Shirley said, stopping to face her. "What happened to Fido—or rather, Fidey?"

Arial took a beat before looking up to meet her eyes. "Fidey did what puppies do. Got bigger, had accidents, started to shed. My grandmother stepped in a puddle of pee one morning and said he had to go."

"And your mother?"

"Ruth? Her one act of courage was giving me that puppy in the first place. But she was a single mother and it was my grandmother's house." She shrugged.

"I'm so sorry." Shirley had tears in her eyes too.

"Thanks," Arial said, reaching over to squeeze her hand. "But there's a happy ending. My aunt Sarah can come off as an opinionated pain in the butt, but she saw how much Fidey meant to me. She took him in and gave him a wonderful, long life. Let me stay with them whenever I wanted. By the time I was in middle school, that was practically full time."

"So you did get love," Shirley said. "From Sarah and from Fidey."

"I did," Arial said, nodding, and then flashed a grin. "Though Fidey was the only one who made it unconditional."

Shirley smiled back. "You said Fidey had a long life?"

"Thirteen. I was in my freshman year of college when Sarah called me." They'd started to walk again. "Edna had a fit when I drove home from school mid-semester, of course. Said I'd pampered that damn dog his whole life and he could die very well without me."

"Bitch."

"You're telling me," Arial said, throwing her a grin. Then she sighed. "I made it to Sarah's in time to say goodbye and never went back. That's when I started to walk dogs and dog-sit for people in Sarah's swanky neighborhood. Amazingly lucrative." She held up a hand as Shirley opened her mouth to comment. "And, yes, I'm sure I was trying to fill the hole Fidey had left."

Shirley took a beat before she said, "Will you get another dog?"

"I will, but . . ."

"It's hard, I know." Shirley reached down to pat her own dog before clearing her throat. "So, your dog-sitting. How is it going here?"

"You're my only client," Arial admitted, toeing a crack in the sidewalk. "I mean, I haven't really had the time to get it up and running. Figure out the marketing. Back in Brookhills, it was mostly word of mouth because Sarah had a real-estate company and knew everybody. And now she owns a coffee house and knows even more people."

"Word of mouth is king here, too," Shirley said. "You should post on the neighborhood board, much as I hate to say it. It's great for finding service providers and the occasional lost dog or cat. That's the only reason I belong, but I think for somebody like Emily, it provides company. You know, a form of social contact since Mark left."

"Mark?"

"Mark Bennett, Emily's ex. They split about a year ago. I'm honestly surprised he lasted that long with her, though."

Arial hadn't realized Emily was a single mother. "So was Emily always like this? Maybe she started sticking her nose into everybody's business because she's lonely."

"Wow." Shirley stopped and raised an eyebrow. "And here I thought *I* was the bleeding heart."

Not much chance of that. "Or maybe we're just nice people," Arial countered, leaning down to give Monty's other ear, which he'd turned toward her, a matching ear rub.

The dog put his paw on Arial's arm, pushing her hand down. "Doesn't he like getting his ears rubbed?" Arial asked. "I thought all dogs did."

"He absolutely does, which is why he's showing his appreciation by trying to hold hands," Shirley said. "Awkwardly, I admit, without opposable thumbs."

"What a sweetie." Arial resumed the ear rub and Monty dissolved onto the ground and rolled over. "Belly rubs are nice, too, huh?" She complied.

"You really are good with him," Shirley said, watching. "And people love people who love their animals. Do you have a catchy name for your business?"

"Not really," Arial said as they resumed their walk. "I've always just been Sarah's niece who dog-sits."

Shirley stopped. "What were you planning to do eventually? Before you inherited the property here, I mean. I can't imagine somebody like you being satisfied with taking care of other people's pets for the rest of her life."

Arial held up both hands. "Whoa. I'm only twenty-five. Lots of life left to decide."

"Unlike oldsters like me," Shirley said with a rueful grin. "Sorry. I went to work as an insurance underwriter when I was your age and my mother expected me to stay there forever. Security."

"Did you?"

"Of course not, which I realize makes your point," Shirley said. "So back to a name for your business."

"How about something like Sit-Stay?" At Arial's words, Monty sat. And seemed prepared to stay. She drew up short. "What a smart puppy. How old is Monty again?"

"Our boy just turned five." Now it was Shirley who was getting choked up and she stopped to clear her throat. "Sorry, but we almost lost him last year."

"Oh, no . . . I'm sorry," Arial said, touching her arm. "What happened? An accident?"

"I guess you could say that." Shirley had started walking again, head down. "It was one of our really foggy mornings, and when I opened the door to get Frank's newspaper, Monty got out like he did today. But that day there was a deer in the front yard and Monty took off after it. I was panicked—for the deer and for Monty, of course, but Frank kept saying not to worry. The deer would easily outrun Monty and he would come home. But when he finally did come back, something obviously wasn't right. That's why I'm so compulsive about keeping him on a leash."

"Had he been hit by a car?"

"No, but he was vomiting and falling down in pain. I had no idea why he was so sick, but I rushed him to Christopher." She managed a grin. "He figured it out, thank God."

Christopher Buck was a veterinarian. "Chris is a good vet then?"

"The best," Shirley said. "He had a hunch Monty had gotten into something poisonous, maybe in an alley or garage. His first guess was window-washing fluid or anti-freeze, so he started Monty on fomepizole, which has to be administered within eight to twelve hours of the poisoning."

"And he's all right now?" Arial found it painful to think of the dog—now prancing happily in front of them—writhing in pain on the floor.

"Yes, thank God his kidneys weren't badly damaged." Shirley shook herself, as if to shake off the memories. "But back to your business, Arial. You could put the location into your name, if you wanted. Like we did with Monty."

Monty. "Monty was named for Monterey?"

"Yes, he's Monterey Jack," Shirley said, as the subject of

their conversation stopped to prove his kidney health by watering a tree. "Named for his favorite cheese."

"That's fun," Arial said. "Though your boy Monty here is so much more exciting than the cheese. Aren't you, buddy?"

Both Monty and Shirley gave her side-eye.

"You don't like Monterey Jack?" the human one asked.

Apparently, Arial had touched on a nerve. "Don't get me wrong. Monterey Jack is great for grilled cheese and on tacos and stuff. It's just kind of a blank slate, though, isn't it? The vanilla of cheeses, you might say, rather than the . . . the—"

"Stop now, you're only digging the hole deeper."

"I . . . umm, OK," Arial said. "I just—"

Shirley held up her hands. "I'll give you young Monterey Jack is a mild, unpretentious cheese in its usual form, but Monty prefers Dry Jack—in very small amounts." She waved her finger in admonishment as the dog's nose lifted and swiveled her way at the mention of his favorite treat. "Right, Monty?"

"I've never heard of Dry Jack. Though I guess I'm not necessarily up on my cheeses." Which is why Arial should have kept her Monterey Jack opinions to herself.

"Dry Jack is aged and eats like a good parmesan. You should try it."

"I will," Arial promised, then changed the subject. "I like the name Monty. Or I guess you could have called him Jack. I like that, too."

"I thought about it, but for whatever reason, he doesn't respond to Jack." Shirley laughed. "Not that he responds to anything if he's got a scent. "Which is why," she waved a warning finger at Arial, "if you're taking care of him, you make sure to hang onto him for dear life."

"Absolutely," Arial promised. No way was she going to let Monty disappear into the fog on her watch.

Shirley seemed reassured. "Anyway, a little local lore for you: the Jack in Monterey Jack is actually David *Jacks*, with an 's.' Jacks bought up the land around here in an auction in 1859 and then either foreclosed on the original tenants or charged exorbitant rent. By the time he was done, Jacks owned everything—ranches, vineyards, dairies and everything they produced."

"Including the cheese?" Arial guessed.

"Including the cheese, which was being produced as Queso Blanco by the Franciscan friars at a nearby mission." She snorted. "Didn't stop Jacks from slapping his name on it and making a fortune—or another fortune—off it."

"That . . . oof!" Monty had spotted a squirrel and crossed in front of Arial, nearly tripping her up. "I see what you mean."

"Sorry," Shirley said, reining him in.

"So is there controversy over the Jacks legacy?" Arial asked. "I noticed his name on a park—or I assume it's his name. Jacks Peak?"

"Correct," Shirley said. "And, if you want to look at the other side of the argument, Jacks did some good things, including donating the land that became Pacific Grove to the Methodists for their religious retreat."

"After he took it from somebody else," Arial mused.

Shirley dipped her head. "A lot of somebody elses and more somebody elses before that. Different groups settled here over the centuries—Spanish, Mexican, Chinese, Italian, Portuguese, Japanese, British, French—and that doesn't even count the indigenous tribes who inhabited the area for thousands of years before any of the interlopers came along. There are bound to be disagreements about who did what to whom when where."

So much Arial didn't know—including how to punctuate Shirley's last sentence.

"But," her friend continued as they turned onto Lighthouse Avenue, "the fog has lifted and the sun is out, so let's talk about happier things."

"Like the name of my company?"

"Exactly. I think Sit-Stay is clever, but maybe a little too much so. You don't want to keep having to explain it."

"So you're saying I'm too clever?" Arial said.

"Be grateful. Most people don't even approach clever in my estimation," Shirley said. "But I think you should choose a name that means something to you. Even if it's not immediately apparent."

Arial's brow had been furrowed as she thought, and now she brightened. "What about Pampered Pooches Pet-Sitting?"

"Exactly what your grandmother *didn't* want you to do." Shirley grinned, raising her eyebrows. "And I do love me a good alliteration."

"And the 'pet' leaves the door open for sitting for other kinds of animals."

"Cats, of course," Shirley agreed. "But don't forget the turtles, snakes and backyard chickens. We have a lot of those here, too."

If Shirley was trying to put a dent in Arial's new enthusiasm, she wasn't succeeding. "We could even add a tagline: 'Your place or ours.'"

"You'll need a fence first."

"Absolutely." After she got done paying for this extermination, of course. But then her experience was that most people preferred in-home care anyway. "You're right—I like that it reminds me of Fidey."

"He did inspire your love of dogs. And your dog-sitting business."

"He did, didn't he?" Arial shook her head as they crossed the street. "Thank you."

"For what?" Shirley asked, looking sideways at her.

"Saving me thousands of dollars and hundreds of hours in therapy later in life." Arial's cheeks were tinged pink. "In twenty minutes, you drilled down on what makes me tick. Things I never really thought about."

"Well, you can pay me in Monty-sitting," Shirley said. "But while we're on the subject of names and psychology, I've been wondering. Have you considered using Mayes as part of your name? Like Arial Mayes Kingston? Or vice versa."

Arial wrinkled her nose. "Mayes Kingston is definitely better than Kingston Mayes. But why? Do you think it would mean something to people here? Get me more sitting gigs?"

"It would mean something, definitely, but not dog-sitting. More like old money. And art, of course."

Arial's grandmother Edna had been a painter and quite a well-known one, at least locally. It was her mother,

Gretchen—Arial's great-grandmother—who had owned the Pacific Grove property and left it in trust for Arial on her twenty-fifth birthday.

"Well, I don't paint, and I don't have a whole lot of money, old or new. Just the house, like I said." Arial swept her hand toward the shops and restaurants ahead on Lighthouse as they made a turn onto Central Avenue past Chautauqua Hall. "But I do love it here and plan to stay. So beyond this tenting and probably the fence, any improvements I make on the house will have to be done gradually as I have the cash."

"Absolutely take your time," Shirley agreed. "That house isn't going anywhere. Built in 1911, Gretchen told me, and the guest house before that."

"Really?" Arial said. "The guest house predates the main house?"

"By a decade or two, from what your great-grandmother said. You should visit the PG Library down here on Central Avenue, or the Historical Society. I'm sure you could find plenty of historical information."

"Why would I do that, when I have you?" Arial grinned at her friend.

Shirley shook her head. "You kids these days. Can't be bothered to read."

"I love reading, as I told Emily. But there's something to be said about oral history. You know, passed down by the elders?"

Shirley elbowed her. Hard.

Monty glanced back at them.

"Don't worry, she's too frail to hurt me," Arial assured him before turning back to Shirley. "Speaking of the Historical Society, I noticed there are no date plaques on either my main house or the guest house, like there are on a lot of homes in Pacific Grove."

"I imagine Gretchen didn't care two shakes about any plaque if it meant somebody telling her what she could and couldn't do with her property. Stubborn, even at ninety."

Unsurprising, knowing the other women in the family. At any age. "Was the guest house rented out when my great-grandmother was still alive?"

Shirley wrinkled her nose. "Not that I remember. But after Gretchen died about ten years ago, there was a renter or two in there. And an older couple, the Sevilles, leased the big house until they both died a couple of years back. I've never met anybody in your family, so I wondered if the line had died out."

"From what I understand, my grandmother—Gretchen's only daughter Edna, the artist—moved to Denver when she married my grandfather and then she and my mother Ruth moved to Brookhills, Wisconsin, where Ruth had me. I never even knew about Pacific Grove until Edna died about six months ago and her lawyer told me about Gretchen's trust."

"And your inheritance?"

"And my inheritance," Arial said. "Gretchen hopscotched right over both my grandmother and mother and left the property in trust to me."

"Gretchen was a woman who knew her own mind. I was reminded of her when you were talking about your aunt Sarah stepping in for you and Fidey when you were young." Shirley frowned. "Do you think your grandmother and mother resented you because Gretchen passed them over?"

"It's possible," Arial said, lifting her shoulders. "They certainly would have known about the will after Gretchen's death, and maybe even before that. But I knew none of this, so I just assumed it was . . ."

"That it was you," Shirley finished for her.

"Because I was a bastard." Arial was nodding. "You know, my birth had ruined their lives. My grandmother had to support us. My mother never married. Never really had a life of any kind."

"Bullshit!" Shirley snapped, startling Monty, who stopped and turned around.

"It's OK, baby," Arial told him. "Your mom's not angry with you."

"No," Shirley said, giving him a scratch. "I'm angry with Arial's mom. This isn't Victorian England, for God's sake. A lot of women raise their children alone and have lives. And they certainly don't take it out on the kids."

"I know. Believe me, I know." Arial inhaled deeply, consciously slowing her breathing to match the rhythm of the waves pounding just a few short blocks below them. "But whatever my path was, I'm grateful it brought me here. One visit, and I was hooked."

"Of course you were." Shirley seemed a little ashamed for dredging up the past. "What's not to like about a place where the ocean is practically at your doorstep and the average high temperatures range between sixty and seventy degrees?"

"Like autumn in the Midwest year-round." Arial sighed. "I'm so glad to be here."

"And we're glad to have you," Shirley said, shifting Monty's leash to link arms with her neighbor.

"I second that," a voice at Arial's opposite ear said.

FOUR

"Geez, Chris, you scared me." Arial had her hand over her pounding heart.

Christopher Buck was close to six feet tall, to Arial's five foot two, and had dark hair to her fawn-colored. At the moment he was wearing his white lab coat and had a to-go cup in his hand. "I saw you walk past toward Lovers Point," he said, gesturing back toward his office on Lighthouse Avenue. I've been trying to catch up."

"You couldn't have been trying very hard," Shirley said dryly. "Monty's been stopping at every tree."

"Glad to see all systems are working," Chris said, falling in step with them and leaning down to give Monty a scratch. "How's my favorite patient today?"

"He's just fine," Shirley said. "But can you please tell Lucy to stop texting me all those stupid reminders? Time for Monty's rabies shot! Time for Monty's exam! Time for Monty's dental check! Each one with a smiley face and party popper emoji. I hate to break it to you, but none of us are all that excited about seeing you."

"She doesn't mean that," Arial told Chris.

"Yes, I do," Shirley sniffed. "What is that you're drinking?"

"Chai latte," he said. "Where are you three headed?"

"Away from the fumigation," Shirley told him. "They're just getting started, and Arial is a little freaked out."

"She'd be more freaked out if she had to listen to the termites sharpening their fangs every night."

Arial's eyes narrowed. "Termites have fangs?"

Chris held up his hands. "We can call them mandibles, if you prefer. Big, strong mandibles."

"I'll take your word, you being a veterinarian and all, but I'm a little surprised that you're fine with their wholesale slaughter. You caught the spider crawling across my kitchen counter this morning and put it outside instead of squishing it. But you're OK with termites being poisoned?"

"I know it's a paradox. But termites destroy our dwellings. Spiders, on the other hand, serve a purpose—they eat pests like mosquitos and roaches."

"Which also apparently deserve to die, unlike the spiders." She had him.

"You tell him, Arial," Shirley said. "But remember there's still the natural order of things to consider. You know," she took a deep breath and cupped her hands to form a megaphone. "Naaaan-begoniaaa . . ."

The opening call of *The Lion King*. Or a facsimile thereof. "I don't think that's quite—"

"Naaaaaan-injo-naama . . ." Chris was grinning at her as he took up the chant. Correctly, at least to Arial's ear.

"OK, OK," she said, holding up both hands. "'Circle of Life,' I get it—"

But she was interrupted again, this time by Monty, who jumped up to put his big paws on her shoulders and howl along with the other two.

"OK, OK," Arial said, laughing as she struggled to stay upright. "You three win. I get the point."

Shirley and Chris shared a grin while Arial stared Monty in the big brown eyes. "Could you hop down now?"

He complied with a harrumph.

"Anyway," she continued. "As far as the guest house is concerned, I appreciate you moving into it, Chris, so I could live in the main one. I'm just sorry about the termites."

"Aww," he draped his arm over her shoulders. "You know I was happy to do it for my sis."

She shook him off. "I'm not your sis. You are my half-sister's half-brother. There's a difference."

"I'm not sure if that makes it more inappropriate or less for me to be living with you," Chris said.

The truth was that both of them were finding it hard to define their relationship. Seven months ago, the two had never met and Arial, at least, had had no idea that Chris and his half-sister Melinda existed.

"What do you think, Shirley?" Chris continued.

"I don't judge," she said, holding up her hands. "Consenting adults."

"We're not—" Arial cut herself off, not wanting to rise to their bait.

Chris grinned, straightening his coat. "Please, I'm an upstanding member of the Pacific Grove community. A beloved veterinarian. Lover of animals, kids and people. And eternally grateful that you're letting me stay while my guest house is being fumigated."

Now it was *his* guest house, Arial thought. Maybe Shirley was right and this shirt-tail relative wasn't going to be easy to get rid of.

Arial wasn't quite sure how she felt about that.

"I can cook dinner tonight." It was two days later, and Chris was standing in the kitchen of the main house, one eye closed as if he expected to be punched in it.

Arial cocked her head. "You can cook?"

"Sure, why would you think otherwise?"

"Maybe it's because you've been staying here since Monday; the house was fumigated Tuesday, and only today, Thursday—your last night—are you making the offer."

Chris cleared his throat. "Yeah, about that. I—"

"Oh, by the way," Arial said casually as she took a bag of espresso from the cabinet. "I told Shirley that you're sleeping on the couch, so don't make a liar out of me."

"She knows there are two bedrooms in the house," Chris pointed out. "If you didn't want her to know the truth, why not say I'm in the guest bedroom?"

Arial grimaced. "I'm not used to having a guest bedroom, so this just popped out."

"Afraid to admit the truth?" Chris took two mugs out of the dish drainer and handed her one. "That you're sleeping on your own couch."

Arial put the mug under the spout and pressed start. "Because it sounds weird."

"Maybe because it is weird," Chris told her. "Humans have nesting instincts, just like animals do."

"That's the point." Arial turned. "My nest has always been a couch. At my grandmother's house, at my aunt Sarah's, at friends' houses. I don't feel comfortable sleeping in a bed."

Chris leaned over to remove the finished cup and slid the next mug in. "Think of it as a big flat couch. Without buttons. Or maybe you could start by sleeping on the floor of the bedroom and gradually move up to the bed."

"It's just that . . . a bedroom is so far removed. Shut away from everything."

"From everything what?"

"The front door, maybe?" Arial wasn't sure herself, so she shrugged and went to get the cream. "I don't know. On a couch, I could always leave whenever I wanted. Not be in anybody's way." This last was almost swallowed up by the refrigerator as she reached in.

"You still can leave anytime you want, do anything you want, you know. This is freedom. This is your house. No tiptoeing around necessary."

"Intellectually?" Arial closed the refrigerator door and turned, her face a little pink. She wasn't used to being so honest with someone. "Of course, I realize that. But in practice, it takes a little getting used to. Except for the nights I dog-sat, I'm not used to being alone in a house. And even then, when I dog-sat, I had the dog for company."

"And now you have me, at least you have for the last few days." Chris handed her one of the filled mugs and took the other for himself. "Listen, about that. Maybe I could stay another night or two beyond tonight?"

Arial added cream to her coffee and looked up. "I'm fine, really. I didn't mean to make you think I'm lonely. Or a freak." That ship had sailed.

"I don't think you're either," Chris said, taking a sip. "Though 'weird' still stands." When Arial grinned, he continued. "This is more for my benefit than yours. I know the tent is down and they're testing the air tomorrow. But I must admit you've made me think twice about the fumigation process."

"Just the fact they advise removing your clothes from the house, not to mention the mattress and stuffed furniture." She nodded to the living room, where the mattress stood against the wall, secured by the couch from the guest house, which was piled high with black garbage bags of clothes, linens and goods from Chris's pantry, "It has to make you wonder how long the poison lingers and what it seeps into. Besides, you haven't been a half-bad guest, if you forgive the fact that you've apparently been suppressing your cooking abilities."

"You haven't tasted it yet." Chris leaned back against the kitchen counter with a grin. "So don't get your hopes up. But the fact is that I just can't do delivery pizza four nights in a row."

"Looking a gift horse in the mouth much?"

"I appreciate your letting me stay here and I did offer to pay for the pizza—or pizzas—you know."

"If I pay, I get to order what I want." Arial had to admit she'd taken a liking to Chris. The man cleaned up after himself, didn't complain, and—at least so far—hadn't left the seat up.

And now, apparently, he could cook. Or was willing to try. While Arial wasn't looking for a relationship, the guy wouldn't make a half-bad roommate. If she wanted one. Which she didn't, of course. Because she wasn't lonely. Or a freak.

"Have to maintain toppings control, huh?" he asked, returning the cream to the refrigerator. "Well, if you'll let down your guard long enough to eat my food without a taster, I'll pick up the makings today down at Grove Market."

"What are you going to make?" Arial asked, sitting down at the table.

"Pasta, what else? I'm a guy." Chris sat down across from her.

"Now if I said that, I'd be stereotyping."

"There's a reason, as they say, that it's a stereotype." Chris was tap-tapping on his phone, presumably a shopping list. "I'd also grill out if there was propane or charcoal. Or a grill."

"Should we get one?" Arial asked without thinking.

Chris's eyebrows went up. "We?"

"As your landlord, I could provide a grill that we both could use. Separately."

"That would be great," Chris said, draining his coffee cup

before hopping up to wash it out and put it in the dish drainer. "Gotta get to work."

"It's only seven thirty." Arial stifled a yawn. "Veterinarians start this early?"

"Frenchie with a broken tooth. We do surgeries first thing, and then I start seeing patients about ten."

Arial had to admit she liked the idea he cared about animals. And she especially liked that he had saved Monty's life. And had likely done the same for countless other critters, large and small.

But then she glanced out the window.

"What?" the vet said, pausing at the door.

"What, what?"

"A shadow crossed your face," he said, coming back.

"It's just this stupid fumigation," she said, standing up herself. "I keep thinking what if some animal wandered in and got . . ."

"Don't think about it," Chris said, looking a little stricken now himself. "Didn't they tell you they seal everything before they started the work?"

"They did, but . . ." Arial waved. "I know, I worry too much. You go to work, save Frenchies and buy groceries. I'll be fine. And Chris?"

He'd made it to the door again and turned. "Yes?"

"You're welcome to stay as long as you want."

As Chris started down the street through the early morning fog to his clinic, Arial went to the sink to wash out her cup and put it in the dish strainer next to his.

"Welcome to stay as long as you want?" she repeated to herself. "Arial Mayes Kingston, what in the world were you thinking?"

"Pasta, huh?" Shirley asked as she stepped out onto the porch to take Monty's leash back. Arial had taken the big dog for a late afternoon walk on the coastal trail since Shirley and Frank had been out this afternoon. "And how about a little Chianti, Clarice?"

Arial regarded her new friend. "I honestly thought you were

going to tease me about a romance, but then you make a detour into . . . was that *Silence of the Lambs*?"

Shirley was punching at her phone. "It was, but damn . . ." Frank was calling her name from inside the house. "Somebody apparently wants his dinner. Maybe we'll have a nice Chianti, too." She wiggled her eyebrows. "And fava beans."

FIVE

Arial was still smiling as she stepped into her kitchen. Chris was already there stirring red sauce in her largest pot. "You look happy."

"I am, actually," Arial said. "Shirley makes me laugh, you're making me dinner, and"—she caught motion out of the corner of her eye—"there appears to be a French bulldog in my clothes basket."

"Sorry," Chris said. "He tipped it over and climbed in there himself, so I just kind of left him there so I wouldn't step on him. Figured it was the next best thing to kennel rest."

"Is this the Frenchie you were doing the dental surgery on?" Arial asked, going over to sit on the floor next to the little dog in a basket.

"Yes, this is Beau. His parents are out of town, and I didn't want to leave him at the clinic alone. I was hoping you wouldn't mind."

"Of course, I don't mind," Arial said, helping Beau out of the basket.

The nose on his little pushed-in face was going a mile a minute as he gave her the once-over, snuffling loudly.

"You smell Monty on me?" she asked him, giving him a good rub on his butt. "You'd like him, but he's a lot bigger than you are."

"Not in Beau's mind," Chris said, turning to look at the two. "He's a big dog in a tiny, snuffly body."

"Is his mouth OK?" Arial asked, trying to get a look. "Is he in pain?"

"He's probably a little high at the moment," Chris said. "But it was just one extraction and a cleaning. He'll be fine."

"What a cutie." Arial said, snuggling her face close to the bulldog. "I'd love to adopt a rescue here, but it would complicate things with dog-sitting for the time being." She brightened. "I did come up with a name for my—"

But Chris's head was in the refrigerator. He emerged with a bunch of fresh basil. "You're still planning to dog-sit? You're a land baron now—and a landlord, I might add."

"Much as I appreciate the rent you pay," Arial said, "it doesn't begin to cover the work that needs to be done on both houses, not to mention the garage. Starting with this fumigation. Everything is so expensive, and the only way I can come up with cash is selling this property. Which kind of defeats the purpose."

"It does," Chris said. "You also inherited your grandmother's house back home in Brookhills, didn't you?"

"I did, but my mom is still living there, and I can't very well evict her to sell it."

"And you can't charge her rent—"

"Because she's lived there since I was born," Arial filled in. "And she nearly died there a few months back, if you'll recall."

"There is that," Chris said, coming over to give Beau a scratch. "So you'll still dog-sit at other people's houses despite having a place of your own?"

"Meaning now that I don't need a place to stay?" Arial asked, with a sheepish grin. "Absolutely. When people need to leave their dogs, they prefer to keep them in their own environment if they can. Familiar place, familiar routine."

"Rather than a kennel." Chris got down on the floor with them. "I get that. I don't even like leaving the animals on their own at the practice."

"I noticed," Arial said with a grin at Beau. "I mean, I'm sure there are some fine kennels around here, but not every dog—or cat either—does well in that situation. Back in Wisconsin," she continued, "it was a win-win."

"They had somebody to look after their pets and you had a couch to sleep on."

"Absolutely." She glanced at him and then away.

"You couldn't possibly have been booked every night."

"No, but, like I said, I flopped at my aunt's or a friend's house if I needed to. Anyway, I met a guy the other day delivering bagels and he said—"

"You were delivering bagels?"

"The guy I met was delivering bagels," she said, turning to Beau. "You might want to reconsider your choice of physician. Dr. Buck seems to be being purposely obtuse."

"What do you mean?" Chris gave Beau one last scratch before getting up to wash his hands. "I thought you might have added food delivery to your repertoire."

"Not yet, though I'm not ruling it out either. Anyway, this guy said dog-sitting should be fairly lucrative here. And, by the way," Arial eyed him, "he agreed with you about rents here being high. We have a month-to-month lease. Just how long are you planning to stay? Renting the guest house, I mean."

It was Arial's way of partially rescinding—or at least clarifying—her "welcome to stay as long as you want" of this morning. Chris was still her renter. In the guest house, once it was safe to return to.

"Honestly?" Chris said, taking a fresh spoon to taste the sauce. "As long as I can, before you kick me out. Why? Are you planning to move your bagel guy in?"

"Nah, I got the impression he lives with his folks, which is going to be even cheaper than the rent you pay." Beau hopped off her lap and went to sit at Chris's feet.

"No sauce for you," the veterinarian told the Frenchie. "Bland diet tonight."

Arial stood to wash her own hands. "It's just that my initial idea was to redo the main house to rent and move into the guest house myself."

"Well then, maybe I'll rent the main house from you again. After all, that's where I was before you kicked me into the guest house so you could move in."

"You just come with the property, is that it? Grandfathered in?" Arial cocked her head. "You know, I never thought to ask, but you've obviously had your veterinary practice longer than the ten months or so you've rented here. Where did you live before that?"

Chris glanced around, as if not wanting to be heard.

"Don't forget to check Beau for bugs," Arial suggested. "Beyond fleas, of course."

"No fleas, no ticks, no parasites," Chris assured her. "And no listening devices. I'm more worried about neighbors. The houses aren't very far apart and the walls are thin. I can hear a lot more than I'd like over at Shirley and Frank's." He lifted his eyebrows meaningfully.

Arial didn't ask. Didn't even consider asking. Sex amongst our seniors is best left to the imagination. Or, preferably, not.

"I'm sure you don't have to worry about them now, way over on the other side of the guest house. And as for Emily," she pointed out the back window to the house beyond the alley, "she won't care unless you used the wrong type of lightbulbs, wherever it was you rented."

Nonetheless, Chris grimaced. "You see, that's just it. I have been in PG for five years, but I didn't exactly rent. Or I guess I did rent, just not technically as a living space."

"You slept at your office with the puppies and the kitties," Arial guessed. "And here you said I was weird, sleeping on couches."

"Sleeping on couches when you have a bed available," Chris corrected. "And, for your information, I have a futon in the office."

"Which I'm sure you unfolded each night and made into a bed with the requisite sheets, blankets and pillows?"

"Sometimes," Chris said defensively. "And sometimes I was tired enough that I fell asleep without unfolding it. Watching Netflix. On my phone."

"Well, well," Arial said, trying not to laugh. "We're not so different after all, are we? And now I understand why you feel bad about leaving the animals alone overnight."

"I don't bring all of them home with me," Chris said, picking up Beau. "But Frenchies have breathing problems, so I wanted to keep an eye on this guy post-anesthesia."

"You are a good vet." And man, but Arial didn't say that. "But why don't you want anybody to know? It is your office, after all. You're the boss, aren't you?"

"Yes, I own the practice, but I don't own the building, and I'm fairly certain it's only zoned and insured for business."

"What about other staff?"

"There's just my receptionist, and she goes home at five, while I routinely stay and catch up on things. You know, finish my notes and such."

"And she buys that?" Arial asked dubiously. "Never noticed your toothbrush hanging next to your stethoscope?"

"Hey, good oral hygiene is a twenty-four-hour pursuit," Chris said, grinning. "But no, Lucy wouldn't tell anybody even if she did suspect. And I don't think my landlord would have truly minded either. But knowing might have put him in a tough position with the city if something had happened."

"So it was one of those don't tell, don't ask things."

"Don't ask, don't tell." Having checked out the little bulldog's mouth, Chris set Beau down to skitter across the tile floor to the water dish. "And, yes. People are pretty live-and-let-live here, with a few notable exceptions."

One of whom shared a back alley with Arial.

Watching the little dog slurp and snort his way to the rose pattern on the bottom of the bowl, Arial gasped. "Is that my good china?"

"Oh, I'm sorry," Chris said. "I . . ."

"Messing with you," Arial said, getting up to get a towel to mop up. "I have no good china. So what do you want to drink?"

"I bought a nice bottle of pinot noir. It's on the cabinet if you want to open it."

"No 'nice Chianti'?" Arial said, thinking about her conversation with Shirley.

"Would you prefer Italian?" He glanced out the window at the guest house. "The tent is gone, but I'm not sure I want to go in to retrieve my sangiovese at least until they come back to test tomorrow."

Arial decided it wasn't worth explaining the Hannibal Lecter quote. Nothing like a cannibal to put a damper on dinner. "You left your wine in the house? Is that safe?"

Chris's eyes opened wide. "They said the unopened bottles would be fine."

"What if the poison seeps in? Like through the corks?"

"The corks are covered with foil," Chris said, turning around to face her. "But now you've got me thinking that I don't want to take a chance. I'm going to end up trashing my whole collection."

"I could be wrong." Arial felt terrible for maybe making Chris unnecessarily paranoid about his wine. But then again, she wouldn't want him or anybody else to get sick. "How many bottles do you have in your collection?"

"Three," he said with a wicked grin. "And, quite honestly, two of them were there when I moved in."

"They belonged to the former tenant?" Arial asked. "How old are they?"

"Late nineties. I assumed either Robbie was a wine collector or the bottles had been left behind by your family." He turned up the flame on a kettle of water.

"My mother said they would stay in the guest house when Edna brought her and my aunt Sarah to visit Gretchen when they were little girls."

"There were some odds and ends in the cabinets—maybe your family's, maybe Robbie's, I guess—when I moved in."

"What did you do with them?"

"There was a lot of expired food and broken dishes, so I tossed those. Everything else I boxed up and put it in the back hall closet. I didn't want to throw anything away until you looked at it. It is yours, after all."

Other people's junk. Not Arial's favorite thing. But she appreciated his consideration. "That was nice of you. If I'd known, I'd have gotten somebody to clean up the guest house."

"Before you kicked me out of here to go live there?" Chris gave a good-natured shrug. "It was no problem. I'm just grateful I could stay at all."

Arial was trying to get the timeline straight. "This Robbie was already living in the guest house when you moved into this one?"

"Yes. I moved into this house in June of last year."

"So I was right. In a couple of months it'll be a year," Arial noted.

"This being the first of April, yes," Chris confirmed. "Robbie still had a couple of months on his lease for the guest house, or I honestly would have rented that."

"You would have preferred the smaller one?" So maybe Arial didn't need to feel guilty about kicking him down to the guest house.

Chris flashed her a smile. "It was cheaper, so yeah, I'd have moved there if it was an option. But as you'll recall, Melinda was with me, and she became the driving force behind my move here."

A driving force was an excellent way to describe their half-sister.

Melinda had wanted Chris to rent the Mayes property so they could nose around for answers about the death of Melinda and Arial's father. They'd found them, but that was another story and now, less than a year later, it seemed like a lifetime ago.

In a life that Arial was starting to put behind her.

"But back to wine," she said brightly. "Pinot noir is perfect. And it is what this area is known for, isn't it?" She was rummaging through a drawer for a corkscrew to open the bottle Chris had indicated.

He, too, seemed to welcome a change of subject from family matters. "It is. And this one is from Santa Lucia Highlands, which is one of my favorite areas."

"You'll have to show me . . ." Arial started and then stopped, cork halfway out of the bottle. "I mean you don't have to. I—"

"I want to," Chris said. "We're family, after all."

"But we're not."

"Then extended family. And family is a good thing."

"Not my family, except for my aunt Sarah," she said. "You've met them."

"I thought you said you and your mother were doing better." He dropped the pasta in the now boiling water.

"Let's say we're a work in progress." She took two large wine goblets from the cabinet, one pinging as she accidentally tapped it on the edge of the door. "You know, I kidded about the china, but my great-grandmother did have some nice crystal and such. It's a miracle it survived."

"I think all the really good things were packed away when Gretchen died," Chris said. "I helped Catherine unpack some of it for you before you arrived."

Catherine Smythe was the real-estate agent who had managed the property.

"That was kind of you," Arial said, coming to the table with the glasses and bottle, as Chris went to drain the pasta. "That can't be cooked already."

"Sure, it's fresh angel hair, so it only takes a minute."

"Please don't tell me you made it yourself." Arial didn't pride herself on her cooking prowess, but still, a man should only be so perfect. Especially if he was just related enough to make things uncomfortable.

"What? You don't make your own pasta?"

"I've often thought about it." Along with many other things, like building her own house or performing brain surgery. "Flour, eggs, olive oil—all things I keep on hand."

He turned with a cup of the reserved pasta water in his hand. "After three days, I can attest that you have none of those things here. In fact, when I made the sauce, I had to fish the olive oil from the box of cupboard items I brought from the guest house."

"I haven't had time to shop," she said in her own defense. "I do try to keep pasta on hand, just not things for *making* pasta." Or making much of anything else. In fact, her go-to meal was penne (store-bought) and peas (frozen), tossed with olive oil and red pepper flakes (dehydrated). Which meant that, "I do, too, have olive oil. It's right . . ." She swung open the cabinet door. "Hmm, maybe I put it in the refrigerator. Yes, here it is."

She pulled the bottle triumphantly out of the fridge and frowned. "It's a little cloudy, maybe it has to warm up."

"Olive oil shouldn't be stored in the refrigerator."

Arial frowned at the label. "It says cool, dark place."

"I think the next words you'll find on the bottle are 'do not refrigerate' and maybe even 'do not freeze,' for those really intent on maximizing its shelf life. And just for the record," he reached past her to pluck a tall green jar from the refrigerator shelf and hold it up, "this is not real cheese."

Arial grabbed it back. "You can denigrate my method of storing olive oil, but I'll defend with my life my grated cheese. The perfect food—never clumps, never gets stringy."

"Because it doesn't melt," Chris said mildly and turned back to the pasta. "And the answer is no."

Either she'd lost the thread or he had. "No?"

"No. Much as I, like you, have thought about making pasta, I have not." He was tossing the angel hair with his red sauce. "Bought this at the farmer's market this morning."

That was a relief at least. And Arial counted shopping as one of her greatest talents. "I love a good farmer's market, assuming they have all locally grown produce. Where is it?"

"This one was in Carmel-by-the-Sea, but there's a market every day of the week somewhere on the peninsula. Right here in Pacific Grove, downtown Monterey, Carmel, Seaside, Del Monte, Carmel Valley. And everything is local because we are right next to the Salinas Valley, which is the salad bowl of the world." He added a touch of pasta water to the angel hair and tossed it one last time before plating.

Realizing food was imminent, Arial poured the wine and sat down.

"I'd love to go sometime." Damn it, she was doing it again. "I mean if you just tell me what days it's where, I can . . ."

"I would love to take you," Chris said, turning with two plates of pasta in his hands. "No strings attached."

"Thank you," Arial said, feeling a little ashamed. "That's nice of you. As is making dinner."

"What can I say?" Chris slid one plate in front of her and sat down with the other. "We tend to be nice here."

"You are," Arial said, studying his face. "I mean people here in general."

"Of course, that's what you mean." He raised his glass. "To nice."

Arial raised hers. "And to family. Extended or not. Now can you pass me my cheese, please?"

The air in the guest house tested safe on Friday, but it wasn't until Saturday afternoon that Arial and Chris started to move his furniture and clothes back in.

"Do you have office hours every Saturday?" she asked, shuffling across the yard under the weight of her end of the sofa.

"No, but people call and . . ." He shrugged as he backed across to the front porch steps of the guest house.

"Probably was a lot easier to work weekends when you slept in the office," Arial teased.

Chris threw her a warning look. "Shh."

She grinned but relented. "Should we set this down so you can open the door?"

But Chris apparently had planned ahead.

"No need. I left the door ajar this morning before I went to the clinic to let out any residual killer toxins while I was away." He gave the door a backward shove with the sole of his shoe.

It didn't budge.

"Maybe the wind closed it," Arial suggested. "Or the killer toxins wanted privacy."

Chris groaned. "OK, let me set down my end."

As Arial tried not to drop hers, Chris turned the knob and swung open the door into the living room before reclaiming his. "OK, in we go."

"Where do you want to place it?" Arial asked, following him up the steps. "I was thinking—"

"Just here on this front wall," Chris's voice said from inside.

"But that's where it was." She made a face that she knew he couldn't see. "Why don't we create a conversation area with a couple of chairs? You know, shake things up a bit."

"Nope. It has to be on this wall because it's best for seeing the TV." He was well into the living room now. "Just follow me in and then swing left when you clear the door so I can bring the end around."

"This door jamb is a little tight," Arial said, giving the couch a shove. "You sure this is the way you brought it out?"

"Yes, I'm sure. The termite guys helped me, though, and they're—"

"Stronger than I am?" Arial asked as she cleared the door. "I agree. In fact, I'm losing my . . . oops." The couch hit the floor. ". . . Grip. Sorry."

"It's your couch and your cottage," Chris said, setting his end down a little more gently than she had. "But I think you might have cracked that floorboard." He pointed.

"Oh, dear," Arial said, shoving the couch a little further to one side so she could bend down and inspect the floor. "It is kind of dented, isn't it? And you're right; there's a crack." She straightened up. "The fumigation guys said the floor was mushy, but I thought he was exaggerating."

"Mushy?" Chris repeated, coming over to check. "Do you think you might have mentioned that before we—"

CRACK. Chris stopped, one foot still in the air.

Arial's eyes were wide. "Is there a basement under here?"

"Very few basements in California—not like in the Midwest." Chris was whispering like his voice might crack the floor further. "But there is a crawl space. Maybe three or four feet high?"

High enough to break a leg if Chris fell through. Arial backed away from the now visibly bowed section of pine planks.

"You're leaving me?" Chris squeaked.

"No, I'm just going to come around and help you," she said, edging along the wall to Chris's side of the room.

"Help me how?" His planted leg was starting to tremble. "I'm thinking if I put my other foot down gently and slide sideways."

"Gotcha!" Arial grabbed his arm and pulled.

"Wait!" Chris's other foot went down not so gently, but Arial's yank combined with their weight took them down and away from the potential abyss.

"You OK?" Arial mumbled from under Chris's body on the floor.

He pushed himself up on his palms to regard her. "I think my less aggressive plan would have worked, but probably not half as much fun."

"Only fun for the guy on top," Arial said. "Ouch."

"OK, maybe not so much fun," Chris said, rolling off her, "as . . . exciting?"

"That, I'll grant you." Even as she said it, Arial pulled him back down.

Chris looked surprised. "I thought you didn't—"

"I don't." She slid out from under him to sit up herself. "Look."

He twisted to see the floorboards broken away and hanging not two feet from where they lay. "Mushy, huh?"

Arial shrugged. "I thought the guy was just trying to sell me his service. You know, he's both the inspector who tells me there's damage and also the one who can fix it."

"You have trust issues."

He didn't know the half of it.

Still on his rump, Chris edged closer to the abyss, pulling out his phone.

"That's smart," Arial said. "Take pictures to document this, and I can send them to—"

"The company you wouldn't let fix the problem they informed you about," Chris said. "Good idea."

"The insurance company." Happily, her aunt Sarah, a real-estate agent in Wisconsin, had made sure not only that the taxes were paid but that the property was fully insured before Arial had taken possession of it.

"Also, a good idea." Chris had shoved the couch back and was shining the light from his phone into the hole. "But you may have something else to worry about."

"What's down there?" Arial scuttled closer. "Please don't tell me some poor animal got asphyxiated during the tenting."

"Logically, I'd say a hard no," Chris said, holding up his hand. "But you might not want to—"

Arial ignored him, pushing forward to hang over the edge with him. "I can't see—wow, it's all sand under here. What is all that? Was somebody using the crawl space as storage? Why would you do that, with just a sand floor?" She glanced back at him.

"Don't look at me," Chris protested. "I don't have enough to fill the house, much less overflow to the crawl space. But I think you're missing the—"

"I might not miss it if you hold the light steady already."

"I—"

"Well, I have to be able to see," Arial persisted, taking the phone from his hand and angling the light through the opening. "There are clothes and a shoe . . . Oh."

"Oh," Chris echoed.

She sat up to face him, her face white. "There's a foot in the shoe."

SIX

"It looks like an entire body." Arial had called 9-1-1, and now they were both on their stomachs, peering through the hole. "I'm surprised animals didn't take it apart."

"Partially skeletonized," the veterinarian assessed. "So it's been here for a while."

"But not *old* old."

Chris swiveled his head to squint at her.

"I mean, Shirley told me about all the different settlers and the indigenous people before them. I'm just saying it isn't an ancient burial ground or anything."

"You've deduced that because there's a sneaker on that foot?"

Arial sat up. "I do realize the sneaker makes 'ancient' implausible, but can you confirm that—to your knowledge—this should be the only body we find under here?"

"What would I know?" Chris said, shrugging. "It's your family that lived here for generations."

He had a point. "Maybe that's why my great-grandmother left the property in trust to me," Arial said.

"So she didn't have to disclose the random body in the listing contract?" Chris asked facetiously, and then shook his head. "I doubt that whoever this is was here before your great-grandmother died. Was that ten years ago?"

"A little over," Arial confirmed. "The property was held in trust until I turned twenty-five this past year."

"Yeah, it hasn't been down here a decade," Chris said, taking another look before he sat up. "But discoveries like this could have an effect on any sale and renovation plans you have."

Arial gestured to the corpse. "Not to be insensitive or anything."

"I'm just saying," Chris continued pedantically, "that a buddy of mine had to stop construction on his house in

Monterey because they found the legless lizard on the property, and it's endangered."

"Legless lizards?" Arial repeated. "You mean a snake?"

"No, they . . . well, yeah, they could be mistaken for a snake."

But apparently not by nature boy here. "You say not a decade. So how long would it take for a body to become partially skeletonized, as you put it?"

The veterinarian shrugged. "A year? Six months? Hard to say. Most of the time it would be dry and cool under here. And then there's the sand. Animals don't seem to have gotten to it, as you said, at least nothing big enough to carry body parts away."

"So . . . your best guess?"

A shrug. "Somebody a lot smarter than me will have to tell you."

She patted his hand. "You're smart. You know all about legless lizards."

"I do." He suppressed a smile.

"So, Mr. Know-It-All, what *do* we know about this body? Besides that it's wearing sneakers?"

"And jeans. Denim does hold up well, doesn't it?" He adjusted his position so he could see further into the hole. "I can't tell what they're wearing above the waist."

"Can you see how long the hair is? Not that it'll necessarily tell us anything. Doesn't it continue to grow after death? Like fingernails?"

Chris sat up. "Should I be worried that you are so informed—or misinformed, in this case—about death?"

"Particularly because we're hovering over a body dump? Or is it because my family has a history of killer women?"

"And not killer in the good sense."

Arial grinned. "You know, it's situations like this when you realize how easy it would be. All I'd have to do is hit you over the head and give you a shove."

Chris didn't seem concerned. "The doing is easy; it's the 'not getting caught' that's tricky."

"I certainly wouldn't have called the police if I was going

to add you to the body count," Arial admitted as sirens ramped up in the distance. "Now what were you saying about my being misinformed?"

"Hair and fingernails. They don't grow after death. The skin and soft tissues shrink, giving that appearance."

Well, that was disappointing. Arial stuck her head back into the hole. "I can't see the hair anyway. Maybe an animal took it for nesting—like a squirrel or possum."

"More likely rats or mice. Possums find a hollow and then line it with leaves and twigs. And, turnabout, it's birds that like to use discarded possum fur to line their nests. In fact, possums are beneficial in a lot of ways—shy, generally peaceful, and more likely to play dead than fight. Or even when they're startled. Hence the expression 'playing possum.'"

Dr. Doolittle said all this with his head back in the hole.

"You said the last tenant in the guest house before you was this Robbie?"

Chris pushed himself up on his elbows. "Henry. You're thinking he took a wrong turn on his way out the door?"

"Of course not," she said, as the sirens got close. "Whoever it is, somebody obviously put him in here. When was the last time you saw Robbie?"

"I honestly can't remember." Chris sat up. "You're assuming the man was murdered?"

"Of course." Arial sat up to face him. "The body has been here more than a few days, so the extermination was a fluke that allowed us to find him, not the cause of death. At some time—which, you're right, smarter people will have to tell us when—either he crawled under the house and inexplicably died . . ."

"Or somebody killed him and shoved him under."

"I know which my money is on." She pulled out her little flashlight and beckoned him to look. Because the light was less diffused than that of Chris's phone, the contrast in the sand was more visible.

Chris followed her gaze. "Drag marks."

"There must be an opening to the crawl space from the backyard," Arial said, getting up. "You meet the police, and I'll go see."

"Be careful where you walk," Chris warned as Arial skirted the hole. "There may be other weak parts. And as the owner, don't you think you should be the one who—"

But Arial was already out the front door and circling the house as the squads pulled up out front, sirens fading. Once the police took over the scene, she knew there would be no opportunity—at least short-term—for poking around.

Out of sight, Arial slowed down. The guest house backed up to the property's garage, with the guest house facing the street and the garage facing the alley. Given that Gretchen had told Shirley the guest house predated the main house's 1911 build date, it made sense that both the garage and guest house had been built around the same time, though left as separate structures mere yards apart. Attached garages probably weren't in vogue at the time.

The walkway between the two buildings provided privacy for Arial as she poked about, as they would have for somebody, say, stuffing a body under the foundation. The space was made even narrower by the overgrown bushes planted along the house's foundation up to a set of concrete steps and the back door. But no obvious access to the crawl space, and she couldn't quite place the scent in the air.

As Arial hesitated, trying to square what they'd seen inside with the outside dimensions, she heard the radios and the sound of voices coming closer.

Taking her best guess, Arial pushed between two bushes about two yards to her side of the back door and spotted a section of latticework backed with rusted wire mesh over a two-foot wide by three-foot high opening.

Most of the screws intended to hold the lattice in place seemed to be missing or hanging loose. Arial would blame it on the exterminators if the body in the crawl space didn't prove they had never checked the space for woodland critters as they'd said.

So how long had it been like this?

"Piece of cake to drag a body from the house to here," she murmured to herself, trying to see inside the crawl space without using the flashlight and giving herself away to the officers she had to assume were inside the house. "Just prop the lattice back up and who's the wiser?"

"You apparently."

The voice made Arial jump, but it was also familiar.

"Sergeant Dan," she said, straightening. "Are you with the Pacific Grove police force now?" Dan Sotherly had been with the nearby Sand City police when Arial met him on her first visit to Monterey.

"I am," Dan acknowledged. "I grew up in Pacific Grove, so when a position opened, I jumped at it."

"A detective position," she said, taking in his plain clothes and badge. "Congratulations!"

"Thank you. And, by the looks of it, just in time. You weren't about to go messing around a potential crime scene, were you?"

"Heavens no," Arial said, backing out of the space between the bushes. "I . . . well, we saw the drag marks, and I assumed there had to be an entrance here."

"Dr. Buck told us about the drag marks and showed us where the body was," Dan said. "All from the doorway of the house, so as not to disturb the crime scene."

"I figured I'd be asked where the access was and that I should know." She lifted her shoulders. "Being the owner and all."

Dan had pushed aside the branches. "Rosemary."

"Rose . . . Oh, the plants," Arial said, sniffing her hands. "I knew I recognized the smell."

"Hard to miss," Dan said, leaning down to peer into the space. "And much more pleasant than decomposition, though it's likely this body stopped smelling a while ago."

"How long would that take?" she asked, maybe a little too eagerly.

Yup, too eager. Dan's eyes narrowed, but his words pretty much echoed Chris's. "Depends on the conditions, I would think, but the coroner will tell us more. And, for the record, it's not drag marks until crime scene says it is. And even then, it's not for public consumption. Remember, this is somebody's father or mother, son or daughter."

So they weren't making a guess at gender yet either. "Um, Chris—Dr. Buck—was staying in the main house while the cottage was being fumigated. We were just moving him back in. He told you about that? The fumigation, I mean?"

There went the babbling again.

"He did," Dan said. "But I don't think the termite fumigation has any bearing."

"I know, but it was the termites that caused the floor to cave in. Who knows how much longer he"—she glanced at the detective—"or she might have been down there otherwise."

"True," Dan said. "And, like I told Dr. Buck, you can stay in the main house. Just honor the crime scene tape, and don't go poking around here."

"Of course," Arial said.

The detective waved to a uniformed officer coming around the side. "I'm going to have Officer Norris—"

"Oh, is that Ned Norris?" Arial asked, stepping around Dan to see the young officer.

Arial had met Ned with Dan about six months ago. She'd flown out to Monterey to inspect her new inheritance with her aunt Sarah and Maggy Thorsen, Sarah's partner in their Wisconsin coffee house, Uncommon Grounds. Unsurprisingly, the first thing on Sarah and Maggy's agenda in a new city was to track down a good cup of coffee. They'd found it at Acme Coffee Roasting, along with Dan, Ned, and an assortment of other happily caffeinating locals.

"Officer Norris came over to the PG department at the same time I did," Dan told her. "He'll take a preliminary statement from you and crime scene will be here for as long as their job requires. Meanwhile, I have another investigation—"

"Oh," Arial said as Ned Norris joined them. "The robbery in the Beach District? I heard it's part of a series of burglaries?"

"Beach Tract," Norris corrected, giving her a hello smile. "But, yes. Five of them now, spread over the last year."

"With the last occurring on Ocean View just this past week," Arial said to Ned, as Dan moved away. "I was walking Tuesday morning and heard the sirens."

"You must have been walking early then," the blond officer said, flipping open a notebook. "We were called out just after six, as I recall."

"It was early," Arial said. "And before you say anything, I've already been chastised for walking alone in the dark."

"Wasn't going to chastise you," Ned said. "Just be careful."

"I am—or I will be in the future. Got my whistle." She held up the whistle/light combo. "But then this happens—a body right here under my rental house." She hesitated, brow furrowed as she tried to pull up a memory.

"Just shows crime can happen anywhere," Ned said, not seeming to notice her preoccupation as Chris joined them. "And we don't know this was a crime. This poor guy may have just crawled under there and died. Whatever it was, though, looks like it happened well before you got here, Arial. That was what? A month ago?"

"Yes, March first," Arial said, glancing back up to see Ned writing it down. "Then how long has the body been down there? I mean, it has to have been there before Chris moved in."

"And how long has that been?" Ned asked, turning to the veterinarian.

"That I moved into the guest house? Just before Arial got here, so maybe five weeks?"

"But Chris rented the main house before that," Arial informed Ned.

"Ten months ago," Chris said, watching Ned write. "June of last year."

"And you never saw anything?"

"Certainly not bodies being shuffled under the guest house next door." Chris glanced at Arial, obviously uncomfortable with being questioned. "But there was a guy renting the place at the time, so you might want to ask him."

"You have his contact information?" Ned looked expectantly at Chris.

"You should ask Catherine Smythe, the rental agent," Arial interjected. "Since neither Chris nor I was here at the time the lease was signed."

Chris threw her a grateful look as a van pulled up in front.

Ned caught the movement. "Crime scene is here, but I may have more questions later."

"We'll be at the main house," Arial said.

"Is that new?" Ned asked as a man and woman got out of a van and proceeded to pull on white coveralls. "I mean, you two being a couple?"

"We're not," they chorused.

Not that it was anybody's business. "I let Chris sleep on my couch while the fumigation went on," Arial explained, nonetheless. "It was my responsibility to provide lodging as his landlord."

"Looks like it's going to be a bit longer," Ned said, making one last note before closing his notebook.

"Make sure you're careful if you walk in there," Arial warned. "The floor is mushy."

"Termite damage," Chris explained.

"We'll be careful," Ned said. "Now if you two will move back to the other house, I'm going to get these guys going."

"Of course," Chris said, turning.

But Arial stood for a moment, staring at the crawl space opening as the officer briefed the crime scene team.

"Are you thinking you left DNA on the rosemary bushes?" Chris's voice asked in her ear. "And here I thought I was the one being paranoid."

"What? No, I was wondering . . . You said the last tenant was Henry. Did you mean his last name?"

"Of course," he said studying her. "You already knew his first name was Robbie. Why do you ask?"

"Robbie Henry." And she'd just met Aaron Henry. Could that be a coincidence?

SEVEN

"Coincidence? Of course it's a coincidence," Chris told her as they stood on her back porch watching the crime scene folks. "You live in a small town. You have to get used to people being related in some way or another. Siblings, kids, parents, cousins, exes. Besides, why are you assuming the body is Robbie Henry? It's far more likely that Robbie moved away and somebody else—maybe somebody homeless—crawled under there, like the officer said."

"And died? And I'll remind you of the drag marks."

"Or crawl marks."

Arial couldn't see the crawl space entrance from where they were, so now she was hanging over the rail to get a better perspective. "Do you think they're still in there? I suppose they could have taken the body out the other side—closer to Shirley's house—but then wouldn't we have seen them out front?" She nodded to the windowless coroner's van that had joined the crime scene vehicle on the street.

"You could call Shirley," Chris suggested dryly. "Set up a drum signal so she can let you know if they make a break for it out the other side."

"Funny, but Shirley's Prius isn't here. She must be gone, or she'd be calling me."

"Anyway, what I meant was drag marks or crawl marks—could we really tell the difference? Officer Norris is probably right that this could be a natural—or at least accidental—death. Nothing sinister, just somebody hurt or sick who crawled under the house for shelter."

"Instead of coming to any of the houses around here for help?" Arial asked. "And did you notice Ned used the word 'guy'? I bet they know it's a male but aren't ready to say so yet."

"What I do notice is that you're on a first-name basis with

the cops—Dan, Ned—and meanwhile, they're practically asking me for my whereabouts."

"I think Ned actually did ask," Arial said, grinning. "I mean, best he could without knowing the time and date of death. You were likely living right here next door." She shrugged. "And heard nothing."

Chris rubbed his chin. "You're messing with me, right? There's no way the police can think I was involved in this death."

Arial liked getting under Chris's skin—his being so self-possessed and all—but now she relented. "Listen, they don't know anything at this point: not when he died, not how he died, not even if he's a 'he,' if we can believe them. The questions the police are asking you are routine, and the only reason they're not asking me where I was is that I've only lived here a month."

"I suppose," Chris said reluctantly. "But back to why somebody would hide rather than go to one of the houses around here, I was thinking. Maybe he was high or involved in something criminal."

That got Arial's attention. "Criminal, like the burglaries maybe? Ned said they started around a year ago, which could fit."

"But they obviously didn't stop when this guy died," Chris said. "And let me just state now that you're on your own if you want to breach the police tape to search for the loot."

"I would think the police would do that, wouldn't—"

"Helloooo," a voice called.

They turned to see Emily emerging from Arial's own back door onto the porch where they were standing.

"Forgive me," her neighbor said. "I rang the doorbell, but nobody answered."

"So you came in anyway?" Arial was feeling more violated about her neighbor's intrusion than she probably should be, considering the dead body under her other house.

But at least Emily had the grace to be embarrassed. "Sorry, but I heard the sirens and then I saw you out here from Dickie's window when I put Casper down for his nap." She held up a receiver for a baby monitor.

"Don't you mean when you put Dickie down for a nap?" Arial asked, glancing sideways at Chris.

He shook his head and put a finger to his lips.

"Oh, no," her neighbor was saying. "Dickie is four and has made it perfectly clear that he's done with naps. He's off on a play date."

Arial glanced across the alley to the back of Emily's house, wanting badly to ask more about Emily's relationship with her second, furrier child.

But then, Emily's house—or at least the backyard—looked to be well-tended with drought-resistant plantings. And yellow lights. In contrast, Arial's own house was wood frame with peeling paint and cops crawling all over it. Or at least crawling all over the guest house, which had a sinkhole in the living room and a body in the crawl space, to boot.

Best to mind her own dysfunctional business.

"The front door was unlocked, and I could hear you back here," Emily was saying, taking out her phone. "I just walked through and didn't look at a thing, I promise."

Arial didn't believe her, and now the woman had her phone up and was hanging over the porch rail. "What are you doing?"

"Just trying to get a shot—"

"Uh-uh." Shirley had come around from the front yard and managed to snag the phone from Emily's hand as she passed her to mount the porch steps. "No posting from here."

So that was why Emily was paying this neighborly visit. "Couldn't see anything from your house?" Arial asked mildly. "Or the alley?"

"Your garage is in the way." Emily snatched her phone back from Shirley, who was scrolling through her photos. "Though it's not much better from here, I have to admit."

"Why didn't you just walk right into the guest house?" Arial suggested. "Like you did here?"

Emily grimaced. "I tried, but that nice young officer stopped me."

Chalk one up for Ned.

"Not much to see in front, just crime scene tape and the

coroner's van where I usually park," Shirley said. "Which is why I walked *around* your house to see what you knew."

She turned to Emily. "And for the record, if you ring our doorbell and we don't answer, it's because we don't want to talk to you. Don't even think about snooping around my house."

Emily sniffed. "I wasn't snooping. I was worried."

Shirley turned to Arial. "And as for you, lock your doors."

"We've never had to lock our doors," Emily said, settling on one of the two chairs of the patio table set. "But in this day and age . . ." She shivered.

"Strange women walking straight into homes, I hear." Chris had been standing by quietly until now.

Emily blushed. "Anyway, I am sorry. But just what is going on?"

"Don't tell her," Shirley said. "She'll just post it."

Emily's chin went up. "You can't blame people for wanting to know what's happening practically in their own backyards."

"Yes, I can." Shirley collapsed in the other seat. "And for the record, I did go into my own backyard and couldn't quite make out the deal. They're at the back of the guest house?"

"And inside." Arial bit her lip. Dan had asked her specifically not to mention the drag marks, but the facts would be public soon enough. Probably already were. "There's a body in the crawl space under the guest house."

"Oh, no," Emily said. "A human body?"

"I don't think they call out this kind of manpower for a squirrel," Shirley retorted. "Who is it? How did they find it?"

"Did it smell?" Emily's eyes were wide and unblinking.

Arial glanced uncertainly at her and then turned back to the normal people. "Chris and I found it."

"You went crawling under the house?" Emily asked, her nose wrinkling. "And right after a fumigation? Ugh."

That did give Arial pause, but she shook it off. "No, we didn't go crawling under the house." Arial turned to Shirley. "Remember when I told you that the termite guy said there was a problem with the floor?"

"He said it was mushy, right?"

Arial glanced apologetically at her tenant. "I didn't believe it."

"So you said," Chris said, going to the door of the house. "Anybody want something to drink?"

"A lemonade would be lovely," Emily said. "Or an iced tea."

"I have water," Arial said. "Tap or tap."

"Tap would be lovely," Emily chanted.

Shirley rolled her eyes and turned back to Arial. "You were saying about the floor?"

"Turns out that mushy was an understatement. When we carried Chris's couch in," Arial purposely neglected to mention she'd dropped the thing, "the floor collapsed."

"Oh, my God," Emily said. "Did you fall onto the body? Was it all yucky and disgusting like on TV? You've showered, haven't you?"

Arial was starting to appreciate that her own habit of nervous babbling might be annoying. "Neither of us fell onto it. But the hole was big enough that we could see down into the crawl space under the house."

"You're telling us the floor just happened to break through, and there it was?" Shirley asked incredulously.

"But how did it get there?" Emily asked.

"I checked the entrance to the crawl space." Arial pointed to the back of the guest house. "The lattice hadn't been fastened over the opening. It was just leaning there."

"The exterminators?" Shirley guessed.

"Maybe," Arial said. "The main termite guy—Kenny, I think it was—said they check for animals, but I find that hard to believe under the circumstances."

Shirley pursed her lips. "They probably just stick their heads in and make noise. If something doesn't run out, they assume it's clear."

"That's a terrible assumption," Chris said, coming back with a tray of four glasses of water. Tap. He set the tray on the table. "A frightened animal is much more likely to hide than to run out in the direction of the noise."

"Or a frightened human," Emily said. "Do they think this person was killed by the chemicals?"

"No," Chris and Arial said in unison. All they needed was for that particular rumor to make the rounds.

"Whoever it is has been dead for quite a while," Chris added.

"Partially skeletonized," Arial added. "Isn't that what you said, Chris?"

"I did. Not that I'm an expert." He picked up a glass and took it to the corner of the porch closest to the guest house.

"Have they brought it out?" Emily asked breathlessly, joining him. "Or is that what they're doing now?" Her tone said she hoped so.

"They could also go out the opposite direction, toward our house," Shirley said sourly. "If you'd like to set up a camera there."

Emily seemed ready to take her up on that. "I . . . oh, never mind."

Arial was thinking. "Maybe they could lift it through the floor if the opening is wide enough. Or they could widen it."

"I'm not sure they'll risk the weight of his body—and the technicians—on that floor," Chris pointed out.

"You said 'his body,'" Emily said. "Do you know it's a man?"

"No, not from what we were able to see." And even if Arial were dead certain, she wouldn't share it with Emily.

"Did you take photos?" Emily asked, and they all turned to look at her. "I'm just thinking that you two haven't lived here long, but Shirley and I have. Maybe we'd recognize him. Or her."

"No photos," Arial said stonily. To be honest, she had thought that maybe she and Chris should have snapped a couple, but that was more for . . . research purposes? Being able to examine what was left of the clothes or whatever. Emily's interest somehow seemed almost voyeuristic.

Or maybe Arial was just making excuses for herself, but not for her neighbor.

"Were there clothes?" Emily continued, like she'd read Arial's mind. And then a thought seemed to strike, the freckles on her nose standing out against the sudden pallor of her face. "Oh. Could it have been a sexual assault?"

Now Arial felt sick. She'd never considered that. Maybe

because there were still jeans, at least, on the body. And she'd been assuming it was a man.

Shirley threw her friend a concerned glance and then turned on Emily. "Leave it to you to make a bad situation worse. How about we wait to see what the facts are?"

"But how long will that be?" Emily asked, turning to Chris. "How can you even think of living there without knowing what went on under that house?" She shuddered.

Arial opened her mouth to reply, but Chris held up a hand. "I'll be fine. And Shirley is right. We just have to wait until the police have an identity and cause of death, and that may take a while."

"That bad?" Those big eager eyes again.

"Chris did say the body was 'skeletonized,'" Shirley reminded her. "They'll probably have to do DNA, dental records—see if they can match it to any known missing persons."

Meanwhile, Arial escaped to the table to get a glass of water and compose herself. She didn't want Emily to get into her head, and she certainly didn't want to let her know that Chris was staying with her. Or that, too, would be all over the neighborhood.

Returning to the group, Arial set her glass on the porch rail and turned to Emily. "Since you have lived here quite a while, did you know the previous tenant?"

"Of the guest house?" Emily asked. "There was only one I knew before Chris—Robbie Henry. He rented the guest house maybe three years ago."

"Was it just Robbie?" Arial asked. "No wife or kids?"

"Robbie is divorced," Shirley told her. "He moved into the place after he and Simone split."

"Do Robbie and Simone have a son?" Arial asked. "An *Aaron* Henry?"

"Yes, my youngest sister went to school with Aaron," Emily said. "And I have to tell you, I always thought he was a troublemaker. Why are you asking? Do you think he killed whoever it is?"

Wow, Emily really didn't like the guy. "No. It's just that I met Aaron a few days ago and thought he was very nice. I didn't realize at the time that his father had rented the guest house."

"Robbie and Simone lived a few blocks away before they divorced," Shirley said. "She got remarried to Charles—"

"Rowan," Emily supplied eagerly. "I told you, didn't I, that it was their house that was robbed Tuesday?"

She had. "So Robbie lived here after the divorce, and then where did he go?"

"Sacramento, I heard," Emily said, lifting her chin. "His mother's health isn't good."

"We're sure he got there?" Arial pressed.

Shirley eyed her. "You mean, instead of crawling under the foundation to die? I think somebody would have noticed, don't you?"

"I'm not so sure," Emily said. "Simone and Robbie don't talk. And God knows about Aaron."

"Surely Robbie's mother would have notified them if he didn't show up," Chris pointed out.

"Assuming she's in good enough health," Arial mused. "But have either you, Emily, or Shirley been in contact with Robbie since he left?"

The two women exchanged looks. "I certainly haven't," Emily said. "You, Shirley?"

"No, but maybe Frank has," Shirley said. "I can ask him."

"Would you?" Arial asked.

Emily's lips pursed. "You said you liked Aaron. Why don't you ask him? Or Simone?"

"I'd talk to Catherine Smythe, Arial, like you suggested to the police," Chris said. "As the rental agent, Catherine should know his last month of tenancy and have a forwarding address."

"Genius," Arial said.

"It was your idea originally," Chris pointed out.

"And like I said, I'm genius." Arial lifted her glass to clink with him.

"Don't get your hopes up," Shirley said sourly. "Tenants come and go. As long as the rent is paid, who would notice?"

EIGHT

"For the record," Arial told Chris after Emily and Shirley gave up the death watch—the former to get the dog up from his nap and the latter to make a late lunch. "I'd notice if you died under the house."

"Thanks. Back at you."

Arial waited a beat. "The Pomeranian takes naps?"

Chris dipped his head. "Wouldn't you, if it meant a few hours without Emily yapping at you?"

"Smart dogs, Pomeranians," Arial said gravely.

They had changed their viewing position, moving down from the porch to the backyard in order to get a better angle of the back of the guest house. It was Arial's property, after all, and they were well away from the forensic team working in the crawl space.

Arial's arms were crossed tightly over her chest again, like they had been when the exterminators were setting up. Chris stood next to her, thumbs hooked on his jean pockets, his expression unreadable. The air still held the scent of rosemary, plus maybe disinfectants and something else Arial couldn't place. Inside, they could hear voices but not make out any words as the technicians went about their jobs.

Floodlights had been set up inside the crawl space and they could see shadows shift and stretch as the forensic team moved the remains closer to the opening.

Arial shivered, despite the late afternoon sun. "It's surreal, isn't it?"

Chris nodded slowly. "You think you're ready for something like this until you see it in person."

"More drag marks," Arial said softly, as the body, now wrapped in a blue bag, was pulled from the crawl space. "I hope they took photos before they trampled all over the ones we saw."

"I don't think it's their first rodeo," Chris said as the technicians lifted the body gently onto a gurney and secured it with straps. Their movements were careful, almost reverent, and Arial couldn't help but contrast them with whoever had dumped a human being under the floorboards.

Dan hadn't returned, but another detective approached them, flipping a small notepad closed. "We'll transport the remains to the coroner's office. They'll start the identification process, but it might take time, given the condition of the remains."

Arial nodded. "How long do you think he . . . or she has been down there?"

The detective's face was carefully neutral. "Hard to say. The environment under the house could have slowed decomposition, but we'll know more after the autopsy." He glanced at Chris. "I assume neither of you will be going anywhere?"

A squeak emerged from the veterinarian's throat. He cleared it. "No, we're both locals."

Arial glanced at him as the detective followed the gurney to the waiting coroner's van. "I'm a local?"

"You are now." He turned to face her. "Did you notice he was looking at me when he asked that? I don't suppose you know this guy personally, too? Maybe you can put in a good word for me."

"Sorry, no," Arial said. "But remember. You're already a respected member of the—"

The sound of the rear door of the van clicking shut made them jump.

"Guess we're both a little on edge," Chris said sheepishly.

Arial watched as one of the technicians stepped out of her coveralls and bundled them into a hazardous waste bin before climbing into the coroner's van. "And to think I made you move into the guest house."

"You're telling me." Chris glanced at her, his expression softening. "Neither of us could have known. Whoever put that body there didn't expect it to be found."

"And yet, here we are, thanks to a fluke. I suppose we should be grateful to the termites. God knows how long you might have lived above . . . him or her."

"And you, next door," Chris said. "Let's just hope they find out who it is. They deserve that much."

"They do." The van pulled away, leaving only one technician and two uniformed officers behind. Arial turned to Chris. "What do we do now?"

Chris offered a small, wry smile. "Maybe call your insurance company about that floor?"

Arial couldn't help but laugh. "Yeah, because that's the real nightmare here."

With a glance toward the crawl space where the technician had disappeared again, presumably still processing the scene, Arial sighed. "I think I'd like a glass of wine, if we still have some from dinner the other night."

"We do," Chris said, leading them back to the main house.

While Arial retrieved the bottle of wine, Chris took two glasses out of the kitchen cabinet. "Want to sit outside or in?"

"I'm torn between wanting to see what's going on and my certainty that Emily and little Dickie are probably at the window watching. She's a bit of a ghoul, isn't she? I wouldn't have expected it."

"Because you're a bit of a ghoul, too?" He waved for her to follow him to the living room. "If we sit on the couch, we can keep watch out front and see when they leave."

"If they leave," Arial said, waiting for Chris to set down the glasses on the coffee table before pouring them each a glass of wine. "I know it's only three thirty, but it seems much later."

"It does," Chris said, checking his phone. "I guess I could go back to the clinic."

"Don't you dare abandon me," Arial warned.

"I won't," Chris said, taking his glass before sinking onto the couch. "And I certainly can't after I drink this."

"No drinking and veterinary-ing?" Arial asked, settling next to him.

"Absolutely not, even if I were to walk there."

Arial cocked her head. "You always walk. It's like two blocks away."

"Unless I have an appointment or house call that day." Chris took a sip of wine before setting the glass down.

"You make house calls."

"Kind of have to with horses and such," Chris pointed out. "Hard to fit in a Prius or Tesla."

They did seem to be the cars of choice around here.

Chris stretched. "Finding bodies is exhausting."

"Especially, I imagine, when you're afraid the police will think you put them there." Arial gave him a toothy grin. "You didn't have any appointments this afternoon, did you? Something important I'm keeping you from?"

"No, I figured moving my stuff back into the guest house would take all day. And I was going to offer to take you out to dinner for your help. And for letting me stay here, of course."

"Which was my responsibility since I'm your landlord."

Chris grinned. "And here I was thinking we were actually becoming friends."

"We are, I think," Arial said, regarding him. "But time will tell."

"I'm not quite sure how to take that."

"That makes two of us." Arial waited a beat before changing the subject. "I think I will try to talk to Aaron Henry."

"And what are you going to say to him? 'Hi, Aaron, I found a body under my guest house and just wanted to make sure it's not your dad'?"

"Pretty much," Arial admitted, chewing on her bottom lip. "I suppose I could go down to Ocean View tomorrow morning. This bagel delivery seemed to be a daily thing."

"Tomorrow is Sunday. If it's not seven days a week, you could spend a lot of time waiting."

There were worse things to do with one's morning than a nice brisk walk to the bay. But it would be early—and dark— and Arial couldn't remember exactly where the house was. She picked up her phone. "Now, let's see which house it is."

Chris looked over her shoulder. "You're using street view to see the houses? What did it look like?"

"Big," Arial said, which she knew wasn't exactly helpful. "And white brick."

Chris had cocked his head. "So down at the bottom of this street to Ocean View and maybe a block east?"

"Yes, I think so," Arial said, still searching. "You know it?"

"Their golden retriever is a patient of mine," Chris said.

"That's Simone and Charles Rowan's house."

"That's what Emily said," Arial said, looking up. "Which I don't get. Why would Aaron be delivering bagels to his own house?"

"His mother and stepfather's house," Chris reminded her. "Maybe it was just luck of the draw or coincidence. Simone orders, Aaron accepts the delivery."

"Coincidence." Arial turned sideways to face him. "Again."

"And again, I say, don't read too much into that."

"I know, I know. But that's not the last of them." She turned to face him. "Emily told me that the Rowans' house was robbed that night."

"What night?"

"Monday night into Tuesday. Aaron and I met on the street in front of the house Tuesday morning at five forty-six."

"And you know about this robbery how?"

"Emily told me about it first," Arial said and felt her face get warm. "I would normally take that with a grain of salt, but I did hear sirens as I continued on with my walk, and both Dan and Ned—"

"Your police buddies . . ."

Arial refused to engage. "Confirmed it."

"Are you saying you think Aaron Henry robbed his mother's house?" Chris asked. "What are you basing this on?"

"Him being there just before the robbery was discovered."

"You were there, too."

There was that. "He had a . . . well, like an insulated bag. You know, for hot and cold? He said it was to keep the bagels warm, but the whole bagel thing seems a little lame now."

"You think he was using this bag to keep the loot on ice instead?"

Arial shook her head. "I'm being serious."

Chris held up both hands. "I know you are. But I'm having trouble keeping up."

"In what way?"

He gestured out the window, where an officer had retrieved

a roll of yellow and black crime scene tape from the squad and was approaching the guest house. "What does the body we just found under the guest house have to do with a robbery that was committed four days ago? We know that skeleton has been there much longer than that."

"But the robberies didn't just start with Simone's house. As we said, they've been going on for a year. And running into Aaron Henry in front of Simone Henry Rowan's house, just before we found Robbie Henry's body, seems like one too many coincidences." And a whole lot of Henrys.

"But we don't know it's Robbie's body, as you said yourself," Chris protested. "We don't know anything really, at this point. I think we need to let the police do their work."

"Aren't you curious?" Arial demanded. "You've been sleeping above that body for more than a month. And before that, living next to it."

Chris's face twisted. "Please. That's the last thing I want to think about."

"I'm not sure that's true," Arial said, cocking her head." I imagine the last thing you want to think about is the police suspecting you."

"Do you think they do? Or are you just saying that to get my help nosing around?"

"A little of both," she admitted, feeling guilty for not being more reassuring. "Like you say, we don't know how long ago the person died. If it was ten months ago or less, you were living on the property. More, you're probably off the hook."

"Probably?"

"You still lived in the same town." Arial shrugged. "Maybe you killed him earlier and moved the body in with the rest of your things."

"Now you're just messing with me."

"I am," Arial said. "But my point is: we both want to find out what happened. Me, because I own the body dump, you because you're—"

"A suspect, you don't have to say it. But we don't know who it is. We don't even know for sure if it's male or female."

"Not officially, but I think we do know that much, at least," she said, studying his face. "I think it's a man. And given that you slip occasionally and use 'he,' I think you concur."

He raised his eyebrows. "And you believe that I've deduced that from my intensive study of doggies and kitties? Maybe I'm just sloppy and imprecise in my language choice."

"You're anything but that." Arial suppressed a grin and picked up her wine glass. "And I'm betting you had to study basic human anatomy in order to move on to animal species in your veterinarian studies."

"Perhaps," Chris admitted. "But it was a long time ago. All I can really say is that I had a general impression of male."

"From the pelvis or . . .?"

"I'm not sure. He"—he glanced at her—"or she still had jeans on, as you know. And since the body was decomposed under them, I didn't get a sense of width."

"For the sake of simplicity," Arial said, "let's use the male pronouns."

"With the stipulation, I could be wrong."

"So stipulated," Arial said, before frowning. "He wasn't huge, though, was he? I didn't get the sense of a six-foot weightlifter."

"Muscle and tissue are mostly gone; it would be tough to tell. But I agree he wasn't real tall."

"And how tall was Robbie . . . or is Robbie?" Arial corrected herself.

"I knew we'd get back to him," Chris said ruefully. "I'm five foot eleven and Robbie was shorter than me, I think. But I'd be just guessing."

Arial rubbed her chin. "You need to introduce me to Simone."

"What am I going to do? Knock on her door and tell her I'm making an uninvited house call and you're my vet tech?"

He had a point. "I don't suppose the golden has anything scheduled . . . oh," A thought had struck her. "I don't need you."

"Thanks a lot." It was said sarcastically, but Chris did look grateful.

"No really. I'm a dog-sitter and dog-walking is a necessary subset of that. Since I know they have a dog—"

"You can't tell them I told you that," Chris warned.

"What? Doctor–doggie privilege?"

"Something like that." Chris was stone-faced.

"Oh, lighten up. I heard a dog barking myself the other morning." Not that she could tell where it was coming from.

"Anyway," she continued, "I'll just go and knock on a few doors on either side of the Rowans' house and drop off flyers advertising my dog-sitting services. I am a legitimate dog-sitter." She made a face. "Or illegitimate, before you say it."

"I would never kid about that," Chris said, chucking her on the shoulder. "My stepfather and your mother's marital status at the time of your conception are nobody's business."

"It's complicated."

"It's complicated," Chris agreed. "But we are family after a fashion, so if you're intent on . . ."

"Investigating?"

"I was trying *not* to say that," Chris said. "Sounds too much like a made-for-TV movie."

"My whole life has been a made-for-TV movie," Arial said. "But you were saying?"

"I was saying you can count on me."

Arial patted his shoulder. "And you can count on me to get you off this potential murder charge."

"I . . ." Chris started to protest and then settled on. "Thank you. What can I do to help?"

"Right now?" Arial thought about it. "You could whip up some of that pasta you made the other night."

Chris grimaced. "Sorry, my red sauce takes all day. But I could do a quick cacio e pepe, if you like."

Arial hesitated, not knowing what cacio e pepe was and, therefore, whether she liked it or not. "I . . . um—"

"Cheese and black pepper," Chris said, standing up to go to the kitchen. "You're going to love it, trust me."

Shockingly, Arial found that she did. Trust him, that is.

And the pasta was good, too.

NINE

On Monday morning, Arial gave the veterinarian another duty. "Would you print out my dog-sitting flyers at your office?"

"Like so many young people of your generation," Chris said, adjusting his lab coat, "I assume you don't own a printer?"

"My generation being Z? You're showing your age, Dr. Millennial." Arial handed him a memory stick. "And I didn't even own a bed until very recently. Or a table. Do you really think I'd have a printer to set on it?"

"Absolutely not." He opened the door and held up the memory stick. "Give me a half-hour and come down to the office. I'll have these ready for you."

"Perfect." Just enough time to shower and get dressed. "You're in the gray building on Lighthouse? The one with the futon in the back room."

Chris turned back with a menacing grin. "That's right, sweetheart. And if you know what's good for you, you'll keep your mouth shut about it."

"You got it," Arial said, making a zipping motion across her lips.

It was closer to an hour when Arial finally made her way to the gray frame building on Lighthouse Avenue. She'd showered and pulled on clean jeans with a tank top, a sweater over that and, finally, a light jacket to be taken off as the day warmed. "Layering," she said to herself. "It's all about layering here."

The bell on the clinic door jingled as she pushed it open. The scent of antiseptic and fur greeted her, mingling with a faint hint of coffee. A receptionist glanced up from her desk.

"Hi, I'm Arial Kingston," Arial said, offering a smile. "Here to see Chris."

The receptionist gestured toward the back. "He's in surgery

at the moment, but he left these for you." She handed over a neat stack of trifold flyers, crisp and perfectly printed.

On the front panel the words "Pampered Pooches Pet-sitting" were stacked—each word starting with a stylized "P"—above a photo of two puppies curled up together on a throw pillow.

"It's even better than I could have imagined," Arial breathed. The receptionist saw her smiling. "You like?"

"I *love*. I assume you laid this out?" The memory stick Arial had given Chris had all of the information but none of the pizazz of the finished version.

"I did." The receptionist was a strawberry blonde and her face flushed. "I hope you don't mind."

"Heavens no," Arial said. "I'm eternally grateful, in fact. I'm not artistically inclined, despite my . . . pedigree?"

"Dog joke—I like it." The receptionist grinned. "Your grandmother was Edna Mayes the famous painter."

Famous in Pacific Grove, at least. "I didn't even know she painted until after she died."

"Families. Filled with all sorts of secrets, I'm finding." The young woman stuck out her hand. "I'm Lucy. Lucy Martin."

"It's a pleasure to meet you, Lucy," Arial said, a little ashamed she hadn't asked the receptionist's name in the first place. "And thank you for the assist."

"My pleasure," Lucy said. "I enjoy doing that kind of thing, especially when it involves animals, as you might guess."

Arial slipped the flyers into her bag. "Mind if I wait for Chris?"

"Not at all." Lucy motioned toward a row of chairs near the window. "We don't take appointments until we're done with surgery, so you have your pick of seats."

"But sadly not of puppies to play with while I'm waiting."

"I know, sorry. Best I can provide for now are pictures to look at." Lucy waved at the walls. "I used a couple of these images on your flyer, in fact."

Arial glanced around, recognizing slightly older versions of the Australian shepherd and Lab puppies from the brochure. A framed poster of a golden retriever also grinned down at her. "Is this the Rowans' golden?"

"Max," Lucy confirmed, as Arial moved on to a bulletin board covered in thank-you notes and photos. One caught her eye—a French bulldog with a slightly crooked tooth, smiling as if the world revolved around him. "And this must be Beau."

"It is," Lucy said. "He broke that tooth, so Doc had to extract it last week."

A door swung open, and Chris stepped out, still wearing his surgical garb. He looked surprised to see her. "Arial. I thought you'd just grab the flyers and be on your mission."

"I didn't want to knock on doors too early," Arial replied. "Besides, I wanted to thank you and Lucy both, in person."

"All thanks should go to her," Chris said.

"I gathered that, so I wanted to thank you for being smart enough to hire her." As Lucy grinned and went to answer a jangling phone, Arial lowered her voice. "I didn't want to put Lucy in an awkward position in case it was against policy, but would it be OK if I left a few of the flyers here?"

"Of course," he said, leaning against the reception desk, arms folded. "You're not going to just hand them out on Ocean View, are you?"

"Simone's house, you mean? No, these are way too good to waste on just a ruse." She slipped a few flyers out of her purse and stacked them on the counter. "But I'll start there and work my way up from the water, go house-to-house."

"Good plan. Just stay away from Emily's house unless you want to be interrogated. Or hear about her composting methods."

"I've already been subjected, sadly." But speaking of neighbors. "The photo Lucy used on my flyer—the Aussie and the black Lab. Might their owners object?"

"These guys, you mean?" Chris tipped his head to their framed images on the walls. "They're both Lucy's, so she obviously is fine with you making them famous."

As if. But yet another reason to be thankful to Lucy. "Please thank her again for me."

"I will," Chris said, giving Arial a mock salute. "Now go forth and be nosy."

With a wave to Lucy, Arial headed out the door to be just that.

Flyers tucked safely in her bag against the wind, Arial made her way down toward Ocean View Boulevard. The marine layer was already clearing, the air crisp over the vibrant dark blue of the bay. She stopped at a few houses along the way where she suspected dogs or cats lived, slipping a flyer in a door or tucking them neatly under doormats.

Turning onto Ocean View, she caught sight of the white brick house in the next block. It looked larger than she'd imagined it in the dark a few days earlier. It also looked newly painted, with expansive windows on both sides of the door positioned to make the most of the ocean view. Like most of the houses on the peninsula, the landscaping was drought-resistant but beautiful and natural all the same. The house was set back from the street, and Arial hesitated for a moment before opening the gate to follow the path to the porch steps and press the bell.

The sound set off barking inside and it was a minute or two before the door opened. The woman was as classy as the house—red-haired and in her late forties, with piercing gray eyes and an elegant style. Arial couldn't see much resemblance to Aaron, but then it had been dark and he'd been wearing a hoodie.

"Hi," Arial said, going for perky. "I'm Arial Kingston. I just moved to the area and have a dog-sitting business. I heard a dog barking as I walked past here the other morning and thought I should introduce myself." She held out one of her flyers.

The woman glanced at Lucy's work, her expression softening. "I'm Simone Rowan. Nice to meet you, Arial. Are you going to school on the peninsula?"

Arial figured that the local cost of living, paired with her young age, probably sparked the assumption from Simone. While Arial could fib and say she was attending nearby Monterey Peninsula College or Cal State Monterey Bay, the truth was easier. Besides, Arial was betting it would have more sway with Simone. "No, I recently inherited my great-grandmother's house in Pacific Grove—did you know Gretchen Mayes?"

"The Mayeses, of course." Simone stepped back, opening the door wider. "A storied family name on the peninsula."

Storied. She didn't know the half of it.

"Do come in," Simone continued. "We do have a dog, as you just heard. A golden retriever named Max."

"Thank you," Arial said, stepping inside. The house was just as crisp and perfect inside as it was out, with irritatingly tasteful decor and a faint scent of lavender.

"Have a seat and let me get Max and introduce you," Simone said, gesturing to the couch in the front room. "I put him out in back when the bell rang."

A few moments later, the young golden bounded into the room, tail wagging furiously.

"Oh, you're beautiful," Arial said, leaning down to greet him. Max immediately flopped onto his side, offering his belly for rubs. "What a lover."

Simone chuckled. "He is, and he certainly knows a dog person when he sees one. I assume you have one of your own?"

"Not yet," Arial said, scratching Max's belly. "But soon, I hope. In the meantime, I get my fix by dog-sitting for others."

They chatted for a while about PG, with Arial asking the older woman's advice on markets and clothing stores. Simone preened, seeming to glory in giving Gretchen Mayes's great-granddaughter a leg-up on local society. In fact, for a moment there, Arial thought Simone was going to flip over for a belly rub, à la Max. Eventually, though, Arial brought the conversation back to the flyers again, explaining her services. Simone seemed genuinely interested and promised to pass along the information to friends and neighbors.

As they talked, Arial decided to take a chance. "You know, I think your ex-husband Robbie might have rented the guest house on my property before I moved in. At least, that's what one of the neighbors mentioned—Emily, I think?"

Simone let out a long sigh, shaking her head. "Emily Bennett.

She's in my book club, though I think she's much more interested in gossiping than she is in reading."

"She does seem to keep her finger on the pulse of the community," Arial said, smiling.

"More like her knee on its throat," Simone said, a little wearily. "But we all deal with things our own way." She seemed almost sorry for the woman.

Arial tilted her head, gauging Simone's reaction. "And Robbie Henry was your ex? You've remarried obviously."

"Oh, yes." Simone shuddered, her red hair bobbing. "Charles and I married last year and bought this property."

"It's absolutely beautiful." She waved toward the windows framing the bay. "And what a view."

"Thank you." There was that preening again. "The location was what attracted us first. We actually considered scraping the lot and designing something new, but it is such a classic structure. And as we remodeled, we managed to put something of ourselves into it. We just moved in a couple months ago."

Arial wondered whether by classic, Simone meant historical, and that was the real reason they'd remodeled. "Scraping?"

"Tearing down the old house and building from the ground up?" She tittered. "Technically, it still would have been considered a remodel because we'd leave part of one foundation wall buried somewhere. But we knew we could do something fabulous with the existing structure. And besides, as you said, it's the view that's really the star."

Arial didn't want to guess how much Simone and Charles had paid for a house directly across from the bay.

"You have quite a large piece of property yourself," Simone continued. "Pacific Grove Business district, which isn't as valuable as beach tract, of course. Scraping might be just the thing there, so you can build exactly what you want."

"Maybe," Arial lied. "But for now, I'm just trying to clean up the existing buildings. Which is why I mentioned Robbie. Would you have any idea where he is living now? I found a few of his things while clearing out the guest house and thought I should forward them."

"No clue, and if you'll take my advice, you'll trash them. Everything that man touches is inconsequential."

Inconsequential. Interesting word. Simone seemed to forget that she was one of those "things." And that she and Robbie had a son together. Also not inconsequential.

"He told people he was going to Sacramento to take care of his mother. Would you have an address for her, by any chance?"

A nerve above Simone's right brow ticked. "I'm afraid not."

Arial sensed she might be pushing too hard, but she didn't need a bestie, so what the hell. "Apparently, Robbie had a son—Aaron Henry. I assume Aaron is also *your* son?"

But Simone had stiffened, her warm demeanor cooling noticeably. "Yes," she said after a moment, her voice guarded. "But why are you talking about Robbie in the past tense?"

Oops. "I . . ."

The other woman frowned. "Wait. Did I hear something about a body being found"—she fluttered her hand—"somewhere?"

Sheesh, it was a small town, as everybody kept telling Arial. She should have known news would travel. "Yes, under my guest house."

"Where Robbie rented."

Arial opened her mouth to ask another question, but Simone cut her off. "I'm sorry, but I really need to get back to some things. It was nice meeting you, Arial."

Taking the hint, Arial stood and gave Max one last scratch. "Thanks for letting me stop by. And for the chat."

Simone walked her to the door, her smile polite but distant. As Arial stepped onto the porch, the door closed behind her. Hard.

TEN

"You know," Arial said, propping her feet up on the coffee table, "maybe I've got this all turned around. Maybe Robbie wasn't the victim. Maybe he was the killer."

"You're talking to yourself now?" Chris's keys jangled as he closed the front door behind him.

"I'll have you know Monty here is the finest of conversationalists." She swept her hand toward where the dog lay, upside down, and propped against the living-room wall, snoring.

"Hey, puppy," Chris said, going over to give him a gentle ear rub, lest he disturb him. "Are you dog-sitting?"

"I am," Arial said, "or I guess we are. Shirley took Frank up to the airport in San Jose for a flight out, and when she was whining about driving back in the dark, I told her she should stay over in San Jose. She took me up on it. I think she's planning to do some shopping."

"And you're not staying over at their house? I thought that was your MO. Nights spent dog-sitting on the couch at other people's houses."

"That's before I had a couch of my own," Arial said, sliding off said couch to sit on the floor next to Monty to scratch his belly. "Besides, Monty knows me well enough to be comfortable here."

"I think Monty is comfortable anywhere he can find a wall to hold up."

As Chris said it, the big dog opened one eye and then closed it with a sigh.

"So what do you think?" Arial asked.

Chris settled on the vacated couch, looking tired. "About?"

"About Robbie being the killer rather than the victim."

"Possible, I guess. Did this come from something you learned from Simone today? I'm assuming you saw her."

"Oh, I saw her," Arial said. "Very gracious, especially when she found out I was a Mayes."

"I'm sure you didn't hide that nugget of information."

"Just making use of what I have." Arial shrugged. "The moment I met Simone, I realized my family connections would be helpful."

"C'mon, Simone's a nice woman. And she's not going to be the only one impressed by your family."

"Only because they really don't know them," Arial muttered, getting back up to sit on the couch. "But yes. Even though I've never lived here before, the Mayes connection does make people feel like I belong somehow. Which is good. Not that Simone actually told me anything."

"No?"

Arial ticked it off on her fingers. "Let's see. I found out that Emily is a gossip, big news. That Simone and Charles married a year ago and remodeled the house rather than 'scraping' the lot."

"Don't know that they'd have gotten permits for that," Chris interjected.

"That's what I thought. Also got great advice on where to shop, but when I got to the important things—"

"Like Robbie?" Chris guessed.

"She shut down. Doesn't know or care where Robbie moved and doesn't have contact information for his mother in Sacramento. She even came that close to denying they had a son."

"That close?" He held up his thumb and index finger an inch apart.

Arial made a face. "She didn't confirm or deny. Instead, she focused on the fact that I used past tense when I was talking about Robbie."

"So she'd heard about the body, no surprise. Not hard to put two and two together."

"More like one and one, it's so obvious," Arial said ruefully. "But her reaction did make me think that I was focusing on the wrong thing. Sure, the body could be Robbie's, but it's just as likely that he's the killer. You know, panicked, stashed the body under the house and took off."

"To think we're discussing either of the possibilities as reasonable boggles my mind."

"You said you moved into the main house because he was renting the guest house. What do you think? Killer or victim?"

"Does it have to be either?" Chris rubbed his chin. "Like I said, he was just in the guest house for a month or two after I moved in. Nice enough guy to say hello to in passing and then he was gone."

"Kept himself to himself," Arial mused. "So you didn't see anybody over there that—"

"Who might have murdered him?" Chris asked. "Not that I can think of offhand, assuming present company excepted."

"For now. But what about Robbie as the killer? Can you think of anybody else who," she made air quotes "'left town' around that same time? What about Mark, Emily's husband? What's the story on that break-up?"

"Mark Bennett?" Chris stifled a yawn. "From what I heard, Emily wanted another baby. Mark, on the other hand, already had a couple older kids and . . ." He shrugged. "They just went their separate ways."

"Was Mark a customer?" She frowned. "Or whatever you call the pet-owners."

"Clients. And their animals are patients. And, yes, Emily and Mark were clients. Emily still is. And Casper is a patient."

"And Mark confided that to you," Arial mused. "About not wanting more kids and all?"

Chris actually blushed. "No, apparently that's the consensus in Lucy's book club."

Lucy, his receptionist. Arial liked her even more now. "Would that book club be the same one Emily and Simone are in? Emily is hosting tomorrow night and invited me to come."

"One and the same, I assume. Are you going?"

"I am now." Arial already had her phone out, texting Emily's number. "By the way, Dan Sotherly—you know, the police detective?—texted to say he'd be here tomorrow morning."

Chris's eyes went wide. "Did he say he wanted me here?"

"No. In fact, my plan is to grill him for information, so it's probably better you're not. I'll also ask when they'll be taking down the tape and releasing the crime scene."

"Is this your subtle way of saying it's time for me to move back into the guest house?"

Arial felt a twinge. "Probably not until we get that floor fixed, but what I really want . . ."

"Is to grill Dan, you said." Chris yawned. "Sorry, long day."

"Take your shoes off and put up your feet," Arial suggested. "I'll get dinner."

"Meaning you'll order in?"

"Exactly. I'm thinking Greek?"

"Sold."

The police and forensic team were already at the guest house when Arial dragged herself out of bed—or off the sofa—and into the kitchen Tuesday morning. There was no sign of Chris, probably having made an early escape to the office. Monty, however, was there and gave Arial a big ol' morning-breath kiss tinged with salmon. He had slept on the rug next to Arial on the couch overnight but must have roused when Chris got up and convinced the veterinarian to get him breakfast.

"I'm happy to see you, too," she said, pulling on the thick socks, sneakers, sweatpants and hoodie that had become her morning at-home outfit. Padding onto the back porch, she descended the steps with Monty on the leash to do his morning business on a nearby tree. Several nearby trees. And bushes.

As he finished up, she saw Dan emerge from under the guest house and waved. "Coffee?"

"Absolutely," he said, coming over to follow them up the steps. "Though I assume there will be a price."

Arial glanced back with narrowed eyes. "Everything has a price, Detective. I don't have to tell you that."

Dan laughed and hitched himself up on the porch railing as she went inside to make the coffee. "Can't the dog stay out?"

"I've been instructed not to let him off leash," Arial called back. "At least not until I get a fence back here."

"In Carmel-by-the-Sea dogs can be off leash all the time,"

Dan told her, taking the mug she proffered. "Assuming they're—quote—'under control.'"

"Well, Monty loves to chase, and I wouldn't want him running through your crime scene," Arial said, settling on the edge of the table to be eye-level with her friend. "If it is still a crime scene."

Dan blew on the hot coffee and took a sip. "Way to steer the conversation back. We're releasing the house to you; the crawl space still has the tape on it and is off-limits. We tacked a few boards over the hole in the floor so nobody can fall in, but I wouldn't be surprised if the city building inspector pays you a visit. It may not be habitable, legally, until you get a professional in to replace the floor and it's inspected."

Ugh. But truth was, she was enjoying having Chris—and his occasional cooking—around.

"Anything else you want to know?" Dan asked.

"Only everything," Arial told him. "Have you identified the body yet? Cause of death? How long has he been dead?"

"One question at a time." The detective pulled out his notepad and flipped a few pages before settling on one. "Preliminary forensics confirm the body is that of a middle-aged male."

So their instincts had been right.

"No immediately apparent cause of death," Dan continued, "but the postmortem and tox screens aren't complete. As for time of death, best estimate right now is somewhere between eight months to a year ago."

"So between April and August of last year." Arial still needed to talk to Catherine Smythe to find out exactly when Robbie's lease was up.

"Hopefully we can narrow that down."

"And as for 'middle-aged'—what is that exactly?" Arial peered at him. "Forty-ish?"

The detective—probably solidly into middle age himself—gave her a sour look. "Forties to sixties."

Again, not exactly precise. "That's a twenty-year range. What good is that?"

Dan shrugged. "It's more than you knew ten minutes ago."

That was true. And presumably Robbie Aaron would fit into the range. Maybe even Mark Bennett, if Chris and Lucy were right about his having older kids. But first things first. "Could it be Robbie Aaron? He was the tenant before Chris, and he seems to have disappeared."

"Which you know because you've been asking around, I presume?"

Her turn to shrug. "My guest house, my crawl space, my—"

"Body?" Dan grimaced. "That's not really the way it works."

It was in Arial-world. "His ex-wife Simone doesn't know where he is—"

"She talked to me, by the way." He set his mug on the rail. "Said this dog-sitter had been around asking questions, and was her ex-husband really dead?"

"Some dog-sitter?" Arial repeated. "Nice. She does have my name."

"Should have told her you're a Mayes," Dan offered with a grin.

"I did; fat lot of good it did me."

Now he laughed out loud.

"Did she actually call the station to complain about me?" Arial was half-proud.

"No, their house was one of the ones robbed; I thought I mentioned that. We were discussing the robbery, so I used the opportunity to ask her about Robbie. That was when your name—or lack of name—came up."

"We're on the same track then," Arial pointed out. "I mean Robbie has to be either the victim or the killer, right?"

Dan didn't answer, instead asking a question of his own. "How well do you know Christopher Buck?"

Arial's heart gave a thud. She'd been teasing Chris about being a suspect, but now Dan—a friend, perhaps, but still a police detective—was questioning her about him. "I'm his half-sister's half-sister. You know that."

"And it never fails to confuse me," Dan said, shaking his head. "But I also know that's a fairly new revelation. What do you really know about the man?"

"I know that he moved here from Portland a few years back

now and that he's a respected veterinarian. People in town like him. I like him."

"I like Chris, too," Dan admitted. "But he was living on the property at the time this man died."

"Sometime between June and August of last year?" Arial said it a little more sarcastically than she intended, but she was getting worried.

"Listen," Dan said. "At this point, we don't even have a cause of death, so I can't declare it a homicide. Like any other town, we have the occasional person who is homeless and looking for a safe place to sleep. This poor guy could have crawled under there and never woke up. Drugs, alcohol or just exposure or poor health."

As Ned had suggested, as well. Was this the official police stance? "I met Robbie's son Aaron the other day."

Dan drained his mug and set it down. "When was this?"

Dan seemed to be playing at casual, so Arial did likewise, pretending she had to think about it. "Last Tuesday morning, so a week ago? I was on Ocean View Boulevard, and he was delivering bagels to a house there. I thought it was his mom's house, but that seemed kind of weird."

"They're estranged, I know," Dan said. "Aaron and Charles Rowan don't get on."

"Have you talked to Aaron yourself? I was going to try to find him and ask about Robbie. You know, try to rule him out as the . . ." She glanced toward the crime scene tape.

"Deceased?" Dan said, getting up. "Truth is, we've been looking, and we can't find either Robbie or Aaron Henry."

Arial had that sinking feeling again, this time regarding Aaron instead of Chris. Was he a suspect? And in which—the death of his father or the robberies? Arial didn't want to put ideas in Dan's head that weren't already there, so she just asked, "Why do you want to talk to Aaron? To see if he knows where his dad is?"

"That and some other things." Dan had his pad out again, this time flipped to a blank page. "What time did you see him on Tuesday?"

Arial got up too. "A little before six?"

Dan glanced up sharply. "Was he carrying anything?"

"Just a thermal bag—like food delivery people use to keep things warm."

Dan nodded and flipped the pad closed again. "I know you're going to keep nosing around, so if you do see Aaron, let me know."

Arial was watching him. "You think he's involved in the robberies."

Dan ducked his head. "We're pursuing several lines of inquiry."

"Emily Bennett said Aaron has been in trouble."

"Emily . . ." Dan started and caught himself. "I'll keep you informed, OK? And you do likewise."

When Arial didn't answer immediately, "Promise?"

"Promise," she said.

Dan started down the steps and then turned. "I know somebody being killed—if he was killed—a year ago sounds like a cold case. Like there's no immediate danger. But there are a lot of intertwining lives here and—pull at one thread, you may not like what unravels."

ELEVEN

Dan Sotherly's parting words had sent shivers down Arial's spine, so she was inordinately glad to see Monty as she opened the door to go back inside the house.

Monty had been lying on the floor in the corner of the kitchen cabinets and now got up, giving her quizzical-dog face.

"Sorry, I'm a little weirded out," Arial told him.

Still projecting concern, Monty reared up on his back legs, hovering just a few inches short of jumping on her.

Arial grinned, taking his two front paws in her hands to give him a snuggle before telling him to get down. "Somebody taught you not to jump on people, huh? Not that you don't do the next best thing."

As she said it, Monty hopped down, and she leaned over to give the big dog a butt rub. He swung his head around and gave her nose a flick of a kiss. "What a lover you are. I'm fine, though. And speaking of lovers, should we go for a walk to Lovers Point?"

Monty's happy dance made it tough to get the leash on, but before long they were out of the house and walking down to the park where Arial knew—as apparently Monty did, as well—squirrels were abundant. That would make the canine half of their duo happy, while settling on a bench to watch the bay would help organize the human's thoughts.

But first . . . "We need to make a quick stop, buddy."

Climbing the steps to Smythe Realty, a block away on Lighthouse, Arial tapped on the door and opened it a crack. "Catherine? Are you there? It's Arial Kingston."

"Arial," a voice said. "Come on in, you don't have to rest on formalities."

"I . . . uh," she glanced at Monty, who was peeing on Catherine's bush. "I have the Coopers' dog with me, and I wasn't sure—"

The door opened wide, and a beautifully coiffed white-haired woman grinned at them. "Monty! Please come in."

"Are you sure it's all right?" Arial asked. "I didn't want to leave him outside on the leash, but—"

"Of course, it's fine," Catherine said, waving them in. "We're very dog-friendly here on the peninsula, if you haven't noticed."

"I have noticed," Arial said, sitting down in one of two chairs in front of a sunny window. "Which is lucky for me."

"Oh, your dog-sitting business," Catherine said, opening a drawer to pull out a bag of dog treats. "How is that going?"

"Slowly," Arial admitted, as Monty sat for a treat. "I've had the . . . situation in the guest house to deal with."

"The police came by," Catherine said in a hushed voice, despite the fact it was a one-woman office. "I didn't get a good read on whether they think the body is Robbie's or that Robbie killed whoever it is."

"I'm in the same boat," Arial admitted, as Monty swallowed the treat whole and sat obediently, tail waving, waiting for more. "Were you able to give them a forwarding address for him?"

"I was," she said, pulling a folder from a vertical file on her desk and opening it. "His mother's address in Sacramento."

"Well, that's good. At least they can check and see if he's there, alive and well," Arial said, leaning forward. "Is that the lease?"

"Yes," Catherine said, sliding a thick document across the desk to her.

Arial glanced through it. "A one-year lease then?"

"Actually, two one-year leases in a row," Catherine said. "Robbie knew I managed the property and when Simone kicked him out, he asked if the guest house was available." She shrugged. "It wasn't in great shape even then, but he said he just wanted some place to lay his head temporarily."

"Temporarily turned out to be two years?" Arial looked up in time to see Catherine sneak Monty another treat.

"Yes." She slipped the dog treats back in the drawer and closed it. "He signed the second lease just after the divorce was final. He said he wanted to be close to Aaron, but I felt like he was waiting—like he and Simone might work things out even then." She rolled her eyes. "I don't know why. They were always a mismatch. Robbie is kind and laid-back and Simone . . ."

"Is not," Arial finished for her. "The second lease was up July thirty-first of last year. Did he move out that day?" Which would be toward the end of the April to August window for time of death.

"No, earlier." Catherine thumbed through her folder and came up with a paper. "He paid his July rent in June and gave me notice he was vacating early."

"June then?" Arial asked, to be sure.

"Or early July. I assumed his mother's health had taken a turn for the worse. Or maybe he'd finally given up hope of a reconciliation, since Simone was already with Charles by that point. Whatever the reason, Robbie told me he was leaving and asked that I forward his security deposit to his mother's address."

Arial leaned forward. "Was that check cashed?" Because if it was, it would prove that Robbie had made it to Sacramento. "When?"

"The officer asked the same questions, I'm afraid. And yes, it was cashed in early August. But Robbie asked that I make the check payable to his mother." Catherine grimaced. "I'm not technically supposed to do that unless his mother was on the lease, but he said his accounts wouldn't be set up yet and . . ." She raised her shoulders and dropped them.

"You did the nice thing," Arial said. "I certainly don't have a problem with it."

"That's a relief, thank you."

"No worries, and thanks for the information." Arial stood and handed her the lease. "Ready to go, Monty?"

The dog stood eagerly, nearly clearing a low file cabinet with his tail.

"Where are you two headed?" Catherine asked, getting up to escort them to the door.

"Lovers Point," Arial told her. "Plenty of squirrel-watching there, right, Monty?"

The big dog was already out the door, pulling her down the steps.

"Oh, Arial?" Catherine's voice called. "As the property owner, I think you should know."

Safely on sidewalk level, Arial turned back.

Catherine's face was worried. "Robbie wasn't the only tenant the police asked about."

So Dan's interest in Chris wasn't exactly casual, Arial thought as Monty led her down the sidewalk, big bushy tail waving high. But then the detective was also asking around after Aaron.

"Hell, the police would probably be asking about me if my first visit coincided with the murder," she muttered aloud, drawing a startled look from a woman passing by.

Arial pointed to her ear as if she was on the phone, but the woman didn't seem reassured.

"Probably the mention of the police spooked her," Arial said to Monty when the woman was out of earshot. "Or murder."

The boxer/shepherd mix ignored her, of course, his long brindle coat gleaming as he stopped to sniff every patch of grass, tree or hydrant like it was the first he'd ever encountered. As they got out of downtown PG, the sidewalk was fairly quiet, with the occasional passerby stopping to pet Monty, or doing just the opposite—crossing the street to give him a wide berth.

"Sorry, buddy," Arial told him when he glanced up at her as if asking "why don't they love me?" "You're a big dog and some people are intimidated." She scratched him behind the ear and he did a happy little jig. "Big and adorable. Own it."

The puppy-like joy of the dog made Arial relax a little as they passed by pastel-colored house after house on their trek down to the water. Most of Arial's favorite houses dated prior to 1926 and bore the green date plaques with the original owner's names. Many of them—no, most of them—were women.

Getting to the corner of Seventeenth Street and Ocean View, Arial had Monty sit, and she looked both ways before crossing to the Lovers Point parking lot. Given the name of the park, Arial had assumed it was a popular make-out spot, but it turned out it was originally "Lovers of Jesus Point," named by the Methodists who used it as a retreat and ultimately settled in Pacific Grove.

Today, with the marine layer already clearing, Lovers Point was lively for a weekday. People were lined up at the concession stand or renting bikes or four-person Surreys to pedal down the coastal trail toward the wharf. The kiddy pool was closed, but a few daring souls in swimwear even seemed to be willing to brave the chill of the water. Or at least lie on the sand in the sun.

Which, Arial had to admit, seemed warmer than the sun elsewhere. Not hot, hot, like in the tropics, but when the sun was out, the temperature seemed to rise a good ten degrees. In the shade, though, it would still be downright chilly. And when there was fog . . .

Without warning, Monty crossed in front of her and then stopped short, his nose snuffling furiously at a hole next to a rock. "Whatever you've found, we're not taking it home," she told him, giving the leash a tug. With a glance at her, he lifted his leg and peed on the rock, staking his claim regardless.

"Good thought," Arial said, glancing toward the restrooms. "But what will I do with you while I'm in there?"

"Arial," a voice called from the tables in front of the coffee stand, and her stomach did a little somersault. Aaron Henry.

Sometimes you just had to go with fate.

Bladder forgotten, Arial led Monty to the sea wall, where Aaron stood with a foil-wrapped cylinder in one hand.

"Hey," she said. "What brings you here?"

It was a lame question, since they were only across the road and down a few blocks from where she'd met him in the first place.

But Aaron didn't seem to notice. "Had to have my fix." He held up what Arial could now see was a wrap of some kind. "Breakfast burrito."

"I'll have to try one," Arial said. "I've only had coffee here."

"Scrambled eggs, cheese, tater tots and bacon is the way to go," Aaron said, unwrapping one end and taking a bite. "Ooh, sorry. Did you want some?"

"No thanks," Arial said, though the dog sitting obediently next to her gave out a polite bark to indicate he was game.

"Hey boy," Aaron said, pulling off a small piece of egg for the big beggar. "You dog-sitting for the Coopers?"

Arial was past being surprised that everyone seemed to know everyone. And their dogs. In fact, it gave her the opening she needed.

"I should have realized you would know Monty," she said. "Your dad lived right next door to Shirley and Frank."

Aaron's turn to be surprised. Or at least act surprised. "My dad?"

"Yes, Robbie Henry. Or I guess I just assumed Robbie is your dad." Arial could play stupid, too. And this time she didn't make the mistake of referring to Robbie in the past tense. "I didn't put it together when you and I met that morning, but I own the guest house Robbie was renting."

"Robbie. Yeah, no," Aaron said, taking another bite to mask his confusion. "Lots of Henrys in the area." This last was said around a full mouth of burrito.

"Well, if Robbie isn't your dad, I'm very glad." She leaned in conspiratorially. "Did you hear that a body was found in the crawl space of the guest house?"

Aaron's face was white. "No, I . . . um, haven't been feeling well, so I've been lying low." He let out a weak cough. "Hadn't heard a thing."

Arial moved back a hygienic pace, just in case that was true. "Listen, Aaron. I know Robbie is your dad because I talked to your mother."

In truth, their talks had broken down before Simone had actually confirmed that Aaron was her son. But Arial had plenty of other ways of knowing, including the red hair that had been hiding under Aaron's hoodie when she met him.

"My mother?"

Even Monty let out a groan at that. Or maybe he just wanted another bite of burrito.

"Please. As everybody keeps telling me, this is a small town. Everybody knows that your dad, Robbie, moved into the guest house when he split from your mom, Simone. She got remarried a year ago to Charles Rowan and they live in the white brick house down the street." She waved her hand in that direction. "The house that you said you were delivering bagels to on Tuesday morning."

"So?" Aaron had gotten down on one knee to let Monty lick the burrito wrapper and now he looked up at her. "You've tumbled to the fact that I'm so poor I have to deliver bagels to my mom and her new husband's mansion overlooking the bay. Is that a crime? Some of us didn't inherit property from their grandparents."

So Aaron did know who she was, even if he hadn't when they first met. "I didn't say it was a crime."

He got up and cocked his head, standing just a little too close to her for comfort. "Then what are you saying?"

She took a step back. "Listen, you're right that I'm lucky to be here and to actually own something. But I'm not some kind of heiress. I spent most of my life flopping on other people's couches."

"I suppose you even have your own dysfunctional family." Aaron was studying her.

"You have no idea," Arial said truthfully, and then hesitated, struggling with how much she should say. "I think you should know that there's talk going around that you may be involved in these robberies."

"Now I've not only sunk to delivering bagels to my mother, but I'm robbing her?" He leaned down to grab the dog-mangled wrapper and toss it in a trash can. "I suppose you said you'd seen me in front of her house?"

"I don't believe you robbed your mother." The coffee earlier was making its presence known. Arial had to go, literally, but she also could use a moment alone to decide how much she should tell Aaron.

A bathroom break seemed just the thing, but Arial also needed to keep Aaron there until she came back out. She held up the leash. "Can you hang on to Monty for a second while I use the restroom?"

Aaron hesitated, looking surprised at her abruptness, then nodded. "Sure, take your time."

"Right back." She handed over the leash and hurried around the corner and into the women's restroom to stand in front of the mirror, hands braced on the sink as she tried to think.

It was true she couldn't picture Aaron as a robber. But it was also true that she *had* told Dan about seeing Aaron in front of the Rowan house. She didn't want to lie about it. Or withhold information from Dan, for that matter.

Running her hands quickly under the water, Arial wiped them on her jeans and dashed out of the restroom. "Hey," she said, rounding the corner. "I have to be honest—"

She stopped. Monty's leash was looped neatly around the leg of a table. Aaron, however, was gone.

TWELVE

"My own damn fault," she muttered, untying the leash. Monty wagged his tail as if nothing unusual had happened. "I never should have left you alone with him. I should have known he'd abandon you."

Monty thumped his tail twice.

"Or worse, steal you because you're so handsome." The dog licked her face. "But you're not much of a guard dog, are you?"

She got a ruff in response.

They'd made it past the children's wading pool when another thought stopped her. "Damn. I never used the toilet."

As if to torment her, Monty lifted his leg yet again.

In the end, Arial had taken Monty into the restroom with her.

"Oops, sorry," she said to a woman washing her hands as she and Monty emerged from a very crowded cubicle. "I didn't want to leave him outside."

"No worries." The woman had a youthful face with blonde, nearly white hair framing it. She was maybe forty and didn't seem at all startled by Monty's sudden appearance. "Isn't that the Cooper dog?"

At the sound of his last name, Monty smiled and danced over to the woman.

"Oh, yes, you are," she said, scratching him behind one ear, "yes, you are."

"Shirley and Frank are my neighbors," Arial told her. "I'm dog-sitting."

"Oh, that's right," the woman said, straightening. "Shirley had to take Frank up to the airport for his flight." She shook her head. "I don't know why he doesn't just fly out of Monterey. It's such a nice little airport. But you can't tell Frank Cooper anything. Anyway, I'm Olivia Marin." She stuck out her hand.

Arial shook. "Arial Kingston."

"Arial Mayes-Kingston, from what I hear," the other woman said. "You should really hyphenate. I understand you're coming to book club tonight and, even though most everybody is nice, there are one or two snooty ones."

Arial laughed. "I'll keep that in mind. I'm still getting used to everybody seeming to know me."

"And everything about you," the woman said grinning. "PG's slogan is America's last hometown. For good and occasionally for bad, at least privacy-wise."

"It's nice, though, to feel a sense of belonging. I guess that's my great-grandmother's doing, not mine. But I am happy to be here."

"See you tonight?" Olivia asked, giving Monty a last pat.

"You will," Arial said as the woman left.

Arial looked down at the pooch. "I'm going to wash my paws. You?"

Monty woofed.

Leaving Lovers Point, Arial and Monty headed west, farther out on the peninsula toward Asilomar State Park on the very tip. Unlike the wide paved walking and bike trail leading toward Cannery Row, Old Fisherman's Wharf and beyond, this section was narrower and gravel, some parts veering onto Ocean View Boulevard momentarily and then back again.

It was already Arial's favorite part of the trail, less busy and wilder in both foliage and water. It also took her past Simone's white brick house and Arial wanted another look. Being careful to check both ways, she and Monty trotted across the street from the trail, slipping between two cars to the sidewalk.

"There was a car in front of the house that morning, too," Arial said to herself. In fact, she'd first seen Aaron reflected in the car window as he approached, presumably after delivering the bagels. Assuming he had delivered the bagels.

"Just the one car parked on the street and . . ." she squeezed her eyes closed to picture it, "it was a dark-colored sedan—either blue or black—with maybe an Oregon license plate?"

Arial was still standing there with her eyes closed as she heard the front door of the white house. Opening her eyes, she saw Simone's head poke out, the woman leaning down and then resurfacing with a package in her hand.

"Hi, Simone," Arial said. "See you tonight?"

The woman frowned, seeming confused. "What are you doing with the Coopers' dog?"

"We'll have to get you a fake mustache if you ever want to go incognito," Arial told Monty before turning back to Simone. "I—"

"Oh, that's right," Simone said, waving off her own question. "You're a dog-sitter."

"And the Coopers' neighbor," Arial reminded her. "Arial Kingston?" Just in case she wanted to complain to the police again.

"Oh, yes," Simone said and went to shut the door.

"Will I see you at book club to—" The door closed before Arial could get out the last syllable.

She was starting to think Olivia was right and Arial should use the full weight of her hyphenated name. But even that might not unplug the gigantic stick that Simone . . .

With a sigh, Arial turned to Monty. "Enough. Let's go home."

As they approached their block, Shirley's red Prius pulled up in front.

"Mom's home," Arial told Monty.

"Monty," Shirley called, opening her arms wide as she knelt.

Unwilling to let go of the leash, Arial was dragged down the sidewalk by the big puppy.

"And here I thought Monty and I were doing just fine," she told Shirley on arrival. "Guess I know where I stand."

"He acts like I've been away for weeks, even after an overnight like this," Shirley said, standing to wipe a Monty kiss off her face. "Thanks for taking care of him. Everything go all right?"

"He was perfect," Arial said. "I was half-hoping you'd decide to stay over another night, so I could get more Monty-time. But tonight is book club. I assume you're coming?"

"I'm exhausted," Shirley said, going to the front door to let Monty in and then back-tracking to the car to pull out shopping bags. "I had a great time shopping at Westfield Mall and Santana Row and had a lovely big lunch. Traffic was bad going through Morgan Hill, as usual, but now I plan to kick back and binge-watch a few of my shows."

Sounded lovely to Arial, too, but she had a mission to complete. "You're really not coming? I could use the moral support."

"I'm afraid you're on your own, baby," Shirley said, looping the bags over one arm in order to close the car door. "Even if I wasn't tired, it's Emily's turn to host, and I'm not in the mood for a night of Little Miss Perfect."

With a wave, she disappeared into her house with her shopping and her dog and her binge-watching.

Arial sighed and continued down the street, glancing at the front of the guest house as she passed. The police tape across the front door had been taken down, as Dan had promised, but there was a notice taped on the door. Arial mounted the steps.

"Stop work order from the city of Pacific Grove," she read to nobody, since she no longer had Monty for cover. "Essentially I have to have the place inspected for structural damage and have it repaired. And then inspected again."

Not surprising, given what Dan had said just hours earlier, but still . . .

With another sigh, Arial disappeared into her own house to change for book club. And Little Miss Perfect.

THIRTEEN

Chris wasn't home from the clinic by the time Arial left, so she didn't have moral support from that quarter either. Not that she expected he would brave the book club even for her. But maybe she'd see his receptionist Lucy there, if she wasn't working late as well.

Not knowing what people would be wearing, Arial paired a short, tailored blazer with skinny jeans, hoping she'd bridged the gap between casual and dressy. With one last look in the mirror, she headed out her front door and took a series of right turns which landed her at the front door of the house directly behind her.

Emily's house—from the front—turned out to be a tidy pale-yellow Victorian tucked behind a white picket fence, the kind of place that belonged on a postcard. White trim framed the door and windows, and the porch was neatly arranged with potted succulents and a rail bench.

Arial heard chatting inside and rapped lightly on the door. Nobody could hear her over the voices, of course.

"Hello?" Feeling like an Emily, Arial stepped uninvited into the house, which smelled faintly of lemon furniture polish and something savory baking in the oven. "Of course it would," Arial muttered to herself.

At that moment, Dickie darted through the living room in dinosaur pajamas, clutching a plastic sword. "Hi, Hi, HI!" he called, waving the sword in what Arial assumed was meant to be a greeting.

"Hi, Dickie. Nice sword," she replied, stepping around him as Emily appeared, a glass of white wine in one hand and the Pomeranian tucked under her other arm. Casper gave a shrill bark and wiggled furiously, his fluffy white coat practically vibrating with energy and the desire to get down.

"Dickie, I told you to stay in bed," Emily said, her tone

sharp but distracted. She turned to Arial, her smile tight. "Welcome. You found the place OK?"

"Hard to get lost," Arial said. "You have a lovely home."

She meant it. The living room looked like a magazine spread, with every pillow perfectly plumped and not a single toy out of place—aside from Dickie's sword, which he'd promptly dropped before disappearing down the hall.

"He'll be out like a light soon," Emily said, though it sounded more like a prayer than a prediction. She deposited Casper onto the floor while she picked up the sword, and the little dog immediately pranced over to Arial, yipping for attention.

"Hiya, Casper," Arial said, leaning down to scratch behind the Pom's ears.

"He likes you," Emily said, seeming surprised. "Wine's in the kitchen. Help yourself and I'll be right back after I settle Dickie back in bed."

Arial made her way to the kitchen to find Olivia Marin already pouring Chardonnay into a stemless wine glass. "Arial! Just in time. Emily's about to launch into one of her stories, I can feel it."

"Should we be worried?" Arial asked, taking a glass.

"Always," Olivia said with a grin.

Back in the living room, the other attendees were settling in. Arial would have bet against it, but Simone Henry was there, perched stiffly on the edge of the couch, expression unreadable but body language screaming reluctance. No Lucy, unfortunately, but there were two other women Arial thought she recognized from around town but hadn't officially met. They waved her over.

"I'm Fiona Sinclair," said the taller of the two, extending a hand. "This is Marta Villanueva. We're the unofficial wine committee."

"Nice to meet you both," Arial said, shaking hands. "I'm Arial Kingston."

Despite her intentions, she couldn't quite bring herself to do the hyphenation business. At least with these two friendly women.

"You're the one with the dog-sitting business," Marta said.

"That's me. And now apparently also the woman with a

body under her house," Arial said, thinking she might as well lay it all out on the table.

Fiona's eyebrows shot up. "We know. You'll have to tell us everything."

"She'll have to wait her turn," Emily interrupted, sweeping into the room to take center stage. "But first, can we talk about the break-ins? Someone needs to start keeping an eye on who is coming and going around here."

"Isn't that what you already do?" Olivia asked mildly.

Simone gave a tight smile but said nothing, her gaze fixed on her wine glass. The woman wasn't generally forthcoming, at least in Arial's most recent experience, but the air of disinterest seemed more pointed tonight. It made Arial wonder whether Simone was there more for information than socializing. But Arial certainly couldn't judge her for that.

"It's not funny," Emily was saying, folding her arms. "Now I know you don't want to hear it, Simone, but I saw Aaron loitering around Lovers Point this morning. You can't tell me that's not suspicious."

Simone's head snapped up, her expression icy. "It's a park. Why would that be suspicious?"

"Aaron was enjoying a breakfast burrito," Arial interjected, earning a startled glance from the man's mother. "We chatted for quite a while."

"I just think it's odd that he doesn't seem to have a home, that's all," Emily said quickly. "No one's saying Aaron is the thief."

"And yet you *are* saying it," Olivia said, her voice sharp. "Why don't we stick to the book?"

The suggestion was met with a brief, awkward silence, followed by a collective shuffle of feet and wine glasses. Emily sighed dramatically. "Fine. Let's talk about the book. Who actually read it?"

No one raised their hand.

"Well, that's just great," Emily muttered. "Why do we even call this a book club?"

"Because calling it a wine-and-gossip club sounds tacky," Marta suggested. "Now what about that body under your guest house, Arial? Maybe you should be writing a book."

"I'd need to know the ending first," Arial said, jumping at the chance to glean information from this not-so-reticent group. "Right now, we don't even know who it is."

"Is it a man?" Marta asked.

"Or is it a woman?" Fiona added, like the two were playing tag-team twenty questions.

"Man," Arial said, since Dan hadn't told her to keep it to herself.

"Age?" This was from Emily.

"Middle-aged," Arial supplied.

Emily frowned, but Simone flopped her hand dramatically before their hostess could ask. "What does that even mean these days? Fifty is the new thirty."

Not in Arial's opinion, but OK. "That's what I asked. Forty to sixty, apparently."

"Well, that's not very helpful," Olivia said. "I heard the police think it might be Robbie."

"Why is that?" Emily asked.

"Because he lived in the guest house where the body was found, duh," Marta answered. "Have they been in touch, Simone?"

"Why would they talk to me?"

The question was disingenuous since Arial knew with certainty that Dan *had* talked to Simone. Albeit it in the guise of the robbery investigation.

"To find out when you last saw him, of course," Fiona said, eyes wide. "Besides, you're his ex. Maybe you have something with his DNA on it."

"Or know which dentist he went to, so they can match dental records," Olivia suggested.

"Robbie never went to the dentist," Simone snapped. "He hated them."

"He's not alone in that," Marta said, shrugging. "But needs must."

Fiona had been thinking. "You know, Aaron could provide his DNA."

"Oh, yes," Marta said, resettling herself on the couch excitedly. "I didn't think of that. To see if there's a familial match."

"Well, I have no idea where Aaron is at the moment," Simone

said, folding her arms. "Thanks to Emily, no doubt, he's made himself scarce."

Except for the occasional need for a breakfast burrito.

"You can't actually think Aaron is the thief," Olivia said to Emily. "What are you basing it on?"

Emily shrugged. "He just seems to be everywhere, doesn't he?"

"He delivers food," Arial said, rolling her eyes. "And does rideshare. Give the guy a break."

"Amen," Simone said, this time throwing Arial a grateful glance before turning to Emily. "And if Arial's body is a middle-aged man, maybe we should be talking about Mark. Didn't he supposedly pack it in and leave one day?"

"Not supposedly," Emily snapped. "And he wasn't that old."

"Twenty years older than you." Marta was nodding. "That would put him past fifty."

The grapevine was amazing. And helpful.

"Well, I'm sorry to burst your delusional bubble, but Mark is alive and well living with his bimbo in Florida." Emily stood up, fists balled on her hips. "Can you be as sure about your ex, Simone?"

"No," Simone said, drawing herself up to face their hostess. "But then I don't stalk him."

The two faced off for what seemed like a full minute before Olivia cleared her throat and stood up. "Well, this has been lovely, but I think it's time to call it a night."

Emily and Simone stayed where they were as the rest of the group mumbled their thanks and retreated to the kitchen with their glasses. Arial wanted to stay but wasn't sure how to do so gracefully.

Besides, she might garner more information from the rest of the group going forward than from the warring parties.

"Wow." Olivia turned, eyes sparkling. "This certainly was one of our best book club meetings."

"It lasted half an hour," Arial protested, going to the sink to rinse out her glass.

"They've been shorter," Marta said, as she followed suit. "Believe it or not."

And Arial had to admit, the thirty minutes had been informative. "Why do Simone and Emily dislike each other so much?"

"That's an interesting question," Marta said, turning to set her glass on the counter.

Really? Arial thought it was pretty basic.

Olivia saw her expression. "Thing is, Arial, Simone and Emily used to be great friends."

"What changed?"

"Simone," Marta said dryly.

"That's not really fair," Olivia said.

"Is too," Marta countered. "And I think it dates back to when she met Charles. Emily wasn't even invited to the wedding. It really hurt her."

Arial was starting to see Emily in a new light. Warm white, of course. "And Emily targets Aaron because . . ."

"She sees him as Simone's weak spot?" Fiona posited, recorking a partial bottle of Chardonnay.

Marta shrugged in agreement. "What else is she going to criticize in Simone's life? The rich husband? The big house?"

"And no matter how rocky Simone's relationship is with Aaron," Olivia said, "Emily knows that Simone still loves him."

"So she also knows her barbs hurt," Arial said as Olivia ushered them toward the back door.

"Exactly," Marta said, before turning to Fiona. "Are you taking that with you?"

"I brought it," Fiona said, holding up the Chardonnay. "And I'm certainly not going to let the rest of the bottle go to waste."

"I'm not sure Emily lets any alcohol go to waste," Marta said, as they stepped out onto the porch.

"Also not fair." Olivia was apparently the group's referee.

"Is it OK to leave them together like this?" Arial asked, as the decibel level in the other room went up again.

"Hope so," Olivia said, closing the door firmly behind them.

"If not," Fiona shrugged in the gentle yellow of the light as they stepped off the porch. "I guess we'll see which of them ends up in your crawl space tomorrow."

FOURTEEN

Fiona, Marta and Olivia circled to the front of Emily's house and, presumably, on to their cars or homes. Arial took the more direct route to her house, cutting first through Emily's backyard—with its swing-set and sandbox—to the alley and then into her own yard, with its overgrown brush and recently removed dead body.

Reaching the porch steps, she paused to make a few notes on her phone before swinging open the back door.

"Shit!" Chris exclaimed, whirling around from the kitchen counter. "You scared the hell out of me. Weren't you at book club? What were you doing out in the yard?"

"The book club was at Emily's, remember?" Arial said, collapsing into a kitchen chair. "I cut through the backyards. Are you cooking something good?"

"English muffins with peanut butter," the veterinarian said, moving aside so she could see the toaster. "Didn't Emily feed you at book club?"

"Wine was drunk," Arial said. "But things imploded before any food came out."

"Imploded how?" Chris asked as the first muffin popped up. "Butter or just peanut butter?"

"Just peanut butter, of course," Arial said, like anything else was heresy. "And quick, while the muffin is still hot, so it melts."

"Hope creamy is all right," Chris said, following directions. "We seem to be out of chunky."

"I prefer creamy anyway, which is why you found it in my cupboard," Arial said, as he slid the plate in front of her. "You didn't have to give me the first one."

"Says the woman after giving me explicit directions on how to prepare her muffin." Chris split another one and put it in the toaster before sitting down across from her. "Besides, you need something to soak up the wine. So what imploded?"

"Well, first, Emily accused Aaron Henry of these burglaries, and Simone went rightfully ballistic." She took a bite of muffin. "This is great, thank you."

"Wait, Simone was there and who else? I want to get the full picture."

"Well, no Lucy, for one. I was disappointed not to see her there." Both because she was nice and had proven she wasn't above sharing information—at least with Chris.

"I'm afraid that's on me," he said now. "We had a last-minute emergency appointment."

"I'm sorry. Is the dog or cat or whatever it was OK?"

"Dog with uncontrollable itching," Chris said. "She was scratching so badly she was making herself bleed."

"Oh, no. Did you figure out what it was?"

"Flea infestation." Chris shrugged. "Turned out they fell behind on her flea meds. So, yes—we got that one taken care of, I hope. Sent them home with medicated shampoo and flea and tick medication, but they'll have to do the rest."

Arial wrinkled her nose as she surveyed him. "You showered, I hope?"

"At the office," Chris assured her. "Now who else was there? Shirley, I assume, since I don't see Monty here."

"Shirley got home late this afternoon but said she was too tired. And that she can't stand being in the same room as Emily for any length of time."

"That's too bad," Chris said. "So no friendly faces there for you?"

"Oh, I wouldn't say that," Arial said, grinning. "Like I said, Simone was there, perched on the arm of the couch like she was ready to attack."

"Or flee?" Chris suggested.

Arial liked that Chris enjoyed . . . well, Arial wouldn't call it gossiping, necessarily, just . . . talking. About other people.

"Perhaps," Arial said, pulling out her phone to consult. "Also Fiona Sinclair, Marta Villanueva and Olivia Marin."

"You took notes?" Chris asked, getting up to check the toaster. Not satisfied with the muffin's degree of brownness, he popped it down again. "Or can I hope you recorded the whole thing for my listening pleasure?"

"Sorry, but no," Arial said regretfully. "Maybe next time. But when I got back, I sat on the porch steps here and typed the names into Notes so I wouldn't forget."

"No wonder you scared me," Chris said, sitting back down. "I thought I heard something, but when I didn't see anything—"

"—In the white porch light," Arial supplied.

"I went back to what I was doing until you burst in."

"Sorry," Arial said, finishing her muffin and getting up with the plate. "Your muffin smells done. Butter or just peanut butter?"

"You're asking that now after you shamed me?"

"I will admit," she said, opening the cutlery drawer to get a new knife for the butter, "that sometimes I do both. But only when I'm feeling needy. Are you feeling needy?"

"No, but I still want butter and peanut butter," Chris said. "Will you get on with it? The story of this evening's book club, I mean. I'm less picky about my peanut butter melting than you are."

"You should be *more* picky," Arial said, moving onto the peanut butter. "Peanut butter on top of cold butter? Ugh."

"I actually like that," Chris said. "But mostly on bread, not toast."

"Well, you're the connoisseur," Arial said, bringing him his muffin.

"I am," he said, taking a bite. "And thank you. This is perfect. Now you were saying?"

"OK, just so you have the full picture," Arial said, turning to lean against the dishwasher. "We're in the living room and we've all got white wine, probably because Emily's house is so immaculate she doesn't serve red." She cocked her head. "It's hard to believe that a boy and a dog live there. You'd never think it if you didn't see them."

"A small boy and a small dog," Chris said. "Though that can mean even more mess."

"I'm sure she cleaned like crazy before we got there. Or had someone clean. There was also something in the oven that smelled amazing." At the thought, Arial's stomach growled, and she swiveled her head to regard the still-open packet of muffins.

"Oh, go ahead," Chris urged. "If you want, I'll go halfsies with you."

"Sold." Arial split the muffin and slipped it into the toaster before sitting down. "So, like I said, we're in the living room, and I'm thinking we're going to talk about the book, whatever it was."

"You don't know what book you were supposed to read?"

"I just decided to go for sure yesterday. Or was it this morning?" She thought about it and shook her head. "I don't know, but either way I couldn't be expected to read the book in that time. Besides, nobody else seemed to have read it either."

"Lucy has mentioned that's a problem."

"Maybe to Lucy, if she likes to read, but nobody else seemed to care. Marta and Fiona wanted to hear more about the body under the guest house—"

"No surprise," Chris said. "It is big news here."

"Or anywhere, I'd hope. Anyway, Emily was having none of it. She wanted to talk about the burglaries and her suspicions of Aaron Henry."

"Right there in front of Simone?"

"Exactly," Arial said. "And Simone must have been expecting it. She was primed and ready to pounce."

"So why would she come at all?"

Arial shrugged. "I didn't expect her to be there, but it probably was smart. You know, to keep tabs on what people were saying?"

"But you said she'd practically denied that Aaron was her son when you first spoke with her."

"I think that was a bluff," Arial said, rubbing her forehead. "Simone is very hard to read. She should take up poker."

Chris didn't follow up on that. "Did Emily say why she suspects Aaron?"

"It's not clear that she does," Arial said. "The ladies think she's just using Aaron as a way to needle Simone."

"But why . . ."

Arial waved it off. "Jealousy. Hurt. Opinions differ. But whatever the reason, she accused him of loitering—specifically in Lovers Point—this morning."

"Is she following him?"

"Got me, but if so, I should have Dan talk to her. The police haven't been able to find Aaron anywhere and here, Emily and I both saw him at Lovers Point this morning."

"You saw him, too?"

"Yup, when I took Monty for a walk. Aaron was having a breakfast burrito, which is exactly what I told—"

"I love those," Chris said, getting up to prepare the last course of their dinner. "Did you talk?"

"We did, though I didn't get much out of him. He's a lot like his mother in that regard—didn't even confirm Robbie was his father until I pinned him down."

"So he didn't give you any contact details either, I assume?"

"No," Arial said. "But I did get some information from Catherine Smythe on Robbie."

"You went to see Catherine today, too," Chris said, twisting around to smile at her. "Busy girl."

"You know it," Arial said. "Walking Monty is a bonus since people seem to open up around him."

"He does have an honest face," Chris said, going back to his slathering. "What did Catherine tell you?"

"Specifics on some of the things we already knew. Robbie's lease was up at the end of July but he may have left as early as June when he paid both June and July's rent. She's not sure when."

"He certainly was there in June when I moved in." Chris turned with his brow furrowed but then he brightened. "I'm pretty sure he was gone by the Fourth, though, because Melinda was here and sent me over to invite him for drinks on the deck."

Obviously the more sociable of the siblings. Or half-siblings. "And?"

"House was dark. I assumed he'd gone away for the holiday, but now that I think about it, I can't remember seeing him after that. Or seeing lights, even."

"That didn't worry you?" Arial had a feeling if Robbie was a golden retriever or cocker spaniel, Chris would have paid more attention.

But now the veterinarian just shrugged. "I knew his lease was up that month."

Hopeless. "Well, Catherine had an address for his mother in Sacramento. Robbie had her send the check for the security deposit refund there."

"So then we know he went to Sacramento," Chris said. "Which means he isn't under the house."

Arial wrinkled her nose. "Not really. The check was cashed, but it was in Mother Henry's name. No way of telling if Robbie cashed it."

Chris groaned. "Well, at least we have an address. Do the police know?"

"They talked to Catherine before I did," Arial confirmed. "So I assume they're following up with the mother."

"Well, that's good," Chris said, coming back with the muffin halves. "I did butter on yours, too, since you looked needy."

"Growing needier by the second," Arial said. "Thank you."

"You're welcome. Can we get back to the book club?"

"Absolutely," Arial said, taking her half. "Anyway, I told the group that Aaron was at Lovers Point for a breakfast burrito and that we talked. I even think I made a few brownie points with Simone by pointing out that Aaron was a rideshare driver and did food delivery as well, so—by nature of his work—would be 'loitering' around town, waiting for the next job."

"Which is true, though it's not really loitering. In return for your support, did Simone spill anything about Robbie's whereabouts?"

"No. And when Olivia asked, Simone said that the police hadn't talked to her."

"Olivia?" Chris said. "Have you deputized her?"

"No need. Fiona, Olivia and Marta are all very interested in our body."

"*Our* body."

"They actually refer to it as my body, but I'm sharing." She took a bite. "Mmm, animal and vegetable fat, all in one bite. Delicious."

"Dairy and legume fat, to be precise, but still delicious."

Arial caught a rivulet of melted butter that was running down her finger. "So here's something interesting: I know from Dan that he did ask Simone about Robbie. Why is she denying it?"

"That's pretty obvious," he said, handing her a napkin. "She didn't want to volunteer the information in front of Emily, the neighborhood gossip. Especially when it has to do with a police investigation."

"She does seem to be all about appearances. But there was another question from . . ." she tried to remember who asked it and gave up. "Anyway, whoever it was had a great point. She asked Simone whether the police had asked for DNA from Robbie to try to match the body."

"Like a hairbrush or clothes?"

"Exactly, which she denied having, of course. But it made me wonder if there might be something like that left behind in the guest house."

Chris gave it some thought. "Maybe. I mean there was the wine and a few other things left behind in cabinets or whatever. Like I said, I didn't feel right throwing anything out without your permission, so I boxed it up and put it in the back hall closet. Nothing in particular that screams DNA to me, though. And even if it did, how could we know for sure that it was Robbie's?"

"Good question," Arial said. "Though if the DNA matched the body, it would prove that person had been in the house."

"Whether that person is Robbie or not," Chris mused before looking up. "Did anybody mention me?"

"Tonight at book club? No, why would they?" Arial asked, puzzled. "I mean you're probably considered a catch—single veterinarian and all, but—"

"I meant in conjunction with the body we found," Chris said, reddening. "I know Emily was speculating about the burglaries, but did anybody—"

"Suggest you killed Robbie and hid him under the

floorboards?" Arial asked, lifting her eyebrows. "No, but I can bring it up next meeting, if you like."

"You think I'm being ridiculous," Chris guessed. "Imagining that I could be a suspect."

Arial thought about lying, but . . . "Not at all. You were here, Robbie was here and then he wasn't. The police know that, and it makes you a person of interest. If"—she held up a finger as he started to interrupt—"they know that the body is Robbie's and that he was murdered. Which they don't."

"That's a relief," Chris said. "How do you know—"

"Oh, Dan and I talked about it."

"Dan Sotherly, your detective friend. He's been asking you about me?"

"Well, to be fair, that detective told both of us to stick around," Arial reminded him. "I'm not much of a suspect, since I wasn't here during the time frame in question."

"Which is what?"

"April, May, June, July and August. I didn't tell you that?"

"You didn't. Is there anything else you forgot to tell me, besides the chief detective is asking about me as a suspect?"

"I didn't say that," Arial protested. "Dan was here this morning—I told you he was coming. It's just that so much has happened and, I mean . . . you were working and all."

"I was." Chris was not pleased. "So when your pal Dan was here, what did he say?"

"Hey," Arial said, holding up her hands. "I'm genuinely sorry that I didn't call and fill you in. Dan confirmed that you were right, and the body is a man. He also said they're placing the time of death between eight months and a year."

"So that's the April through August."

"Yes, but he also said they still have no cause of death and no ID, like I did tell you. They're just casting a wide net. Talking to Aaron, too, obviously looking for Robbie. Fiona—"

"Fiona?" Chris was having trouble keeping up.

"Sinclair, book club member," Arial reminded him. "Anyway, Fiona suggested the police don't really need something with Robbie's DNA, because they have Aaron." Or they would if they could find him.

"Because Aaron would have half of Robbie's DNA," Chris said, softening.

"Exactly. I was so obsessed with finding out if Robbie was alive, that I didn't even think of that. I should have snagged his burrito wrapper, but Monty snuffled all over it."

Chris didn't ask. "Confirming that Robbie is alive would be a much simpler way of eliminating him as the dead man. DNA takes a while."

"True," Arial said. "Ooh, another thing I didn't tell you. Simone got all defensive about Robbie and suggested that maybe the body was Mark's instead."

Chris frowned. "Emily's husband?"

Arial raised both hands in a "go figure" gesture. "According to Marta, Mark is twenty years older than Emily, which would put him right around fifty. Smack in the middle of Dan's 'middle-aged.'"

"The man whose body you and I found under the guest house was middle-aged?" Chris asked casually.

Arial cringed. "Yeah, sorry—another thing I forgot to mention. Dan said middle-aged, which he defined as forties to sixties."

Chris frowned. "The body should have told them more than that, I would think."

"Same here," Arial said, happy to be back on the same side again. "He did say the postmortem and tox screens aren't complete."

"And it is possible they know more than Dan is telling you, I suppose."

"I suppose," Arial said grudgingly.

Chris threw her a grin. "But back to the book club. What did Emily have to say when Simone suggested Mark could be under the floorboards?"

"She said that she knew exactly where Mark was—on some beach in Florida with his girlfriend—and could Simone say the same about her ex? Simone snapped and said, no, because she wasn't some kind of stalker like Emily."

"Let me guess—that was the implosion." Chris was enjoying this now.

"Oh, yes," Arial said, getting up to take their plates to the sink. We left them facing off against each other in the living room and snuck out the back door."

"You didn't want to see what happened?"

Arial shrugged and turned. "I did, honestly. But Fiona suggested we just check under the guest house in the morning to see whose body was there."

"She was kidding, right?"

"God, I hope so. Or I'm always going to need butter with my peanut butter."

FIFTEEN

Arial stepped out onto her front porch Wednesday morning, squinting against the morning sun to wave to Shirley across the yards. No fog today, and her neighbor had texted first thing to say she wanted to hear all about book club last night and ask if Arial would like to drive to their favorite coffee house.

Acme Coffee Roasting in nearby Seaside was a popular spot for locals, including police and firefighters. Which was one of the reasons—besides the good coffee and company, of course—that Arial had jumped at the invitation. Dan would likely be there, and while Arial felt obligated to tell him about seeing Aaron at Lovers Point, she hoped to downplay the encounter—especially Aaron's vanishing act.

I mean, just because Aaron bolted didn't mean he was hiding something, did it?

Yes, pretty much. But exactly what?

Shirley was walking to her Prius, phone in one hand and Monty dancing at her side.

"I'm telling you, Frank, you put it in your briefcase when you left," Shirley was saying, her tone exasperated as she punched a button on her phone.

"I've checked through twice, Shirley," Frank's voice boomed from the phone's speaker. "Are you sure you didn't take it out?"

"Why in the world would I do that? I know how you are about your things and—"

Arial hesitated, feeling like she was eavesdropping. Why was it that the older generation put every call on speaker? Monty didn't care, though. He let out an enthusiastic bark and started pulling on the leash to come greet her.

Shirley held up a finger, lowering the phone slightly. "Sorry about this. Frank is at his conference in Chicago, though I don't know why, given he's *supposed to be retired.*" This last seemed for her husband's benefit.

"Hi, Frank," Arial called, with no real hope of being heard over Frank's diatribe.

"But I need it by five, central time. The talk is—"

With an eye roll, Shirley thankfully switched off the speaker to muffle her husband's voice. "He's misplaced the text of the speech he's giving tonight. Let's just say he's not the most organized person in the world."

"No worries," Arial said, as Frank continued muttering indistinctly on the other end.

Shirley held the phone away. "He swears it's my fault. Typical. I'm going to have to find it on the computer and send it to him. Would you mind going without me?"

"Want me to bring you a latte?" Arial asked, and gestured to the dog, who was sniffing her sneakers. "And Monty? I know he loves the croissants."

Shirley's face lit up. "Would you take him with you? I promised him, and he's been bouncing off the walls all morning."

"Of course. Want to go for a ride, Monty?" Arial asked, taking the leash from Shirley. Monty reared up on his back legs, doing his happy dance.

"Thanks, Arial," Shirley said, already turning back toward the house. "Frank, I'm going to try to find it. Hold on."

As she disappeared inside, Arial glanced down at Monty. "Well, buddy, looks like it's just you and me. Ready for an adventure riding in my car?"

Monty woofed enthusiastically, pulling her toward the Toyota.

The cream-colored brick building with its bold orange 'Acme Coffee Roasting' sign painted on one corner stood out like a beacon. A line of about ten people snaked up to the garage-door-like opening, where two espresso machines hissed and steamed. Next to them, a pour-over counter held four drip coffees going simultaneously.

Arial scanned the parking lot as she brought Monty out of the back seat on his leash. A couple sat on a bench with their newborn in a carrier, while others stood around the small counter-height table and chatted as they waited for their drinks. And . . . yes! Dan was at the far side, sipping from a to-go cup and talking to a man Arial didn't recognize.

"Best manners, buddy," Arial murmured to Monty as they weaved through the small crowd. "No stealing pastries."

Monty wagged his tail, oblivious to her admonition, as they crossed to Dan. The detective noticed their approach, nodding in Arial's direction before excusing himself from his conversation to meet them halfway.

"Morning, Arial. Coffee with you two mornings in a row. How lucky am I?" His tone sounded more suspicious than lucky.

"I know," Arial said, sidling up. "Shirley was going to come with us, but she needed to help Frank with something. Still," she said, gesturing at the dog, who was eyeing a doughnut a little boy was dangling nearby. "Monty wanted his croissant, and I needed coffee."

"You're being awfully casual," Dan said, eyeing her. "You sure you don't have something to tell me? Or, more likely, ask me?"

"You did say we should keep each other informed."

"I did." Dan glanced around, then tipped his head toward where his dark sedan was parked in the adjacent public parking lot. "Let's step over here."

Arial tugged Monty away from the doughnut, and they followed. Dan set his cup down on the hood. "We've tracked down Robbie's mother at a nursing home in Sacramento. Advanced Alzheimer's. Staff says she doesn't get many visitors, and they can't confirm if Robbie's been there recently—or at all."

"I talked to Catherine Smythe yesterday," Arial told him. "She said the check for Robbie's security deposit refund on the guest house was sent to his mother."

"And deposited to her account," Dan said. "We followed up on that, too, but it's possible Robbie never saw it. The check was made out to his mother and there's a local lawyer who holds her power of attorney and oversees her finances."

"So another dead end." Arial sighed. "But Catherine said Robbie paid the July rent for the guest house in June, though she doesn't know exactly when he vacated the premises. So are you thinking that Robbie murdered whoever it is, stashed the body and took off, or that it's Robbie we found in the crawl space? But who would Robbie have wanted to kill? Or, conversely, who would have wanted to kill him? From everything I've heard, he was a regular guy. Chris said he was quiet—that he didn't see much of him."

"But then Chris would, wouldn't he?" Dan asked mildly.

Arial gave the detective stink eye. "Chris had no reason to kill Robbie. Besides he told me yesterday that he's fairly certain that Robbie was there in June, but gone by the Fourth of July."

One eyebrow went up. "And the Fourth is significant because?"

"Because Chris went to the guest house to invite Robbie over for drinks that night, but there was no sign of him. No lights or anything and he can't recall seeing Robbie after that." It belatedly occurred to Arial that she might be raising Dan's suspicions of Chris, not allaying them. "Melinda, Chris's half-sister was there that weekend, too. You can ask her if you want."

"I might do that."

Arial had an urge to punch Dan in the arm not-so-playfully but, given the whole "assaulting an officer" thing, resisted. "Setting aside Chris, who had no motive, who would have wanted Robbie dead?" She looked up hopefully. "His ex-wife maybe?"

"You really don't like Simone, do you?" Dan said, shaking his head.

"No more than she likes me," Arial said. "Though I think she may be warming up a bit, so I may have to adjust."

"Good to know," Dan said. "And as for Simone killing her ex, she should have done it before the divorce was final, not after." He shrugged. "There was nothing to gain."

"Not financially," Arial agreed, and had another thought. "But if Simone was the one with money, maybe she was paying alimony and wanted to get out from under before she remarried."

"So she killed him and then hid the body so nobody knew he was dead?"

Argh. "Good point."

"The only other family member is Aaron," Dan said. "And while I don't see a reason offhand why he'd harm his father, I would like to talk to him. And maybe get a DNA sample to see if he's a familial match to the body under your guest house. I don't suppose you've seen him since the day you met?" He was looking at her like he knew the answer.

Arial dipped her head. "OK, yes. I ran into Aaron at Lovers Point yesterday after I saw you."

"Oh?"

She shifted uncomfortably. "He dodged my questions. In fact, he didn't admit Simone and Robbie were his parents until I backed him into a corner." Denial seemed to run in the family. "But he does know people are talking about him in connection with the robberies." Because Arial had told him, for better or worse. Probably worse.

Dan nodded, his expression thoughtful. "If you see him again, let me know. We're not calling him a suspect, but we're running out of leads, and his cooperation could be key."

"To the robberies or identifying the body?"

"Both," Dan said. "Though we've nothing to pin him to the robberies, except your seeing him Tuesday morning, presumably leaving the Rowans'—"

"After delivering bagels," Arial pointed out. "Surely Simone can confirm that. And how would that work? You deliver bagels to the front door and then run around back and break in while they're toasting and schmearing? Besides," she said, just realizing, "I saw somebody open the door to get the bagels while we were still standing there."

"We have asked the other victims whether they had food deliveries on the dates of the robberies," Dan said. "So far, no pattern, at least not from what they recall."

"Couldn't you get records from the delivery apps?" Arial asked.

"Not without a warrant. But as I said, there's no basis at this point."

"But the robberies—you said there are five now—you believe it's the same person?"

"Or persons. Same MO every time—a door or window that's left open or unlocked, so no forced entry and only small valuables taken, things that won't be immediately missed and can be sold easily. It would appear to be someone who knows the area well."

"Which is pretty much everybody who lives here," Arial said as Monty leaned against her in a dramatic "I'm starving" pose, nearly toppling her. "Steady, buddy."

"I should get going," Dan said, finishing off his coffee. "Keep your ears open, Arial, and let me know what you hear. But please don't do anything reckless."

"Never," she said, holding out her hand for his empty cup. "I can toss that for you. Monty is still in desperate need of his croissant."

"And you still haven't had your coffee. You know, the reason you came."

She grinned. "Can't pull anything over on the detective."

As Dan's car left the parking lot, Arial looked down at her canine companion. "Curiouser and curiouser, Monty. You ready for your croissant?"

Monty practically dragged her back toward the order window.

Shirley was on her porch when they pulled up in front and came to greet them. "Finally got the speech to Frank, thank God. How was Acme?"

"Great as usual," Arial said, handing her the latte as she climbed out of the driver's seat. "I got that extra hot for the drive, so be careful."

Shirley took the top off and blew on the foamy drink as Arial swung open the back door of her car to get Monty. But before she could snap the leash on his collar, he launched himself out, barking furiously.

"Monty!" Arial called frantically, chasing him toward the big live oak. "Stay! Sit!"

"Oh, dear," Shirley said, putting the latte down. "Monty? You come here right now!"

"Croissant," Arial called as he disappeared between the houses. "Monty, croissant!!"

"Do you have one?" Shirley asked breathlessly as she caught up. "He's scent- and food-driven."

"In a bag in the car," Arial said, hesitating. "Want me to go grab them?"

"I will," Shirley said. "You go after him and keep him in sight."

Guilt-stricken, Arial stopped in the backyard, glancing around. There was no sign of the dog, and, of course, no fence, so he could already be out in the alley or, worse, on the street.

Shirley came chugging up with the bag. "Monty? Monty? Where is he?"

"I'm so sorry," Arial said, nearly tearful. "I should have left the leash on him or—"

"No, no," Shirley said. "Never in the car, he could get hung up. I don't know why he took off like that, but when he has a scent . . ." She shook the bag loudly. "Monty? Treat!"

"Wait," Arial said, putting her hand on Shirley's arm. "Do you hear digging or—"

"There," Shirley said, pointing to the back of the guest house. "The crime scene tape."

Sure enough, one end of the yellow and black tape was dangling in the wind, no doubt torn off by a sixty-pound-plus puppy.

"Dan is going to kill me," Arial muttered, shoving aside the loose tape to crawl in.

"Is he in there?" Shirley pushed up behind her to see Monty digging furiously in the center of the crawl space, sending sand flying in every direction. "Monty, no. Leave it."

"That is one monster hole you're digging, buddy," Arial told Monty in a low tone as she half-crawled, half-bottom-scooted some fifteen feet to him. "Don't you think it's big enough though?"

The dog met her eyes, head tilted as if considering.

Shirley appeared at Arial's elbow. "Please tell me that wasn't where the body was," she whispered.

"I'm afraid so." Arial reached for Monty and he dodged her playfully, kicking sand in her face like some four-legged bully on the beach.

"Monty, no!" Shirley said again, reaching past Arial to grasp the dog's collar. "I'm so sorry, Arial."

"You aren't the one who should be sorry," Arial said, doing a modified duck walk to follow the other two out from under the crawl space. "I," she straightened and spit out a mouthful of sand, "pretty much got what I deserved."

SIXTEEN

With Monty safely in hand, Shirley had brightened considerably as she handed Arial the croissant bag and went to snap the leash on his collar. "It was Monty who took off, wasn't it, boy? We just can't listen, can we?"

Arial took a deep breath, setting aside the destruction of the crime scene for now. "Well, I'm glad he's safe. Should I give him the croissant we were luring him with?"

"Because he came so obediently?" Shirley asked. "No way. We did have to pull him out."

"Well, I actually bought these for you anyway," Arial said, holding up the bag. "Though they might be a little worse for wear."

"I'm sure they'll be delicious—thank you," Shirley said. "Why don't you come in and we'll have them and get Monty some water?"

"That would be nice, thanks," Arial said, following her neighbor through the front door and into the cottage's kitchen.

"Here, let me consolidate Frank's junk," Shirley said, gathering a pencil, pink eraser, and yellowed *New York Times* crossword puzzle and placing it on top of a laptop before moving it all to the desk across the way.

"Is this one of those bluetooth speakers?" Arial asked, wandering over to the desk to pick up a red plastic bulldog wearing sunglasses.

"Online purchase," Shirley admitted, her face turning red. "I thought it was cute."

"It is," Arial said, examining the speaker grill hidden in each sunglass lens before setting the thing back down next to the laptop. "The only thing cuter would have been a Monty version."

"Not that he deserves the homage." Shirley gave Monty a stern look before waving Arial to the table by the window. "Can I get you some coffee? Or iced tea?"

"Oh, no," Arial said, sitting down. "Water is good for me. Did you dump your latte in all the confusion?"

"Not most of it," the other woman said. "Let me go grab what's left."

As Shirley went to do that, Arial got up to fill Monty's water bowl.

"Well, that was certainly enough excitement for the morning," Shirley said, returning with the to-go cup. "First, Frank's crisis and then the Great Escape. Do we need to tell the police we violated the crime scene?" She glanced at Monty, now lapping water at a furious pace. "Or Monty did."

"I'll text Dan," Arial said. "To be honest, they should have put up the lattice door or a sheet of plywood if they didn't want animals to get in there."

"Very true," Shirley said as she placed a glass of water in front of Arial and then went back to the cupboard for a plate. "Dogs or squirrels don't respect crime scene tape."

At the word "squirrels," Monty lifted his head, then he went back to drinking.

Arial took out two croissants, one plain and one chocolate, and put them on the plate. At the sound of the paper bag, Monty was sitting practically on her foot.

"No chocolate for you," Arial warned as Shirley moved a neat stack of newspapers from the other chair to the countertop so she could sit down.

"He'll want the empty bag," Shirley told her. "He likes the crumbs."

"What's Chris's take on the croissants?" Arial asked, leaning down to give Monty the bag to snuffle. "I can't imagine croissants are on his list of best foods for dogs."

"They aren't," Shirley said, giving Monty a few moments before taking the torn and already soggy bag away. "But Monty loves them and, given I almost lost him . . ." She shrugged. "Everything in moderation, I say."

For Arial's part, she was glad she hadn't been responsible

for losing him in a totally different way. "Take your pick of croissants. I'm good with either."

"I'll cut them in half, and we can share," Shirley said, getting up to fetch a knife. "Now tell me what you learned from Dan."

Apparently, it wasn't just the detective who saw through Arial's "hey, I'll go to coffee anyway" ruse. "I thought you wanted to hear about the book club meeting."

"I do, but police updates first."

"Well." Arial took an appreciative sip of the water, still recovering from what Shirley had called The Great Escape. "Probably most importantly, they found Robbie's mother."

"With Robbie, I hope?" Shirley chose a piece of the chocolate croissant and took a bite. "Heaven."

"No," Arial told her. "She's in a nursing home with advanced Alzheimer's, and nobody seems to know if Robbie has been there or not. Regardless, he doesn't seem to be living in Sacramento now."

"But somebody has to know where he is," Shirley said and picked up her latte. "His son Aaron, if not his ex?"

"You would think so," Arial said. "Do you know if Robbie had to pay alimony or child support?"

Shirley was shaking her head. "Maybe early on, but Simone is remarried, and Aaron is done with college. I think that all ended."

Arial frowned. "Dan didn't think Simone would have a financial motive."

"Not financial, no," Shirley said a little distractedly as she looked out the front window.

Arial's eyes followed her gaze, but she didn't see anything beyond their quiet street. "Why do you say it like that? Does Simone have another reason to get rid of Robbie?"

Shirley seemed to come back from wherever she was. "No, not really. Sorry."

"You were thinking about something," Arial pressed. "Was it an ugly divorce?"

"Don't most divorces end up ugly, even the ones that start out amicable?" Her neighbor shrugged. "I think Simone was happy at the end to be rid of Robbie—not enough money, ambition, whatever—"

"What did—or does—Robbie do?" Arial realized she'd never asked the question. "Maybe that would be a simple way to track him down." Duh.

"He's a data analyst of some kind or maybe a programmer. Something in tech, I know, because he and Frank were always talking computers."

Or maybe not so simple after all. A lot of people on the peninsula had ties to Silicon Valley in some way or the other. "Tech workers are usually paid well."

Shirley shrugged. "Maybe not as well as they used to be. And I think Charles Rowan—a neurosurgeon," she answered before Arial could ask, "is more Simone's style."

Disappointing. "She was so ticked last night."

"Simone?" Shirley said, leaning forward. "She was at book club?"

"She was," Arial said. "And there was this big blowout between her and Emily."

"Tell me more." Shirley picked up her cup and, finding it empty, set it back down again. "Please."

"Well, Emily—"

"Wait, wait—who all was there?"

This felt like a repeat of her conversation with Chris last night. "Emily, of course, Simone, Fiona, Olivia and Marta."

"The diehards," Shirley said, nodding. "No Lucy?"

"Chris kept her late at work," Arial said.

"Oh, boy," Shirley said. "She's going to be upset if she missed something."

"Well, it was short and not-so-sweet," Arial said. "Emily started the proceedings by accusing Simone's son Aaron of lurking and maybe being involved in the burglaries."

"What did Simone have to say about that?" Shirley said, sitting back in her chair.

"You know, I was surprised. When I spoke to her, Simone barely acknowledged having a son. And Aaron, to be fair, was the same about Simone. In fact, also about—"

"But you digress," Shirley pointed out.

"I do. Sorry. Anyway, Simone went all Mama Lion on Emily. Even suggested that maybe it was Mark dead under the house."

Shirley frowned. "Mark? Really? What did that have to do with the burglaries?"

"It didn't," Arial admitted. "But Simone was obviously stewing and the discussion had shifted to our body—"

"Not surprising," Shirley said. "A corpse is big news, in any size town."

"Exactly," Arial said. "We were discussing whether Aaron might provide the police with DNA for a possible match to the body."

"Oh," Shirley said, her eyebrows going up. "Good idea."

"Fiona's," Arial admitted. "I should have thought of it, but . . . oh."

"Oh, what?"

"Maybe that's why Aaron has made himself scarce. I didn't see why he might object to providing DNA to help identify the body, but I just realized."

"Realized what?"

"If he really was involved in the robberies—and I think that's a big 'if' because Aaron seems like a good—"

Shirley was glaring at her.

"Right, right, I digress again," Arial said. "But if Aaron was inside any of the houses that were robbed—"

"He wouldn't want his DNA on file, even if it were for another reason," Shirley finished for her.

"Exactly." Arial was frowning.

"But back to Simone's accusation about Mark?" Shirley reminded her.

Arial's digressions were having digressions. But that was pretty much how her brain worked. "Simone said Mark supposedly had left town after his divorce from Emily. How did we know the body wasn't Mark's?"

Shirley wrinkled her nose. "Much as I'd love to think Emily guilty of something, Mark and Frank were friends. He knew they were having problems and has stayed in touch with him."

"So not dead."

"Not dead," Shirley agreed. "Alive and well and paying alimony and child support, so far as I know."

"Living with his so-called bimbo in Florida, according to Emily. I guess she would keep tabs, with Dickie being so young and all."

"Please," Shirley said. "Emily would keep tabs, regardless. It's who she is."

"Apparently so." Arial had a thought. "You said Frank might have heard from Robbie. Did you ask him?"

"I did, but no go, I'm afraid. Frank doesn't admit this stuff—typical man—but he seemed a little hurt that Robbie just left without a word."

"Did you tell him there might be a reason?"

Shirley shook her head. "I didn't want to lay that on him. Especially when he's got this speech and all." She took a deep breath. "So did I miss anything else last night?"

"Not that I witnessed," Arial said. "Simone and Emily were still facing off in the living room when the rest of us snuck out the back."

Shirley's eyes were big. "Damn, I should have been there."

"It was quite the half-hour," Arial said, getting up. "Well, thanks for the hospitality, but I should get home."

"So what's next?" Shirley said, standing herself.

"Well, I had to tell Dan that I saw Aaron at Lovers Point yesterday. We'll see if they track him down."

Shirley frowned as she accompanied Arial to the door. "You don't think Aaron's a thief?"

"No, I don't really. But Emily . . ." Arial stopped.

"Is a bitch?" Shirley said, swinging the door open. "Yes, but did you have another point?"

Arial laughed, stepping out onto the porch before she turned. "I get that Emily likes to wind up Simone by picking on Aaron. But I'm wondering if there's another reason she's so hot to pin the robberies on him. I mean, it sounds crazy, but could she be the thief? She's in and out of a lot of houses for book club."

"And she just walked right into yours," Shirley pointed out. "You think she's trying to divert attention to Aaron?"

"I don't know," Arial said thoughtfully. "But I think I'll ask

Dan if there's any correlation between past book club meetings and the break-ins, just in case."

"And do you have a list of past book club meetings?"

"Oh, no," Arial said, stepping down off the porch and turning. "I don't suppose you . . ."

"Of course I do," Shirley said. "I'll dig it out."

"Perfect. I'm going to spend the afternoon going through the guest house. I doubt there's anything of Robbie's still there, but I thought I'd give it a go."

"Would you know if it's Robbie's?" Shirley asked. "Rather than Chris's?"

"Well, no, not necessarily," Arial said, frowning. "But Chris's clothes and personal items are in my laundry room or still in the garbage bags he used to transfer them from the guest house to my living room before the fumigation. Chris said he boxed up a few things he found when he moved in, so they may be Robbie's."

"Want some help?" Shirley asked. "We knew Robbie, so maybe I'll recognize something."

"Great idea," Arial said. "Why don't you grab the book club list and come on over to the main house in about half an hour. I want to shower and change out of these sandy clothes."

"Sounds good," Shirley said, running her hand through her hair. A shower of sand rained down on the table. "I think maybe I'll do the same."

Shirley and Monty arrived at Arial's house a little after noon, Shirley brandishing the promised list of past book club meetings triumphantly as Arial opened the door.

"Found it," Shirley said, stepping inside. Monty bounded past her, his tail wagging furiously as he greeted Arial. "And look who also had a bath."

"You must have gotten a blow-dry," Arial said, snuggling her nose into Monty's soft fur. "You both look fabulous, and I must admit I feel a whole lot better after my shower. Do you want some iced tea before we head out to the guest house?"

"I'd love it." Shirley handed Arial the list and followed her into the kitchen.

Arial scanned the paper while pouring the tea. "OK, so the last five book club meetings were at . . . Olivia's, Marta's, Fiona's, Simone's, and Emily's, in that order." She looked up. "Does that mean it's your turn next?"

"Do I look crazy?" Shirley took a sip of her tea.

Arial didn't answer that. "I don't suppose you know which houses were burglarized besides Simone's? There were five of them, too."

"I don't." She made a face. "But I can't imagine any of these women being robbed and keeping it a secret, much less all of them. Can you?"

Arial couldn't. From what she'd seen, they pretty much spoke their minds. "I suppose it's possible the perpetrator—"

"Can we just call her Emily?" Shirley said hopefully. "Or we can just use 'Karen' as a code word."

"We probably could, but we shouldn't," Arial said with a grin and then shrugged. "I don't suppose the houses would have needed to host the book club recently. Maybe last year or . . ." She trailed off weakly.

"Let's face it," Shirley said. "It would be pretty obvious to rob a house right after it had hosted an event of any kind."

"Besides, didn't you say a lot of people don't lock their doors around here? That would make pretty much anywhere easy pickings."

"I shouldn't have generalized," Shirley said. "But I lock my doors, and we haven't been broken into. Not that we have anything to steal."

"Besides, you have a guard dog." Who had flipped over on his back and was already snoring whilst holding up Arial's kitchen wall.

"I certainly do," Shirley said, draining her glass.

Arial was feeling a little let down. "It's probably still worth asking Dan if there's any pattern between the break-ins and these locations. I've already asked the same thing about food deliveries, since suspicion seemed to be falling squarely on Aaron."

"And?"

"And, no pattern again, at least from what the individual

victims told them." She let out a sigh. "Well, let's check out the death house. Should we take Monty back to your place or leave him here?"

At his name, the overgrown puppy opened one eye.

"Oh, we can leave him here. I should have thought that we wouldn't want to take him next door." Shirley hesitated as Monty resumed his nap. "Do we need to worry about falling through the floor in there? Is it dangerous?"

"Dan's guys patched it up temporarily, but the city posted a notice on the door. The structure has to be inspected for other structural damage, the repair work has to be completed, and then there's another inspection before it's considered safe."

"And habitable, I assume," Shirley glanced sideways as Arial held the door for her. "Does that mean Chris will be staying on with you? Sleeping on your couch, I mean?"

"I guess it does," Arial said, closing the door softly behind them so as to let sleeping dogs lie.

SEVENTEEN

The notice was still on the door, of course, and Arial assumed it would have to remain there flagging the building as unsafe until the work was done. It was kind of embarrassing, but probably no worse than the corpse.

"I need to tell Chris about this," she said, tapping her fingernail on the notice as she stepped in. "I completely forgot last night."

"I'm sure he'll be all broken up." Shirley closed the door behind them.

Inside, the guest house was cool and dim, dust bunnies circling in the light streaming through the front windows. The floorplan was simple: From the front door, you entered the living room which had a single door to the right, leading to the bedroom. Behind the front room was a square back hallway/pantry area with the kitchen off to the left, the bathroom to the right, and the back door straight ahead.

For now, the couch Arial and Chris had so disastrously carried in was on the left wall of the room, along with a dark wood coffee table, both just clear of the boarded-over hole in the floor.

"That is one big hole," Shirley said, standing back.

"Maybe the boarding-over makes it look bigger," Arial started to say, but then shrugged, not feeling the need to make excuses for her hole. "But yeah, it's big. Seems bigger now."

"Or maybe it's like a sinkhole and keeps growing." Shirley was edging along the wall clockwise toward the back hallway. "If the floor was mushy then—"

"Mushy," Arial repeated. "I hope I never have to hear that word again."

"You refused to hear it the first time," Shirley reminded her lightly.

"Point taken," Arial said, following her friend. "I should have let the termite men repair it and then *they* could have discovered the body. Then again, they might have boarded right over and the poor man would never have been found."

"Point taken," Shirley echoed, stepping into the back hallway. She gave a tentative bounce. "Floor feels fine here. Where should we start?"

"Like I said, Chris cleared out the upholstered furniture and most of his stuff before the fumigation," Arial said, going to open a closet. "Anything he found when he moved in, he boxed up and put in here."

Shirley leaned against the kitchen doorframe, watching as Arial pulled out a box of mismatched dishes wrapped in old newspaper. "I hope you're not expecting anything too exciting. Robbie didn't seem like the sentimental type."

"I assume these dishes were washed before Chris boxed them," Arial said, holding up a plate.

"I wouldn't necessarily assume that," Shirley said, coming over to take it. She flicked something hard and brown off it with her fingernail. "Want to check this for DNA?"

"Not especially," Arial said, wrinkling her nose. "I'm not quite sure what I'm looking for. Maybe correspondence? An envelope he licked?"

"Which he then mailed," Shirley said logically.

"True. OK, so maybe there's a clue to where he went when he left," Arial persisted, setting the box aside and pulling another from the high shelf of the closet.

For the next half-hour, they methodically went through every box in the closet before moving on to drawers and cabinets in the kitchen and bathroom.

"Nothing in the bathroom," Shirley said, coming into the kitchen. "Anything here?"

"A sangiovese and two old bottles of wine Chris mentioned, but nothing that screams Robbie. Although . . ." She held up a photo that looked to be of a backyard barbecue. "This was taped inside a cupboard. I think I recognize Simone in this and," she pointed, "is this you?"

Shirley groaned. "Wearing shorts, yes. And Frank," she

pointed. "Have you ever seen legs that white? Thankfully, we don't get much chance to wear shorts a lot in this climate."

"If you did, your legs wouldn't look like that," Arial said.

"You, too, will have embarrassingly white legs in a year." Shirley took a closer look. "I think this was a neighborhood crab-boil at Robbie and Simone's house. Before they got divorced, of course."

"Oooh," Arial said, pushing in to study it over her shoulder. "So which one is Robbie?"

"There," Shirley said, indicating a sandy-haired man placing an oversized pot of water on an outdoor grill with the help of another, bigger man.

"I can see the resemblance to Aaron," Arial said, taking the photo back. "How long ago was this?"

Shirley gazed skyward as she gave it some thought. "Maybe five years ago? Long enough that you couldn't recognize me right off."

"Your hair was different," Arial said quickly.

Shirley punched her. "And I was about twenty pounds lighter. You don't have to lie. I notice you didn't have any trouble recognizing Simone."

"The red hair and the scowl were giveaways." She slipped the photo into her jeans pocket. "I guess that's about all we're going to find, but this was a long shot anyway. Thanks for helping."

"Of course," Shirley said, opening the back door. "We should have come in this way. Sidestepped the whole mushy floor."

"And humiliating notice on the door," Arial said, following her out. "As far as the robberies are concerned, I'll give Dan the meeting list, but I'm starting to doubt if there's any connection." She pulled the door closed behind them.

"Don't give up hope. Emily might still be an international jewel thief," Shirley called back with a grin as she headed in the other direction.

Turning toward her own house, Arial mounted the porch steps and stopped just inside the door, contemplating her next move.

Monty nosed her hand, making her jump. "Geez, Monty. I forgot you were here."

Even as she said it, Shirley reappeared. "Happen to have a spare dog?"

"I do, in fact." Arial gave Monty a scratch as he passed by and then had a thought. "Do you mind if I hang onto Monty for a walk? I want to do some snooping, and he's a good cover."

"Of course not." Shirley nodded at the leash she'd left on Arial's counter. "I'd go with you, but . . . well, I'm lazy. See ya."

Monty, having had his nap, seemed more than happy at the prospect of some exercise. Arial fastened the leash and grabbed the book club list, snapping a quick photo first to send to Dan. "I've already seen Emily and Simone's houses," she told the dog, "so that leaves Fiona, Olivia and Marta. Let's go walk past, see if we get vibes of any kind."

Arial knew full well that she was grasping at straws, but other than passing the list onto Dan, she was out of ideas. "Happily, all three live here in PG and their addresses and phone numbers are on here." She glanced at the club contact information at the bottom. "Lucy put this together. No wonder it's comprehensive."

Monty, who had been waiting patiently up to this point, started to prance.

"You're absolutely right," Arial said. "I'm wasting time—let's go!"

Monty's tags jingled as Arial and her furry cover story threaded their way down the quiet streets of Pacific Grove. The sun was slanting lower and the chill coming off the bay made Arial glad she'd taken the time to go back at the last minute to pull on her jacket. She had also punched the addresses into her phone. It would be a three-mile loop in all—a perfect Monty Walk.

Their first stop was just a few blocks down. Olivia Marin's house was a dark blue adobe with bright white window frames. The cozy Spanish-style structure filled almost the entire narrow lot since the original PG city lots had been plotted to fit campers' tents for the religious retreat, not full-blown houses. The cottages had sprung up on the lots in the early 1900s and

Olivia's was particularly charming, its front yard full of colorful ceramic pots filled with cacti.

"Well, this is cheerful—just like Olivia herself," Arial murmured to Monty, who was thoroughly engrossed in a wide-spreading cactus with spiky orange flowers overhanging the sidewalk. "I wouldn't lift my leg on that one, buddy. One wrong move and ouch!"

Monty glanced back at her doubtfully and lowered his leg.

"Good decision." Arial snapped a quick picture of the house with her phone. "It's lovely and tasteful and reflects somebody who cares for their things. If I were a thief, I wouldn't necessarily consider it a target—certainly not like Simone's big showy house."

But then, what did Arial know? Including which houses had been robbed beyond Simone's.

As they continued on, Arial tapped up Dan's number. He picked up on the second ring.

"Arial," Dan said. "What's up? Have you seen Aaron Henry?"

"Sorry, but no," Arial said, feeling a little guilty for getting his hopes up. "I assume you haven't had any luck either?"

"No, and before you ask, we don't have basis for a warrant to track him through the rideshare and delivery apps he's working for. *And* we can't very well keep ordering food or rides until he turns up."

Arial had considered doing just that, but she had to agree it wasn't very efficient. Or cost-effective. "Hey, I had this crazy idea that maybe—"

"'Crazy' and 'maybe,'" Dan interrupted. "You are already hedging your bets."

"I am," she admitted. "I know it's a long shot, but I just wondered whether somebody from the neighborhood book club could be involved in the robberies. The homes they're held in each month rotate and Simone Rowan's was one." Arial waited a second for feedback, but getting none, plowed on. "It's just that Emily is so determined to pin the robberies on Simone's son Aaron that it has me wondering."

"If she's robbing houses herself? If you're talking about Emily Bennett, and I assume you are, since she's always calling the station about something, I don't believe she has to steal. From what I heard, she got a sweet deal in the divorce."

This last comment was so unlike Dan—practically gossip, in fact—that she had to ask. "Do you know Mark?"

"He's a criminal defense attorney, so our paths crossed."

"If he's an attorney, I'm surprised he wasn't able to negotiate a better settlement," Arial said as a cat crossed the sidewalk in front of them. Monty made a move to follow. "Sit!"

"What?"

"Not you, Dan. Monty and I are out for a walk and he saw a cat."

"Lots of them in PG," Dan said. "You'd think he'd be used to them."

"Lots of squirrels, too," Arial said, as Monty glanced around at the word "squirrel," cat already forgotten. "Doesn't stop him from wanting to chase them."

She cleared her throat, realizing she still needed to tell Dan about Monty's breach of the crawl space. "Speaking of . . ."

But Dan was talking. ". . . suppose you can send me the book club addresses?"

"Of course." She decided to hold off on telling Dan about Monty's escapade, at least until she'd gotten the rest of the information she wanted. "I can send you the list of the last five houses to host, which includes Simone's. Just in case they match up with the robberies . . ." As she spoke, she was firing off the photo she'd taken of the list.

There was a pause as Dan pulled up the text. "No, none of these houses were hit. Except the Rowans', as you say."

"I figured," Arial said, slowing her pace as Monty found another shrub to investigate. "While we're at it, could I get a list of the houses that were robbed? I'm just trying to see if there's a pattern."

"A pattern we haven't seen?" Dan asked.

Arial felt her face grow warm. "I know. I'm just irritated at Emily for targeting Aaron. Everybody is after him for one thing or another. And his mother doesn't seem to provide any support to him—financial or otherwise." This last supposition was a bit of fishing on Arial's part.

"He was always closer to his dad, I understand." Dan hesitated. "You do realize I'm not supposed to share that kind of info—on the robberies, I mean."

"I know," she said, a lightbulb going off. "But it's all public, isn't it? I mean, I could just go back through the *Pine Cone* or the *Herald* or something and find the information. But do you really want to put me through all that work?"

"I absolutely do," Dan said and then sighed. "All right, but I'm not going to send it to you. Meet me at Lovers Point in an hour, and I'll let you take a look."

"Thanks, Dan. You're the best." As she said it, Monty looked up from the bush. "You're the best, too," she assured him. "Next stop, Marta's house."

Marta Villanueva's house was a gray/green bungalow with cream-colored pillars nestled behind a well-manicured hedge. Arial lingered on the sidewalk, taking in the minimalist landscaping and the soft tones of the house.

"Very nice," she said to Monty as she took a quick pic. "But again, it's not ostentatious—not screaming, 'Rob me.'" And Dan had already confirmed that the house wasn't on his list of robberies, at least not to date. So, other than having a nice walk with Monty and snooping on her new friends, what was she doing out here?

Monty let out a low woof and lifted his leg on the hedge. "Not nice," Arial said, pulling him away. "We might as well finish up."

Their final stop was Fiona Sinclair's pink Victorian, a house that could have been pulled straight out of a storybook. Fiona, herself, was in the picket-fenced front yard in a wide-brimmed sun hat and gloves, pruning roses. She looked up and waved as Arial approached.

"Arial!" Fiona called, setting down her clippers. "And is that Monty Cooper with you?"

"It is," Arial said. "I'm starting to think more people know Monty than know Shirley or Frank. And certainly more than know me at this point."

"It's tough being new. But you're doing just the right thing, joining the book club and all," Fiona said. "I was so happy to meet you, and I'm sorry if I seemed overly interested in your body—I mean, the body under your guest house."

Arial laughed. "No more interested than I am, believe me. And before I forget to say it, your garden is amazing. I'll have to do planting at my place eventually, but it's so totally different than back in Wisconsin." Not that she'd ever planted anything in Wisconsin, either. "I haven't a clue what grows in this climate and what doesn't."

"It really depends," Fiona said, brushing dirt from her gloves. "We have a gazillion microclimates, depending on exactly where you are on the peninsula. But your house shouldn't be much different than mine. I'm happy to help when you're ready."

"That's very nice of you," Arial said, gently nudging Monty with her foot as he went to pee on a flowering shrub. "I'd love it."

"Me, too, honestly. I like to keep busy since my husband passed a couple of years ago. Gardening helps. But it's so quiet in the house that I've been thinking about getting a dog myself." Monty, hearing his species, gave her a smile. Fiona grinned back. "It would give me an excuse for talking to myself," she said, squatting to nuzzle him. "Nobody thinks it's crazy talking to a dog, right?"

"Thank God," Arial said. "And dogs are great listeners, to boot. They never judge."

"Unlike some people," Fiona said, rolling her eyes. "And I would say don't judge us by last night's book club, but there's always some sort of drama, I'm afraid."

"I loved it," Arial admitted. "As long as no blood was spilled."

Fiona leaned on the fence conspiratorially. "We were couple friends, you know. Emily and Mark, Simone and Robbie, Peter and me." She flushed. "How things have changed." She shrugged, seeming to try to throw off the mood that had descended on her.

"Olivia and Marta seem lovely," Arial ventured. "I was sorry that Lucy Martin wasn't there."

"How do you know Lucy . . . ?" Fiona started to ask and

then realized. "Oh, of course. Lucy works for Chris Buck, your tenant." Her face asked, "and anything else," but her mouth was too polite to voice it.

Arial grinned. "He is just my tenant. And my friend."

"None of my business." Fiona's face was bright red now, as she changed the subject. "But yes, Lucy is wonderful."

"Shirley gave me a roster of book club meetings and members. I read at the bottom that Lucy put it together. She did my dog-walking flyer, as well." Arial dug into her pocket and came up with one, appropriately dog-eared.

"Very nice," Fiona said, taking it to look over. "Lucy is excellent at these things and volunteered to do our website, too. I think she feels badly that she hasn't hosted."

"Why is that?" Arial asked, despite it not being her business.

"It's difficult because she shares a house with two dogs and a couple of friends and doesn't want to inconvenience them. The friends, I mean, not the dogs."

Having met Lucy, Arial thought it was likely the other way around. "I can see that, especially if a meeting turns out like last night. Bet she's sorry she missed it, though."

"Oh, she absolutely is," Fiona said with a grin. "You know, you should come out with us sometime. Marta's married, but her husband travels, and Olivia, Lucy and I are all single, so we get together sometimes for lunch or dinner. Or First Friday."

"First Friday?" Arial asked.

"First Friday of the month," Fiona said, nodding. "There's music down on Lighthouse Avenue and the shops and art museums stay open later. Restaurants are open, too, of course."

"Sounds like fun. I'd love to tag along," Arial said. "And I probably should host book club at some point, too. When all the crime scene tape is down."

"About that." Fiona lowered her voice. "Like I started to say, I hope you didn't think I was morbid last night, asking about the body and suggesting you might find Simone or Emily under the guest house. I've just been watching a lot of mystery and true crime lately. Makes the world seem a little less scary, oddly enough."

"Bad things might happen, but good people set the situation right," Arial summed up. "I get it. And in fact, I've been nosing around myself. Both about 'my' body, but also the robberies."

Fiona's eyes lit up. "How about lunch sometime at The Grill? Old-school seafood, right on the municipal wharf—that's the working wharf, not the tourist one. We can invite Shirley, too, and Olivia and Marta? Lucy, if she's not working?"

"That sounds perfect," Arial said enthusiastically.

"But no Emily, I'm thinking?" Fiona asked, a mischievous glint in her eye. "Or Simone?"

Arial grimaced. "Probably best to let that volatile relationship cool down a bit, don't you think?"

"Especially in a public place, given we'll likely be talking about exactly what set them off in the first place."

"Exactly."

EIGHTEEN

With all three remaining book club host houses visited and struck off the list, Arial and Monty continued down toward Lovers Point to meet Dan. As usual, Monty was stopping at every bush, wall and shrub that another dog had visited, happily re-marking it with his own particular Monty-ness.

Arial's mood was expansive, too, not so much because she was getting to the truth—because, of course, she wasn't—but because she felt like she belonged here. She liked Fiona, Olivia, Lucy and Marta, and looked forward to getting together with them and Shirley.

By the time they arrived at Lovers Point, the last traces of daylight had faded into a pinky lavender in the distance over Asilomar and, beyond it, the legendary golf courses of Pebble Beach. If Arial squeezed her eyes tight, she could imagine the bagpiper playing as the sun set on the first tee on the Links at Spanish Bay.

"I've only heard about it," she whispered to Monty. "But we should go. Maybe Shirley and our book club friends—"

"You have friends?"

Arial's eyes flew open to see Dan leaning against a picnic table, hands shoved into the pockets of his jacket. A wry smile tugged at his lips. "I mean, besides me and Monty here?" He bent down to greet his pal. "By the way," he said, straightening up, "you're late."

"Blame your friend," Arial told him. "Every tree and bush in Pacific Grove needed his stamp of approval."

Dan gestured to the coffee stand—closed now, its shutters firmly drawn.

"I've been craving one of those breakfast burritos since you mentioned it," he said. "But I guess it's too late for that."

"Now there's a surprise," Arial said. "'Breakfast,' might have been the clue. And speaking of clues, thanks for letting me see the list. It'll save me a lot of time."

Dan pulled a folded piece of paper from his jacket pocket and handed it to her. Arial unfolded it to reveal a list of five addresses, each with a date and time noted beside it.

Arial pulled out her phone and snapped a picture of the list. "Ocean View—that's Simone's, of course. Then Seaside Street, Cypress Lane, Seventeen-Mile Drive, Shell Avenue. They're all in Pacific Grove?"

"Yup and burglarized sometime in the last twelve months. Different times of the day. Four of the five were at night, when the owners were asleep or not there. One—the one on Seventeen-Mile—must have been during the day. The owner noticed things were missing when he came home from work."

"Are they big houses like Simone's?" Arial asked.

"Not really," Dan said. "A little of everything. You can look them up online."

"Or, better yet, I'll run by to see them in person."

"I thought your generation did everything online," Dan said. "If you do go by, please don't bother the homeowners. Promise?"

"Promise." Of course, if one of the owners just happened to be out in the yard . . . "Thanks, Dan. I'm sure I won't come up with anything that you haven't thought of, but—"

"You want to try. I know." Dan stared at her for a second. "If you see Aaron Henry again, you will let me know, right?"

"Of course I will," Arial said, her face getting warm. "Why would you ask that?"

"Because I know you feel sorry for him," Dan said. "But I need to be sure that you'll do the right thing and call me if you see him. I'm not going to slam him in jail. I'm going to ask him some questions and, hopefully, see if we can get his DNA. I'm trusting you not to misuse this information." He held up the robbery sheet. "You need to trust me that I'll do right by Aaron."

"I do trust you." Arial had a twinge, remembering what she'd forgotten to do. "We did have a little accident this morning. I meant to text you."

Dan's eyes darkened. "An accident?"

"As you can see, I've been taking care of Monty—you know, when Shirley took Frank up to the airport in San Jose and such? Well, this morning Monty got away from me when we got out of the car after coffee."

"And?"

"And he broke through the crime scene tape and went under the house."

Dan regarded the dog. "Lots of good smells under there, I'll bet. Especially now that the sand was disturbed."

Monty sat and gave a woof.

"He dug a big hole and kicked around a lot of sand. I'm sorry."

"That's our fault if the lattice wasn't secured across the opening so nobody could get in and hurt himself. Right, Monty?"

Monty wagged his tail. Apparently, the trick for not getting in trouble with Dan was having one.

"I'll tell the techs what happened and give them hell for not securing the space." Dan stretched. "Want a ride back up to your place?"

"We'll be fine," Arial said. "I have Monty and my trusty light/whistle." She held it up.

"I see," Dan said, nodding approvingly.

"Aaron gave it to me," Arial told him, and held up her hands to stave off any questions. "First time I met him. Last week, Tuesday. Then I saw him here, and that's it. I promise."

"I just want you to be careful," Dan said, his tone serious. "Don't go poking around alone."

"Like I said, I have Monty with me," she said with a grin. "He's great backup."

Dan shook his head but smiled. "I think I trust him more than I do you."

Arial lifted her chin. "I'd resent that if I didn't agree that Monty is magnificently trustworthy." When he didn't see a squirrel. Or cat. Or just feel like digging.

Two woofs, this time, and said trusty canine led the way up the hill home.

The house was eerily quiet when Arial opened the door after dropping Monty off with Shirley. "Hello?"

"In here." Chris was sprawled on the living-room couch, a veterinary journal open on his lap. He looked up as she entered and collapsed into the chair opposite him.

"Long day?" he asked.

"You could say that," Arial said, hiking a thumb toward the guest house. "I assume you've seen the 'stop work' order the city posted on the door? Apparently, you can't move back in until we have the floor fixed and inspected."

"We pretty much assumed that, didn't we?" Chris said, looking surprised. "Why? Are you sick of me?"

"No, I . . ." She rubbed her forehead. "It's just this official notice tacked on the door feels kind of embarrassing."

"As embarrassing as a body under the floorboards?"

She thought about it. "Embarrassing in a different way."

"I understand," Chris said, sitting up. "And honestly, I can stay in a hotel if—"

"No, no, no," Arial said. "That's the last thing I want—being here alone."

Chris frowned. "Are you afraid?"

"Not afraid, exactly . . . no, not afraid at all. But I do like having you around. And Monty staying over was fun, too, and having Shirley right next door. I'm starting to think I'm a people person, after all. I've even made some new friends over the last couple of days."

"Imagine that," Chris said with a grin. "Without me even having to set up a play date."

"You jest," Arial said, tossing a chair cushion at him. "But I moved halfway across the country and found . . . family. More family than I had back home." Arial waited a beat for Chris to say something smart. "What?"

"No what," Chris said, leaning forward. "I'm just glad."

"Me, too." Shaking off the sudden onset of sentimentality, Arial reached into her pocket for her phone and the five-by-seven-inch snapshot popped out.

"What's that?" Chris asked, setting his journal aside.

Arial handed him the picture she'd found. "Shirley and I made a search of the guest house, looking for anything Robbie might have left behind."

"And found this?" he asked, taking it from her to examine.

"This and not much more, except the sangiovese and those two bottles of questionable wine you mentioned. The photo was taped inside a cupboard door. Shirley said it was a neighborhood crab-boil that Robbie and Simone hosted when they were still together."

Chris examined the photo closely, his brow furrowing. "That's Mark Bennett helping . . . I think that's Robbie with the pot." He squinted, pointing to the background. "And look—there's Emily. Pregnant, maybe?"

Arial leaned over to look. Sure enough, Emily was smiling in the background, watching the proceedings.

"That does look like a maternity top," Arial said. "And the timing would fit. Dickie's four, and Shirley thought this was maybe five years ago."

"Simone doesn't look happy," Chris said. "I wonder what she was thinking."

"Probably wishing she had a bigger house." The moment the words were out, Arial regretted it, especially after her "we are family" soliloquy. "Sorry, that's not nice. I really don't even know Simone. I just don't like the way she treats her son."

"Have you seen Aaron again?"

"Why does everybody keep asking me that?" Arial said, settling back on the chair with her arms crossed. "Do I look the type to hide a fugitive? Not that Aaron is even *wanted* for anything."

Surprised, Chris held up both hands. "Sorry."

"No, I'm sorry," Arial said, standing back up. "I'm tired and getting prickly. Have you eaten?"

"Yup," Chris said, waving the veterinary journal. "Peanut butter is by the toaster."

Perfect.

Arial was feeling a whole lot more chipper in the morning.

"Sorry I snapped at you last night," she told Chris, handing him a mug of coffee.

"You already apologized," Chris said, going to the cabinet. "And just so you know, I have surgery this morning, so while

I appreciate the coffee, I'm going to have to put it in a to-go cup and head out."

"No offense taken," Arial said, sitting down at the kitchen table with her own mug.

Putting the empty mug in the sink, Chris screwed on the top of the travel cup and glanced out the window. "So what are your plans for this foggy Thursday morning?"

"I told Shirley I'd take Monty for a walk," Arial said. "Then I'm going to do a little internet research on the houses that have been robbed."

"Hmm," Chris said, eyeing her. "Any chance that walk will take you past those houses?"

Was she really so transparent? "I just want to get a feel for the neighborhoods. Which is all I can do, because Dan has already told me not to disturb the occupants."

"But you can't help it if they're outside," Chris said with a knowing grin and nodded to a stack on the desk. "I'd wait a bit for the fog to lift and take your flyers, if I were you."

"You really are a genius," Arial said, getting up to give him a hug. "And so sneaky."

"I . . . well, thanks," the veterinarian said, surprised.

"Sorry, sorry," Arial said, holding up her hands this time. "I guess I'm still feeling guilty for being snippy."

"You weren't snippy," Chris interrupted, picking up his cup. "And you don't have to worry about losing me—or any of your other new friends—even if you are."

"Wow," Arial said, eyebrows knitting. "You should partner with Shirley. You totally psychoanalyzed me in a sentence or less."

"I am a doctor, you know." He picked up his lab coat. "And you're just easier to read than a Siamese."

"Thank you," she called after him as he walked down the sidewalk. "And that was a grateful-friend hug. Nothing more."

He raised his cup in a salute. "Didn't see me complaining, did you?"

NINETEEN

Cups washed and in the dish drainer, Arial showered and got ready to collect Monty for their walk. The fog was still low and thick as she stepped out of the front door, but she didn't want to waste the morning waiting for it to clear up.

As she descended the porch steps, she heard voices from behind the guest house, so she circled back and took a peek. Sure enough, Dan must have gotten on somebody's case because workers were already there, pulling down what remained of the crime scene tape Monty had blown through and securing the latticework.

Arial waved to them and then circled back to Shirley's front door, tapping on it lightly. Monty took it from there, woofing and scrabbling on the other side with his usual exuberance until Shirley opened the door.

"Got time for a cup of coffee before you go?" Shirley asked, standing aside to let her in.

"Maybe just a half," Arial said, a little surprised at her neighbor's early morning sociability. "Is the house quiet with Frank away? I was talking to Fiona yesterday and she suggested we all go out to lunch or dinner."

"Who's all?" Shirley asked, pouring two cups and waving for Arial to sit down.

"You, me, Fiona, Lucy, Olivia and Marta, most likely. No Emily, no Simone."

"Then whoever will you pump for information?" Shirley asked, sitting down across from her.

"I think the idea is to get a congenial group together and chat." Likely about corpses and robberies, but what was wrong with that?

"Wouldn't you rather go hiking in Point Lobos or take a drive over the Bixby Bridge to Big Sur? Those cliffs? That view? It'll take your breath away."

"I didn't know you were such an avid hiker," Arial said.

"I'm not really, anymore," Shirley said, making a face. "I'm just saying I'm not much for . . . chatting."

"You chat with me," Arial protested.

"On the street and in passing. It's formalized chat that bores me. You know, let's all sit or stand around with a glass of wine or a cup of coffee and make small talk. Ugh." She made a face. "I've been dodging book club for months."

"Yet you gave me the list of meetings."

"Which I keep in order to make up reasons I will have to miss. And I haven't hosted for eons."

"So if you don't attend, you don't feel obligated to host."

"Now you got it," Shirley said, swirling her coffee. "Which is probably a good thing, if you still think the book club meetings and the robberies might be connected."

"Turns out, they're not," Arial said, taking a sip and setting down her cup. "So I decided to work the other way around. You know, look for a connection between the houses that have been robbed."

"That probably makes more sense," Shirley said. "But what are you going to see that the police haven't?"

"You sound like Dan when he gave me the list," Arial said ruefully.

Shirley raised her eyebrows. "You snowed Dan Sotherly into giving you a list of the robberies?"

"I could get them from the published police reports," Arial said. "I told him he was just saving me time."

"You're very good." Shirley reached across the table to snap a lid off a bowl of treats and slip one to Monty, who was sitting at her feet, tail swishing hopefully across the floor. "So can I assume that's why you volunteered to take Monty for a walk this morning? Another reconnaissance mission?"

First Chris, then Shirley. Just a few weeks in and they already knew her too well.

"Maybe," Arial said evasively, getting up. "And we should probably get going."

Monty hopped to his feet.

"You didn't drink much of your coffee," Shirley said, taking the nearly full cup from her.

"I only asked for half," Arial reminded her.

"And it's terrible, isn't it?" Shirley said, retrieving hers, too, and taking it to the sink to dump. "I reheated yesterday's."

"Oh, Shirley," Arial protested, wishing she could get the taste of burned pencil lead out of her mouth. "No wonder it's so terrible."

"I know." She gestured to the drip coffee maker on the counter. "With Frank not here, I don't finish a whole pot."

"Speaking of Frank, how did his speech go last night?"

Shirley blinked, clearly surprised by the question. "Fine, I think. I really should call and check. He's not due back until the weekend, and he'll think I forgot about it."

"Which you did."

Her friend grinned. "Which reminds me, can you take Monty on Saturday? I'll be running up to San Jose to pick Frank up."

"And staying overnight?" Arial asked, raising an eyebrow. "Maybe doing some shopping?"

"It is easier without him," Shirley said, considering. "No explanations necessary."

"So go up early and do it," Arial said, claiming the leash sitting on the counter by the door. "I'm always happy to Monty-sit."

"I'll let you know what time then," Shirley said, trying to get past the prancing boxer-mix to open a drawer. "Here's another roll of poop bags," Shirley said, handing it over. "Good luck keeping up with him today."

"Thanks," Arial said, pocketing the bags before clipping the leash on. "I think."

A light mist was coming down now, so Arial flipped up the hood of her jacket as she and Monty made their way to the closest address on the list—Seaside Avenue. The house was a large bungalow tucked behind a new six-foot board-on-board fence. The size and type of the fence screamed "dog lives here!" to Arial and, sure enough, as they approached, a snuffling could be heard at the base of the fence.

Monty immediately took his position on the opposite side and the two canines attempted to sniff each other. Failing to connect satisfactorily, they started to bark ferociously in lieu of.

"Quiet," Arial said, sitting Monty down.

Torn between listening to Arial and playing the game, Monty whined.

"What is it about dogs and fences?" Arial said, pulling out one of the flyers Chris had suggested she bring. She pushed the flyer through an opening in the gate and waited a moment, hoping the homeowner would come out, but no soap. Either nobody was home, or they didn't care that their dog was barking. Which was curious, come to think of it, since the house had been robbed just a couple of weeks earlier.

"So probably nobody home," she surmised, moving on.

Next up was Cypress Lane, just three blocks away. This one was a cottage with a freshly painted robin's-egg-blue door and a historical plaque above the mailbox.

As Arial hesitated, a woman swung open the door to get the newspaper, a baby on her hip.

"Hi," Arial said, holding up her flyer. "I'm a local dog-sitter. I just wanted to introduce myself."

The woman smiled. "Oh, thanks. No dog, but if you're interested in another kind of sitting, let me know." She did a little hip thrust and the baby giggled.

"Afraid I know more about dogs than I do about kids. Sure is cute though." She'd purposely left off the pronoun since she wasn't sure if it was a boy or a girl.

"Thanks." The woman didn't enlighten her. "We just moved in, so we don't have the essential services—babysitters, doctors, dentists, hairdressers—yet."

"I know what that's like," Arial commiserated. "I'm new, too."

"Have you heard about the robberies?" the woman asked, stepping out onto the covered porch to glance around nervously. "That and this fog . . ." She shivered.

"Was yours one of the houses that was robbed?" Arial asked, playing dumb.

"Yes. About two weeks ago, before we—my husband and me and Jimmy—actually arrived. Our stuff was here, though."

"Oh, no," Arial said. "You were robbed before you even unpacked?"

"The night after the movers came." She frowned. "That's odd, don't you think?"

Yes, Arial did think. "Who let the movers in?"

"Our realtor left a key in a lockbox on the door and gave them the code. We've changed the locks since then, of course."

"Did you tell the police?" Arial asked. "About the lockbox, I mean."

"The realtor took care of it with the police, us being new and all." The baby was starting to fuss. "I'd better go in, but it was really nice to talk to you, um . . ."

"Arial," the dog-sitter supplied, holding out a flyer. "My contact info is on here, if you need anything. Like I said, I'm new to the area as well, but I have learned a few things." She had a thought. "Like there's a book club; have you heard of it?"

"No, no, I haven't." She was bouncing the baby now.

"If you're interested, I'll put you in touch," Arial promised. "I'll let you go now, though."

"Thanks," the woman said gratefully. "And, again, nice talking."

"Nice talking to you, too." Arial hesitated. "I'm sorry. What was your name?"

"Heather," she said with a grin. "Heather Vernon."

"Nice meeting you, Heather," Arial said, starting down the walk to the street. She turned. "Oh, and . . ."

"Yes?" Heather was about to close the door.

"The marine layer usually clears by noon and . . . even when it doesn't?" Arial tipped her nose into the air, feeling the mist on her face. "Even when it doesn't, just relax into it."

Arial continued on down the street, as Heather stepped halfway back out onto the porch, turning her face to the sky.

Waiting for Monty to pull his nose out of the hole he was snuffling in, Arial was smiling.

At least at this house, she'd made contact, helped a young

mother, and gotten some information. Maybe even something the police didn't know, depending on how much the real-estate agent had shared with them. It seemed odd that the homeowner hadn't made the report, but maybe the agent was embarrassed about what had happened and wanted to smooth the way for the family.

"I should have asked Heather who the agent was," she said out loud.

Monty ignored her as they turned right onto Seventeen-Mile Drive. The drive was famous, mostly because turning left led you to the scenic Seventeen-Mile Drive in the gated community of Pebble Beach. That part of the drive was known for its golf courses, mansions, and natural scenic attractions along the way, like the Lone Cypress and Bird Rock. Also, for its guard shack and admission fee.

But turning right, the drive was residential and free for all to travel. The house Arial was interested in turned out to be a modern, low-slung build, but more than that she couldn't make out from the street. As they hesitated, a man came up behind them on the sidewalk. "Bag?"

"What?" Arial twisted around to see a smiling man of about fifty with a little fluffy dog on the leash. He gestured. "A poop bag, I mean. Do you need one?"

Arial twisted back to see Monty, indeed, in dump-position. "Oh, I'm so sorry," she said, digging into her pocket for the roll of bags. "But no, I have one."

"No worries," he said. "I just know what it's like to be caught without. You'd be surprised what this eight-pound mutt can put out."

Arial laughed. "I used to walk a Chihuahua that was the same way. Monty here is nothing in comparison."

"Are you a dog-walker?"

"And dog-sitter," Arial said, pulling out a flyer. "Arial . . ." she hesitated, "Mayes Kingston. Call me if you ever need anybody."

"I will," he said, studying her face. "Are you related to Gretchen Mayes here in Pacific Grove? And her daughter, the painter?"

"My great-grandmother and grandmother," Arial said. "I just inherited the property."

The man stuck out his hand. "Well, I'm sorry that you had a loss, but it's good to have you here. I'm sure you'll love the area. Are you heading over to Asilomar and the beach? It's a great place to walk."

"You know I haven't been there, but we should." She looked at Monty, who had finished his business. "Shouldn't we, Monty? After we clean up, of course," she amended.

The man grinned. "Just take a left on Sinex and you'll run right into the park and conference center. There's a gate, but you can walk through." He gave a little tug on the leash of his fluffy dog, who was sniffing Monty's butt. "We should get going, but I'll give you a call if we need a sitter."

"Thanks," Arial said, waiting until they were out of sight to lean down and pick up the poop. "Nice man, and that name trick really worked, didn't it?" Monty, whose face was on the same level as hers, gave her a kiss.

"Thanks." Arial straightened up to tie the bag before surveying the house again. "Doesn't look like anybody's home, but I'll leave a flyer. What do you say we go to the beach?"

Monty danced his approval.

As Arial had promised Heather, the fog was evaporating to reveal blue skies as they walked down Sinex Avenue. It would be a shame to waste what had turned out to be a nice morning, Arial told herself. And if her map app was right, they could visit the beach and then walk up and around the tip of the peninsula, past the Point Pinos Lighthouse and the public golf course to Shell Avenue, the last house on the list, save Simone's.

"It's perfect, right, Monty?"

Monty was too busy sniffing to reply as they passed through the pillars that marked the entrance to Asilomar Conference Grounds. Arial waved at a groundskeeper as they veered onto one of the retreat's winding paths past a trash can, where she deposited the tightly knotted poop bag.

The grounds were serene, dotted with rustic Arts and Crafts

lodges covered in weathered shingles. The woods, from what Arial could see, were mostly made up of the peninsula's native Monterey pines and coastal live oaks.

"I read that Asilomar means 'Refuge by the Sea,'" Arial told Monty in a hushed voice. "Sure feels like that, doesn't it?"

They wound their way around the buildings with no clear plan, but eventually broke out onto a trail edged with scrub on one side and the beach on the other. A couple of surfers sat on their boards in the water, waiting for a wave to ride.

On the beach, a few people sat sunning, and a handful of dogs ran loose, chasing balls or splashing in the surf. Monty wagged his tail enthusiastically at the sight but stayed at Arial's side, pulling a bit and glancing back at her.

"Sorry, buddy," Arial said. "No running wild, especially after yesterday. I'm not sure you'd ever come back."

As usual, Monty managed to attract attention, greeting beachgoers with his big goofy grin and plume of a tail waving enthusiastically. People stopped to give him a scratch or just smile back and dogs came by for the occasional butt-sniff. Monty was in his element.

"You know that your mom is going to kill me," Arial told him as the big mutt had a sand-kicking contest with a Labrador retriever. "Maybe I'll offer to give you a bath."

At the word "bath," Monty's ears flattened and he eyed her suspiciously.

"Or maybe not?"

Monty smiled and pawed the sand, throwing a shower onto her sneakers.

"Well, let's at least get off the sand and onto the boardwalk," Arial said. "I'll empty my shoes and hopefully the sand will . . . blow off you?"

Fat chance.

Arial pulled out her phone to check which direction to go as they started away from the beach. "If we stay along the ocean, it'll be beautiful, but quite a hike to Shell Avenue. So maybe we should cut up through the trees here on one of these streets . . ."

She caught a movement out of the corner of her eye. Monty

did, too, coming to attention as a figure darted into the woods just off the trail.

"Aaron?" Arial called, squinting. It sure looked like him, slipping between the trees with a furtive glance over his shoulder.

Arial wasn't quite sure what to do. If she went after Aaron and found him, she'd have to tell Dan. If she didn't find Aaron, she'd still feel honor-bound to let the detective know that she may have seen him. It wasn't a hard decision—the former might bag her some information while being a snitch. The latter just made her a snitch.

"Come on, Monty," she said, tugging his leash and heading into the trees after the retreating figure.

The woods were quiet, except for the crunch of leaves underfoot and the occasional bird. Monty stayed close, his ears perked as they followed the path worn through the trees. The trail twisted and opened into a clearing, where a small pup tent was pitched under a live oak covered in moss.

"Aaron?" she called softly, stepping closer. She'd always thought it was stupid on television when pursuers called out the name of their quarry, giving them a chance to run. But then again, people also got shot for popping up in the woods, unannounced.

She'd take stupid over dead.

"Aaron?" she called again.

TWENTY

"Arial?" Aaron Henry stuck his head out the tent flap, a meatball and cheese sub in hand.

"You abandoned Monty." Arial had her arms folded.

"Sorry, I guess?" he said, setting the sub aside and going to shove his sleeping bag into the corner of the tent. "I had to leave."

"Why?" Arial shifted to see behind him into the tent. "Your tent missed you?"

He shifted to block her view. "What are you doing here?"

"I could ask you the same thing," Arial said, uncrossing her arms. "You asked me if I was homeless, and here you are, living in a tent?"

"I have a place in PG," Aaron said, lifting his chin. "I'm just . . . camping out."

"You decide to take a camping trip practically in your backyard at the same time people are looking for you. What a coincidence."

"*People* should mind their own business. And you're the one who told me they think I committed these robberies. Which I didn't. What did you think I was going to do?"

Arial admittedly should have known better.

"I know you didn't rob any of the houses," she said now. "The police will know, too, if you just talk to them."

He folded his own arms. "And if I don't want to?"

Arial sighed. "They're hoping you'll provide your DNA to see if the body we found under my guest house might be your dad. Don't you want to know?"

He wasn't buying it. "*Or* they want my DNA to railroad me—prove that I was in one of the houses that was robbed."

"Were you?"

"Of course not," he said. "You just said you believe me."

"And you just said you didn't want to provide DNA because it could be used to prove you were in one of the houses."

He rolled his eyes. "Did you totally miss the word 'railroad'?"

"I didn't," Arial said. "But you can't possibly believe the PG police are going to plant evidence. The only person who seems set on painting you as the burglar is Emily Bennett, for whatever reason."

"Yeah, for whatever," Aaron said. "The bitch hates me and my family."

Arial was going to dispute that for a second and then changed her mind. "OK, maybe. But back to your dad. He's not with your grandmother in Sacramento. Do you have any idea where he might have gone?"

"No." He kept his arms folded. "Maybe he doesn't want to be found."

"Why not?" Arial asked, as Monty started to sniff around the door of the tent. "I mean, the only reason I can imagine for your dad's disappearing is that he killed a man for some reason, then stuffed his body under the guest house and took off."

"That's ridiculous," Aaron said. "Why . . . hey!"

Aaron toppled as Monty pushed past him and into the tent.

"I'm so sorry," Arial said as the dog dove for the sub sandwich. "Leave it!"

Monty looked up, yellow wrapper hanging out of his mouth and tomato sauce on his nose.

"Shame on you, Monty." Arial said, going to take the wrapper away. "That's not . . ." She stopped. "What's this?"

Aaron had wedged himself into the corner in the face of Monty's onslaught. "What's what?"

"Really?" Arial shot back. "This." She held up a hundred-dollar bill. "And if I'm not mistaken, there are more of them sticking out of your sleeping bag."

Aaron hesitated, running a hand through his hair. "Where?"

"Behind you." Arial was trying to keep her voice even, since three in a pup tent was at least one too many for comfort. Or safety. Not that it stopped her from asking, "Where did you get the cash?"

"Not from selling the things you think I stole." Aaron reached past Monty to snatch the bill from Arial. "Because I didn't steal anything."

"And I said I believed you. But you need to tell me where you got the money."

She expected him to say something smart-ass like he got it from the bank or an ATM, or simply that it was none of her business, but Aaron just shook his head. "I'm sorry, but I promised."

"Promised who?" she persisted. "If you got it from your mother or even your dad, just tell me. Otherwise, you're inviting people to believe the worst."

"Arial, please." He was trying to look away, but the small confines of the tent didn't allow it. "Just trust me."

"But why are you hiding?" When he didn't answer, she shook her head. "I have to tell Dan. I promised."

"Dan?" he repeated. "You don't mean the police detective."

Arial was already backing out of the tent, Monty protecting her flank.

"Arial, wait!" Aaron called, trying to extricate himself from the tent. "Come back. I'll explain."

But Arial and Monty were already racing along the dirt trail to the boardwalk.

"Have you lost your mind?"

The question, of course, came from Dan.

"You don't know how desperate he is," the detective continued. "The moment you saw him, you should have called me."

"I thought about it." Arial was sitting on a bench, Monty next to her. "But I wasn't sure it was him."

Dan didn't seem to be buying it.

"And," she continued, "if I hadn't followed Aaron, we wouldn't know where the tent is, and you wouldn't know about the money."

"The tent is gone, and so is Aaron Henry and any money there might have been," a uniformed officer informed Dan as he came out of the woods.

"See?" Dan demanded. "He must have suspected you were going to call us."

"I may have told him," Arial mumbled under her breath.

"What?"

"I told him," Arial said, raising her voice. "I'm not a good liar."

"Then . . . just . . . don't . . . talk." The words were clipped.

Arial opened her mouth and then shut it. Couldn't accuse her of being a slow learner.

"What in the world?" Shirley asked, as Arial unloaded Monty from the back seat of the squad car that had driven them home.

"I can explain," Arial said, as the officer tried to brush the pile of sand Monty had left on the seat into the street. "We were at Asilomar."

"I can tell," Shirley said, surveying her dog.

"I kept him on his leash," Arial assured her quickly.

"And got him arrested?"

"No, no—the officer was just giving us a ride home because it was getting late."

"It's mid-afternoon." Shirley was examining Monty through his bushy fur. "Just tell me there wasn't a dog fight. You didn't get hurt, did you, baby?"

Monty kissed her.

"He's fine," Arial said, collapsing onto Shirley's porch step to empty the sand from her shoes. "We just ran into Aaron Henry, and I called Dan to let him know where."

It was a bit of a summary, but there was no need to go into pup tent/meatball sub and stack of cash kind of detail.

"Ooh," Shirley said, sitting down next to her. "Did they bring him in?"

"No," Arial said. "Because he literally folded his pup tent and slipped away."

"To paraphrase Longfellow. He knew you saw him?"

"Yes," Arial admitted. "We had kind of followed him into the woods."

"You and Monty."

"Yes."

Shirley seemed to be counting to ten. "And he saw you. Is that why he took off?"

"Well, I may have told him I was going to call Dan."

"Have you lost your mind?"

Arial smiled grimly. "That is a more common perception than you might think." She lifted her shoulders and then dropped them. "But when I saw the money, I kind of—"

"What money?" Shirley was frowning.

"Aaron had a pile of cash. I wouldn't have seen it, but Monty pushed into the tent and ate his meatball sub."

"With cheese?" Shirley asked, attention diverted. "What kind? Monty gets terrible gas from soft cheeses."

"He does? What about Monterey Jack?"

Shirley glared at her. "I told you. He eats only Dry Jack. And in small amounts."

Arial was batting a thousand when it came to Monty. Yesterday, he got loose, and now Shirley not only felt Arial had endangered him but given him gas. "I'm so sorry, but it did have cheese. Maybe provolone?"

"Provolone," Shirley spat. "And you call Monterey Jack bland."

Arial believed the word she had used was "blank," as in blank slate, but she didn't think it was the time to argue the point. "I got it away from him before he ate the wrapper," she said meekly.

"Small graces." Shirley sat quietly for a second and then, "So let me get this straight. You and Monty had this adventure but, in the end, Aaron is still missing. Nothing has changed."

Monty sat down to scratch, sending a fine sheen of sand over them.

"Except Monty needs another bath," Shirley amended.

"Sorry," Arial said, swiping at her closed eyes to get the sand away before opening them. "I'd be happy to—"

"No, no," Shirley said, getting up. "You've done enough."

Arial stood, too, feeling forlorn. "Umm, do you still want me to sit—"

"I'll let you know," Shirley said, raising her hand in dismissal.

"Sorry," Arial said, yet again.

TWENTY-ONE

Arial was sitting on the couch feeling sorry for herself when Chris opened the door.

"What happened to you?" he said, setting his bag on the table and sitting down next to her. "You look like you lost your best friend."

"I did." She sniffled. "And her dog."

"What did you do?"

She'd been slumped and now she pulled herself up. "You just assume *I* did something?"

"Hang on a second," he said, holding up a finger before getting up to go into the kitchen. There were noises of cupboards being opened and closed, dishes clanging, and refrigerator doors opening and, ten minutes later, he reappeared with a charcuterie board.

"Where did all this come from?" Arial asked, realizing she hadn't eaten all day.

"I shop," he said. "It's a new concept and results in food and drink being available for consumption at a moment's notice."

"Hallelujah," Arial said, leaning forward to pluck a piece of sausage off the board. "I haven't had anything but coffee today."

"Which is why everything looks worse," Chris said. "Now get some food in your stomach, and I'll open a bottle of wine."

"We have that, too?"

"Yes, another miracle. White or red?"

"White, please. Chardonnay if you have it."

"Now, we're getting picky." Chris grinned and returned a few minutes later with two glasses of white wine. "It's sauvignon blanc. So sue me."

"I like sauvignon blanc, too. And also pinot gris, for future reference." Arial took an appreciative sip. "Thank you. Really."

"You're welcome," Chris said, sitting down again. "Now tell me what happened."

"I've mucked it up with everybody." Arial let out a groan. "And it's not just Shirley and, by extension, Monty. It's Dan, too."

"How?" Chris stabbed a piece of cheese.

"Monty and I ran into Aaron Henry. He's camping out in Asilomar with a tent and—"

"He was camping in Asilomar?" Chris asked. "Why would he do that? I mean, it's beautiful and all, but . . ."

"I asked that very thing." Despite cheese being a bit of a sore subject just now, Arial selected a sliver. "Why so close to home? At first, I thought he might be homeless, but he said he had a place."

"Of course he does," Chris said. "He shares a house with Lucy and another girl."

Arial sat back, cheese in hand. "Now how can you not have told me that? We've been talking about Aaron going missing for days."

"Because it's his legal address on his driver's license and all, so I assumed the police knew and looked there." He scored a mini sausage. "Not that it would have helped. Lucy said he hasn't been there since last weekend."

Last weekend. The Rowan robbery had been the Tuesday before and today was Thursday so Aaron had disappeared . . . Arial looked at Chris. "We found the body Saturday."

Chris dipped his head. "And Aaron Henry disappeared that same weekend."

"Interesting," Arial said, taking a bite of the cheese still in her hand. "Mmm, this is good. What is it?"

"Dry Jack."

Figured. Arial put it down.

"I thought you liked it."

"I like it fine," Arial muttered. "And it probably won't even give me gas."

Chris cocked his head. "Should I ask?"

"No," Arial said. "But back to the cash Aaron had."

Chris's eyebrows shot up. "Cash?"

Oh, yeah. Arial hadn't gotten to that part. "A lot of it, in hundreds."

"So maybe Aaron *is* involved in the robberies."

"He denies it, of course, but I'm not sure what else it could be. Certainly nothing good, because when I told him I was calling Dan, Aaron, his tent and the money all disappeared."

Chris shook his head. "Dan didn't find him?"

"Not yet," Arial admitted. "And he's ticked with me because he thinks I endangered myself."

"You did endanger yourself."

"And Shirley is furious with me because I endangered Monty."

"She's very protective of him," Chris said. "Is he all right? I mean he didn't get hurt or anything?"

Arial suppressed a smile as she reclaimed her Dry Jack. "Monty had a fine time—playing on the beach, running through the woods. He is kind of a mess, though."

"I imagine. Anything else?"

"Well, he ate Aaron's meatball sub. It had provolone on it. And cheese—only soft cheese, apparently—gives him gas. Unlike Dry Jack." She popped the cheese in her mouth.

Chris burst out laughing. "You're a magnet for chaos, Arial."

"Tell me something I don't know," she muttered, grabbing another piece of cheese. "So now Aaron thinks I betrayed him, Dan thinks I'm careless and let a criminal get away. Shirley, likewise, thinks I'm careless . . . oh, did I tell you the police delivered Monty and me to Shirley's house in a squad car?"

"Just keeps getting better and better," Chris said, shaking his head.

"Even Monty probably won't talk to me because he had to have a bath."

"And is farting," Chris reminded her.

Arial sighed. "At least you're not mad at me."

"Not yet," Chris said, settling back with his wine. "But the night is young."

Since Chris had "cooked," Arial cleaned up and they watched a movie. When Chris retired to bed, Arial pulled out the pillow and blanket to make her own bed on the couch.

As she settled in, her phone buzzed on the coffee table and she reached for it, hoping for an update from Dan. Or a conciliatory text message from Shirley. Instead, it was a text from Fiona: Lunch tomorrow at The Grill on the municipal wharf at one? I'm inviting Olivia, Marta, Lucy and Shirley. I hope you can make it!

Arial smiled, her spirits lifting. She typed a quick reply: I'll be there. Thanks for including me!

She set the phone down, feeling a small flicker of hope. This would be a pleasant break after today's "chaos," as Chris put it. And maybe a chance to smooth things over with Shirley.

The Grill was all old Monterey, perched at water level on the municipal wharf, so you had to walk down a flight of steps to reach it. Arial turned the corner into the dining room to be greeted by polished wood and nautical accents, the big windows showcasing the marina. Even at lunch, the place was busy, and Arial spotted the group at a table near the window.

Fiona waved her over. "Arial! Over here."

Arial threaded her way through the tables to where Fiona, Olivia, Marta, Lucy and Shirley were already seated by the window. She was relieved to see Shirley, though her neighbor offered only a curt nod in greeting.

"Hi, everyone," Arial said, sliding into the empty chair across from Shirley and between Lucy and Fiona.

"Glad you could make it," Fiona said. "We were just looking at the menus."

"Here you go," Lucy said, passing Arial the menu that had been sitting open in front of her.

"Sure you're done with it?" Arial asked.

"Oh, yes. I don't even know why I bother looking because I always order the same thing anyway."

"And what's that?" Arial asked, trying to take in the large lunch menu of seafood delights.

"Baby back ribs." Lucy held up her hand as the rest of the table groaned. "I know, I know. Very déclassé to order red meat in a fish restaurant, but they're delicious."

"And admit it," Marta said, "you're not that fond of fish anyway. What's wrong with that?"

"In Monterey?" Olivia asked. "Seafood is everywhere—even the aquarium served sushi at the last event I attended."

"Oh, I know," Fiona said. "I felt so guilty chowing down as the other fish swam by watching."

"It's OK, as long as the seafood is sustainable," Marta said.

"Tell that to the fish," Shirley suggested dryly. "But I always get the same thing here, too. In my case, it's the calamari steak with lemon and capers."

"Oh," Arial said, lasering in on the menu item. "You mentioned that the other day and it sounded delicious."

Shirley leaned back in her chair, arms crossed. "Monty's clean, by the way. Stopped farting, slept like a baby last night."

Arial winced. "Thanks for letting me know. And . . . sorry about the cheese incident."

Shirley's lips twitched, and then she relented. "It's fine. He's forgiven you. I might, too, eventually."

Crisis averted, the group turned their attention to ordering. Soon, dishes of steaming clam chowder, fish and chips, sand dabs, calamari and, of course, baby back ribs arrived, the scents wafting through the air. Everybody wanted to try everyone else's, so the meal turned more buffet than plated lunch. Arial took a sip of her iced tea, feeling relaxed and really happy to be part of this group.

"So?" Fiona said. "Any news on the identity of your cadaver?"

"Nice conversation starter," Olivia said, leaning forward to stab a piece of calamari steak, swiping it through the lemon and caper sauce.

"Sadly no," Arial said. "And Dan still doesn't have the results of the postmortem." Or if he did, he hadn't shared them with her. "I've been trying to find out more about the burglaries in the meantime."

"You think the crimes and the corpse are connected?" Fiona blushed. "Beyond alliteration, I mean."

"You are such a word nerd," Lucy said, shaking her head. "I love it."

Arial grinned. "I honestly don't know if there's a connection.

But yesterday, I took a walk past the houses that have been robbed, just to try to get a sense of why they might have been targeted."

"That was after she gave up on the idea that it's somebody from the book club," Shirley said.

All four of the other book club members turned to regard Arial.

She felt a flush rise. "It did occur to me since Simone's house was hit. But Shirley shared the list of the other houses who have hosted, and none of you have been robbed, have you?"

"You think we'd keep that a secret?" Marta asked, laughing. "So what was your thought, that one of us was casing the houses at book club and then came back?"

Arial shrugged a little uncomfortably. "Yes, honestly. Maybe left a door or window unlocked or saw some vulnerability they could breach at a later date."

"Vulnerability," Fiona said delightedly. "I love that."

"I vote for Emily as the perp," Marta said, raising her hand. "She's way too eager to pin it on Aaron Henry."

"I thought so, too," Arial said, as Lucy sent an unsure glance her way.

"So do you have a new theory?" Olivia asked.

"I'm still working on it," Arial admitted. "Like I said, I went by most of the houses that were robbed yesterday. I only got to talk to one of the owners, though, and they weren't even living there." She leaned forward. "Their boxes and furniture had arrived though, and somebody struck that night."

"One of the movers, maybe," Shirley suggested.

Arial nodded. "Or the real-estate agent. She or he had a key and left it in the lockbox for the movers."

"Who would also have been given the combination to get inside the box," Shirley persisted. "They deliver the furniture, put the key back. What's to stop somebody from accessing the lockbox again?"

"Or making copies of the keys," Arial said. "If we could find out what companies they used, we could see if there are any other parallels."

"And what about Aaron Henry?" Marta asked. "Lucy said he hasn't been at the house, right?"

"I hadn't realized you and Aaron were sharing a place," Arial said to Lucy.

The young woman's face got red. "I don't really advertise the fact that one of my flatmates is a guy. A lot of our clientele is older at the clinic, and they think it's strange for guys and girls to live together. Like we must be doing it or something."

Arial saw Shirley suppress a smile.

"That's those boomers and Gen Xers," Arial hazed before turning to Lucy with a genuine question. "When was Aaron last there—at the house, I mean?"

"Sunday during the day maybe?" Lucy said. "But I don't think he came back to sleep that night."

"You weren't worried?" Shirley asked.

"Boomer question," Arial said, raising her eyebrows.

"Gen X, I'll have you know," Shirley said, eyes narrowing.

"Just by a smidge," Olivia kibbitzed.

"Let's face it," Marta said. "Except for Arial, Emily and Lucy, we all have some gray hair."

"Good to get some young blood in the group," Shirley said in a shaky, faux elderly voice. Then she leaned forward, her expression serious. "Arial saw Aaron camping in the woods near Asilomar yesterday, but he disappeared before the police could get to him."

"What was he doing out there?" Olivia asked, glancing between the two women.

"Yeah," Lucy said, forehead wrinkled. "Why be so close and not come home, at least to sleep?"

"That's a very good question," Arial said.

"You going to tell them about the cash?" Shirley asked.

Arial would have to now. "He had a tent, a wad of cash, and a meatball sub."

Lucy smiled at the sub sandwich reference, but she was obviously uneasy. "Where did the cash come from?"

"He wouldn't tell me," Arial said. "In fact, he said he'd promised not to tell. He didn't get it from you, did he?"

"If the cash was more than a ten for the sub, absolutely not. Nobody I know has wads of cash."

"His mom maybe?"

Lucy looked skeptical. "I don't think they have that kind of relationship. If they did, he wouldn't always be busting his butt to pay his part of the rent. He'd go home to live."

"What about his dad? Are they estranged or . . .?"

"Whatever, he's not on the scene anymore." She shrugged and got up. "Sorry, but I have to get back to the office. This should cover my share and tip." She pulled out a few bills and handed them to Fiona before pulling on her jacket and hurrying out the door and up the steps to the wharf.

Arial frowned, wondering if she had offended Chris's receptionist with all the questions. Lucy had been fine, though, until Arial had brought up Aaron's dad.

As they settled the bill and prepared to leave, Shirley turned to Arial. "By the way, can you still watch Monty while I go up to San Jose tomorrow to get Frank? His plane gets in late, so it'll be overnight."

"Absolutely," Arial said. "I'll take good care of him."

"Come by around three and," Shirley's demeanor softened, "maybe lay off the cheese this time?"

"Deal."

TWENTY-TWO

Arial had parked her Toyota in one of the metered parking spots on the wharf, so she had to wait for the rest of their group milling around outside the restaurant to clear before backing out.

She felt like a huge weight was off her shoulders, Shirley-wise, but a lot of questions still hung over her head. Admittedly, only the corpse under the floorboards was really her problem. Still, Fiona was right that Arial couldn't quite shake the idea that the robberies and body were linked. But maybe that was because Aaron Henry seemed connected to both. "Seemed" being the key word.

There was no reason Arial should feel so personally invested in Aaron's well-being, but he had been kind to her. The whistle/flashlight he'd given her jangled now as she turned over the ignition. In the midst of his getaway from a robbery, did it make sense that he stopped to make sure she was OK that morning?

But then . . . where did the money come from? And why was Aaron hiding? And what might Lucy know about her roomie and his dad that she wasn't saying?

No answers forthcoming, Arial put the car into reverse and waited for a seafood truck to pass by before backing out of her parking spot. Passing Shirley getting into her Prius, Arial waved before pulling out of the wharf parking lot onto Lighthouse Avenue.

Bearing right to take the tunnel under the Custom House Plaza at the foot of the adjacent, and more famous, Old Fisherman's Wharf, Arial followed Lighthouse through New Monterey. At David Avenue she took a right and then a left onto Ocean View, just before the Monterey Bay Aquarium.

Much as Arial would have loved to visit the world-famous attraction today, she had another destination in mind—the

Shell Avenue house. Shell was just three blocks up from Ocean View, almost all the way to the Point Pinos Lighthouse and Asilomar. Windows down and enjoying the view and fresh salt air, she missed the turn-off and had to circle back to the sprawling cream-colored stucco house with a red tile roof.

"Pretty," she thought, grabbing a flyer from her bag before approaching the house on foot to ring the bell. No response; the occupants were probably at work on a Friday afternoon. Slipping the flyer into the crack in the doorframe, Arial returned to her car, waving at a gray-haired woman strolling by as she shifted into gear and drove off toward home.

In retrospect, Arial probably should have taken the opportunity to chat with the strolling woman but, after the luncheon, she was pretty much chatted-out. Shirley wasn't the only one who could turn turtle when she needed her space.

Stepping into the quiet front room of her house, Arial dropped her keys on the hall table and flipped open her laptop on the coffee table.

She decided to search the houses by order of robbery, rather than the order she'd visited. That had been dictated only by their walking route.

As it turned out, the Seaside Avenue address she'd visited was also the first house to be robbed. A photo of the bungalow popped up. Clicking, she was taken to a real-estate site. The house was marked "off-market," but the photos and information from the original listing were still there. The listing pictures gave her a better view of the house, since the fence that had blocked her view wasn't there. Plus, of course, she could see inside the home. No jewels or combination safes were lying about in the photos, but the comprehensiveness of the listing did make her question why she'd left the comfort of her own living room to do the research in the first place—though she didn't underestimate the benefits of a walk with Monty, nor the Aaron sighting, despite how it had ended up.

She scrolled down through the detail—three bedrooms, two baths, garage—and then her pulse quickened. Last sold: just over a year ago.

"Interesting," she murmured, jotting the date into her notebook.

On to Seventeen-Mile Drive. Arial found an image of the sleek, modern house nestled among the trees. Since its low-slung design made it almost invisible from the street, this was the first real view of it she'd had. But the house itself was less of interest than . . . She scrolled. Last sold: eleven months ago.

The next house robbed was Shell Avenue, the one she'd just visited. The picture showed the cream-colored stucco house with a red tile roof, classic and elegant. Last sold: nine months ago.

She leaned back, her excitement building. The pattern was holding.

Next up was Cypress Lane. This was the cottage with its cheerful blue door, which she already knew had been sold recently. The young mother she'd met there—Jimmy's mom, Heather—had mentioned the robbery happened the night between when their belongings arrived and the family physically got there. Arial scrolled down. Last sold: three months ago.

Arial's fingers trembled slightly as she typed in the final address—the Rowans' on Ocean View. The house had been red brick originally, and Arial had to admit that painting the brick white had been a good decision. But that wasn't the thing that stood out for Arial. The last sold date: eight months ago.

She sat back, staring at her notes. Every single house robbed within the last twelve months—including Simone's—had also been sold within the last year.

Talking to Heather on Cypress Lane, Arial had wondered if the movers—or even the real-estate agents—were involved. It was a good theory, so Arial hit "back" for each listing, searching for the selling agent. Yes! The information was included under the price on the date the property had been listed.

But her excitement dimmed slightly as she realized the agents were all different. No single company or person connected the listings, at least on the seller side, and she had no way of knowing who represented the buyers without asking. Same with which movers they'd used.

She pulled up the list of robberies again on her phone, comparing the dates of the robberies with the "sold" dates, which she assumed to be when the transactions had actually closed. Most of the robberies were within weeks of the closings, with the Cypress Lane one being the closest. Simone's house was the aberration. It was robbed nearly eight months after closing.

"But of course," Arial said to herself, since no Monty was available, "Simone and Charles were renovating, so there wouldn't be any valuables in the house until after they moved in."

She sighed, leaning back in her seat as her phone buzzed, jolting her out of her thoughts. It was Dan.

"We found Aaron," he said without preamble.

Arial's heart skipped a beat. "Where? Is he OK?"

"Not over the phone," Dan replied. "Can you meet me at Lovers Point?"

It had become their spot, apparently.

"On my way," Arial said, grabbing her keys and sailing out the door. As she passed the guest house to the car, she glanced at the door with its cursed posted notice.

What a mess, she thought to herself. *Munching termites or not, I never should have let those exterminators—*

She stopped. Not just her thoughts, but physically stopped dead in front of the guest house. Arial had inherited the property, so there were no contracts requiring the buildings to be fumigated. But for pretty much any home sale here, she'd been told over and over again that tenting was almost rote.

"Exterminators," she whispered. "That's the connection."

Dan was sitting at an outside table.

"Did you get here in time for your breakfast burrito?" Arial asked, hiking her thumb toward the café.

"I opted for the Cuban panini. Just waiting for it. Did you want something?"

"No, I had a big lunch," Arial told him, sitting down across the table. "So you said you found Aaron? Is he OK? You didn't arrest him, did you?"

"No, he didn't," a voice said, plopping a wrapped sandwich down in front of Dan. "No thanks to you, probably."

Dan unwrapped his panini as Aaron took the seat to his right with what looked like a bowl of fruit.

"I'm so glad you're OK," Arial said.

"He's fine," the detective growled, taking a bite of his sandwich. "I'm just hoping you can talk some sense into him."

"Me?" Arial asked, looking between the two of them. "Why would anyone listen to me? Especially Aaron, because I—"

"Ratted on me?"

"Well, yes."

"Because I believe you when you say you don't think I robbed those houses." He popped a strawberry into his mouth. "I'm sorry if I scared you. I—"

"Is that acai?" Arial interrupted, twisting around to see the menu boards. "I didn't know they had acai bowls here."

"Yup, with strawberries, bananas, blueberries, peanut butter and granola. Want a bite?" Aaron pulled another spoon out of his pocket.

"I . . . no, I had a huge lunch," Arial said reluctantly. "But I will be back."

"Seems like you're here every day or two," Dan said.

It was true, especially when she was making the rounds of robbery houses or meeting with the cops.

"Anyway," Aaron said, setting down the spare spoon and digging in. "You're my alibi, Arial."

"Your alibi for what? Has there been another robbery?"

"No way," Dan said. "Whole town is buzzing about how some young woman is poking around asking questions. Nobody is going to strike now."

"They're more afraid of me than they are of the police?" Arial asked. "I find that hard to believe."

"Thing is that you, walking your dogs—"

"Dog," Arial corrected. "I only have one client at the moment." And that wasn't going exactly smoothly.

"Walking your dog client all around town," Dan continued, "you see anomalies we might miss. Add the fact that your friends are suddenly hyper-aware as well—"

"Friends?"

"Your book club compatriots. We even had a call from one of the robbery victims who spoke to you. She said you made her realize she should get in touch with us about her burglary. Actually told me a couple of things we didn't know."

"Heather on Cypress Lane?" Arial guessed. "Yes, she started me thinking as well. And I believe I know—"

"That I didn't do it," Aaron interrupted. "You and I were talking when my mom's house was robbed."

Arial cocked her head. "How can you know that?"

"Because there was a car parked on the street. Do you remember it?"

"Yes," Arial said. "Dark-colored sedan, Oregon plates, I think. Why?"

"We found it abandoned in a parking lot along Highway One in Big Sur," Dan said. "And there was a gold chain belonging to Aaron's mother that had slipped into the spare tire compartment."

"Do you know who it belongs to?" Arial asked.

"It's a rental," Dan said. "And the person who rented it used a fake license so we're trying to track him down."

So the car rental company had confirmed a man had collected the car. "Listen, I was checking out these houses—"

"Before we get to that," Dan said, crumpling the wrapper from the sandwich. "I'm trying to convince Aaron here to provide DNA so we can make sure your body isn't his father."

"It's not my body."

"And it's not my father," Aaron added.

"Do you know that for a fact?" Arial asked. "Because if you do, just tell us where he is, so we can check him off the list." The very short list, unless it really was just someone who wandered in and died.

Aaron tugged uncomfortably at his sweatshirt neck. "I don't know. I'm just saying it can't be my dad. The sheriff says whoever it is has been dead for a year."

"And you've seen your dad since then?"

"A year was just an estimate," Dan reminded them.

"Just take my word for it. My father is alive and well."

"If your father doesn't want to be found," and Arial was wondering why not, "why not just provide your DNA and prove the body isn't his?"

"Because I have civil liberties," Aaron snapped. "I don't want my DNA floating around in the system. I'm not a criminal."

Arial looked at Dan. "Could you possibly take his DNA, check it against the body and then destroy it? Does it have to remain in the database?"

Dan shrugged. "Probably not, if it has no bearing on a case."

"And I'm supposed to trust that?" Aaron asked.

But Arial was thinking. "What if Aaron provided his DNA sample to a private laboratory and they compared it to a sample from the body?"

Dan rubbed his chin. "Not sure that would wash—chain of evidence and all that."

"But it's not evidence," Aaron pointed out, suddenly enthused. "It's my DNA and all you want to know is whether there's a familial match to the body."

Dan shrugged. "Worth a try, I guess. I have no way of compelling you to do it, either way."

"I'd be happy to be the go-between," Arial said. "Dan, can you get me a sample from the body? Then I can take it to the lab where Aaron gets his tested."

"I don't think I can just go giving you DNA samples from a possible murder victim."

"So there's *still* no cause of death?" Aaron asked. "Why are we even talking about this then? Poor guy crawled under there to get warm and died. Case closed."

Aaron seemed awfully eager to distance himself from the whole matter. And who could blame him?

"Still," Arial said stubbornly, "I think we should do this. I can always go under the guest house and dig up sand from under where the body was." Like the sand Monty had kicked into her face. And mouth. "There should be DNA."

"It'll be polluted by Monty's DNA, from what you told me," Dan said, and then shrugged. "I'll try to work out something on the other end. Or Aaron could just be reasonable and give us a sample."

"Nice try," Aaron said, getting up. "Now am I free to go?"

"I wouldn't mind getting a statement from you detailing your whereabouts during the other robberies. You know, just to completely clear you."

"These robberies have been going on for like a year?" Aaron said. "There's no way I—or anybody else—would remember where they were back then."

"Unless you were driving rideshare or delivering," Dan pointed out.

"You would need a warrant for that, if I'm not mistaken."

"Unless you volunteered it," Arial tried. "I don't think there would be any harm in it, since I think I know who might be responsible."

"I'll leave you to it then," Aaron said, gathering his acai bowl and spoon. "And so you don't get any ideas, I'll be taking all this with me."

He walked past the trash bin with his garbage and just kept going.

"Too many crime shows on TV," Dan said, shaking his head. "Now tell me what your new theory is."

"I wasn't even sure you heard me," Arial said.

"You think you know who might be responsible. Again, doesn't exactly sound like a sure thing."

Arial ignored that. "Well, as Heather from Cypress Lane told you, that robbery happened the night after the movers delivered their things, but before the family was actually in the house."

"An opportune moment," Dan agreed. "Making you think somebody had information and maybe a key or the code to the lockbox."

"Originally, yes," Arial said. "Maybe a realtor or one of the movers. But I didn't ask Heather who she used and, to be honest, just going past the houses didn't provide me with much information."

"So you went online, like I said."

"Eventually," Arial said a little ruefully. "It's probably where I should have started in the first place. You search an address and you end up on a real-estate site that shows you pretty much everything you want to know, including the last time the house was sold."

Dan was frowning, but not in a disapproving way. More a "did we miss something" way. He took out his notebook and flipped it open to a blank page. "What did you find?"

"Each of the houses has been listed and sold within the last year."

"So you're still thinking an agent or mover," Dan tapped his pen on the notebook. "We can check with the owners and see who they used."

"That's great, because it's something I can't do," Arial said. "I did find the original listing agents online, though, and none of them were the same. There's no way of telling who the agents representing the buyers were, though."

"Either agent would have access to the keys," Dan agreed.

"Thing is, though," Arial continued, "the robberies were all after the house sale had closed, when the new owners were in or, in Heather's case, their stuff was."

"There's no incentive to rob an empty house," Dan said. "And there's nothing saying that the perpetrator couldn't have found an easy access point, but waited until the connection to them wouldn't be obvious."

Arial was grinning.

"What?" Dan asked.

"You said perpetrator. Do you guys actually say 'perp' or is that just on TV?"

"Another thing television has ruined. I wouldn't say 'perp' if my life depended on it."

"Perp walk," Arial said, doing a strut in her seat. "Cool."

"Anyway," Dan continued, closing his book. "Thank you for this. It's a good lead and something we should have noticed."

"I'm not done," Arial said, holding up a hand. "I think it's unlikely all these buyers used the same real-estate agent or mover and nobody noticed. But there's another thing that happens when a house is sold."

"Ah." Dan's face lit up and he opened the notebook again. "Inspectors."

Arial was nodding. "Yes, inspectors assessing the condition of the house and reporting on any issues including . . ." She waited for Dan.

It took him just a second. "Termites."

"Yup," Arial was nodding. "According to my aunt Sarah and pretty much everybody else I've talked to, most every sales contract written out here stipulates the house must be inspected for termites, any damage fixed and the pests eradicated."

"Often under the privacy of a tent," Dan finished for her.

"Exactly."

TWENTY-THREE

"So let me get this straight," Chris said that night at dinner. "You don't think the workers are tenting the houses and then stealing things while it is tented?"

"No," Arial said, sliding a cardboard box of pizza onto the table. It had been her turn to cook. "People don't leave their valuables in the house while it's being fumigated."

"True," Chris said, hiking his thumb toward the pile of garbage bags that contained his earthly possessions. "Case in point."

"Yes, thank God the crown jewels are safe right here in my living room," Arial said, smirking. "But even if there were something to steal left behind, it would be far too obvious if it was missing right after the fumigation."

"True," Chris said, getting up to get napkins. "So, they wait until the new occupants are in?"

"New occupants who most times didn't even hire the company. The sellers did. So the sellers list the property, move out their stuff, have the house tented and eventually the house sells. Buyers move in and days or even weeks or months later, there's a robbery. Who is going to trace it back to the exterminators?"

"You, obviously," Chris said, sitting down.

Arial felt herself blush. "I don't think it's necessarily a big conspiracy concerning the whole company either. It could be just one worker—hopefully one Dan will be able to connect to the car they found with Simone's necklace in it. They could be using the tenting as an opportunity to nose around the houses and find what Dan called access points. He or she could also duplicate any keys they were given."

"Pretty smart," he said, flipping the pizza box open. "Pepperoni again?"

"What? You don't like pepperoni?" Arial asked, taking a slice. "I could add mushrooms next time."

"I like pepperoni, but there are so many more imaginative pizzas. I had this great one with whipped ricotta and fig jam the other day."

"Sounds delicious," Arial said, chewing. "Though I think I'd want that for dessert after I had my pepperoni pizza."

"You're an old soul," Chris said. "An old, boring soul."

Arial tossed a piece of pepperoni at him. "You'll just have to re-educate me."

"I can do that," Chris said, watching her as she picked up her phone to text. "Did Dan say it was OK to talk about your theory while he was still exploring it?"

"You mean with anybody but you?" Arial asked.

"You know I wouldn't tell anybody. And besides, who do I have to tell? A Labradoodle, Persian, or your occasional cockatiel?"

Arial laughed. "You know that's what everybody says when you tell them a secret. Who do I have to tell?"

"And then they blab," Chris said. "Or the cockatiel does. But I promise I'll keep my mouth shut. I'm just not sure everybody has my strength of character."

"Agreed," Arial said, setting down the phone. "I was just texting Shirley to tell her we found Aaron and ask when I should come get Monty tomorrow."

"Frank's flying back?" Chris asked.

"Uh-huh. By the way, I had lunch today at The Grill with Lucy."

"I heard," he said, claiming a slice. "I was surprised you wanted to order pizza after having a big lunch there."

"I ordered it for you," Arial said, putting down the crust and choosing a second piece. "I'm done after this."

"You don't eat the crust?" Chris asked. "It's the best part."

"Especially, I bet, if you don't like pepperoni," Arial said, looking at the orange rounds he'd taken off his slice. "I should have asked what you wanted."

"No worries," Chris said.

Arial hesitated. "Umm, did Lucy seem all right when she got back from lunch?"

"Yes . . . why?" he asked, taking her discarded crust.

"I might have pressed too hard about Aaron, given they're flatmates. Are you really going to eat that?"

Chris had been about to pop the crust in his mouth but stopped. "I was thinking about it. You think it's strange?"

"I think there's more than half the pizza left. If you take a new slice and just eat the crust, I won't judge." Her phone pinged. "And next time, I'll consult you on toppings."

"I also have some pizzeria suggestions," Chris said around the mouthful of fresh crust.

"Oh, good," Arial said, punching in a text message. She looked up. "I mean the pizzerias, too."

Chris grinned. "Shirley again?"

"I pick up Monty at one. Then I asked if she knew a private lab around here that we could have Aaron's DNA done." She set down the phone. "Though I guess I could have just asked you that."

"We do some labs in-house, but when we send samples out, it's to a specialized veterinary diagnostic laboratory, not a human lab. And I don't ever recall ordering a DNA test."

"Paternity isn't a big deal amongst dogs?"

"For the occasional show dog, probably a very big deal. But I prefer not to get involved in those things."

"Smart." Her phone pinged a message. "Shirley says there's a private lab in Ryan Ranch." She looked up. "That's an office park, right?"

"And lots of medical facilities, as well. It's off Highway Sixty-eight on the way to Salinas."

"Got it." Arial texted Shirley back and started to reach for another slice, before reminding herself she was done. "She's decided to go to San Jose tomorrow, like I suggested, and do a little shopping before Frank's plane gets in. I think she's still adjusting to having him home all the time."

"Frank's a good guy," Chris said. "But once an engineer, always an engineer. Shirley probably hoped it would be different when he retired."

"And that they'd take European river cruises like on the commercials?"

Chris seemed doubtful. "I don't see either of them sitting

on a boat for hours, even in retirement. Apparently they met backpacking in the Sierras."

Now that was a side of her neighbors Arial hadn't seen. No wonder Shirley preferred hiking to chatting.

Both tended to exhaust Arial, and now she glanced at her phone and yawned. "Well, I think I'm going to go to bed."

"Is that a polite way of saying I have to get off your couch?" Chris asked, glancing around. "So you can go to bed at nine p.m.?"

"That's exactly what I'm saying."

The next morning, Arial was halfway through brushing her teeth when her phone buzzed with a text from Shirley: **I'm leaving now. Frank took an earlier flight.**

"Wait, what?" Arial muttered, spitting and rinsing. She grabbed her keys, rushing out the door in her yoga pants and sweatshirt to Shirley's house.

"I don't know why I have my car keys," she said to herself, passing the guest house to the Cooper cottage. "I'm not the one driving to the airport."

Climbing the steps to the porch, she heard a familiar voice calling from inside: "Shirley?"

It was Frank, clear as day. Had he gotten in early and taken the shuttle down?

Arial rapped lightly on the door.

No answer, so she knocked a little harder. "Shirley? Frank?"

Arial tried the handle. It was unlocked, which was a surprise. "Shirley? It's Arial."

Stepping into the house, she saw Shirley at the computer with her phone in her hand and her back to the door. Frank's voice was saying, "Slow down, Shirley. We don't want . . ."

"Oh, I'm sorry," Arial said, realizing they were on a call.

Shirley turned sharply, setting down the mobile. "Arial! I didn't hear you come in."

"Sorry." Confused, Arial came closer. "I heard Frank's voice, so I thought he was home. But you're on the phone with him—did he miss his plane?"

"No, I was just replaying his voicemail message about

catching an earlier flight. I was hoping he'd left the flight number, but it's mostly him telling me I shouldn't rush and get in an accident."

"That's sweet," Arial said, peeking over Shirley's shoulder at the list of video files on the screen. "Are these all the speeches he's given? The ones you recorded?"

"Most of them." Shirley flipped the computer closed. "He got someone there to record this last one and sent it to me to watch. Like I don't have anything else to do."

As Shirley stood, Frank's pencil rolled off onto the floor and Arial picked it up, setting it next to his *Times* crossword puzzle.

"This is an old one," she observed. "July twentieth of last year?"

"The one that got away," Shirley said dryly, slipping on her boots. "Frank couldn't solve it, but would he look at the answers the next Sunday?" She nodded to the stack of papers on the countertop. "Never. That was cheating."

Arial frowned, taking in the nearly pristine stack of *Times*. In her aunt Sarah's house, newspapers were taken apart and digested section-by-section. Any attempt to put them back the way they'd been—even by the OCD Sarah—was in vain.

Something felt very wrong. But before Arial could inquire further, Shirley straightened from tying her boots. "I'm glad you're here, though. He'll be landing in an hour, so I need to get going, whether he wants me to rush or not. Monty's leash is here somewhere."

Monty had been standing on his hind legs at the front window, paws resting on the sill, and hopped down at the sound of his name.

Shirley thrust the leash at Arial. "Thanks for watching him. I really have to go."

"Wait, don't you need to give me his food?" Arial protested as Shirley herded them out of the house ahead of her and locked the door. "Or at least leave me a key?"

This last was said to Shirley's back as she climbed into the Prius.

"No time," Shirley said, rolling down the window. "I'll call you later!"

But as the Prius started down the street, Arial heard the faint ringtone of Shirley's mobile phone inside the house.

"Oh, my God, really?" Arial muttered, and then raised her voice to call after her friend. "Shirley! Your phone!"

Too late. Not only had Shirley been in such a rush that she hadn't provided for Monty, but she'd also forgotten her phone, which Arial presumed she'd need to coordinate with her husband. Not to mention calling Arial, as she'd promised.

And both oversights were totally out of character for the Shirley Cooper that Arial knew.

"Maybe we can catch her before she gets too far," Arial said, glancing back at the Cooper house as she loaded Monty into the Toyota's back seat. "If she hadn't locked us out, I could take her phone to her. As it is, she'll just have to come back and get it."

Assuming, of course, that Shirley had left the phone behind accidentally.

The alternative was something Arial was already trying to talk herself out of as she reached the stop sign on David Avenue and looked left. That direction was down the hill toward the bay and Lighthouse Avenue, through Monterey and eventually Highway One north toward San Jose. But even though she could practically see all the way down David to the aquarium, the red Prius wasn't in sight. Confused, she glanced to the right up David Avenue and caught a flash of red.

"She must be going the back way—getting on the highway at the traffic circle," Arial told Monty, lowering the rear windows a few inches to give him some air.

The "back way," as Arial thought of it, was longer in miles, but faster since it took you to the highway earlier rather than going through town. It wasn't Arial's route of choice most days, but she could see how Shirley would prefer it if she was in a hurry to get to the airport.

Arial lost the Prius as she turned left onto Holman Highway, but caught sight of her stopped at the traffic light at CHOMP—Community Hospital of the Monterey Peninsula. Just sliding through the light on a yellow, Arial was about six cars back when Shirley entered the Highway One traffic circle. To Arial's surprise, though, instead of staying in the circle to take the second exit to Highway One North toward San Jose, Shirley veered off at the first exit, south on Highway One toward Carmel and Big Sur.

"What in the world are you up to, Shirley?" Arial whispered under her breath.

Monty, in the back seat, didn't seem to have a clue.

TWENTY-FOUR

As Arial made the circle and took the south exit herself, her phone rang. She punched it up on hands-free. "Dan?"

"Do you know where Shirley Cooper is? I just tried to call her, but she's not answering."

"That's because her phone is on her desk at home, but she's enroute to San Jose to pick up Frank at the airport," Arial said. "Or that's what she told me. I'm supposed to be taking care of Monty, but we're following—"

"I just had Aaron Henry in again. Do you have any idea why Shirley would give him five thousand dollars in cash and tell him to leave town?"

The money in the tent. Arial bit her lip. "I think I'm getting an idea. She didn't want him to do the DNA test."

"But why? What would Shirley care—"

"She wanted us to keep thinking the body was Robbie's. Or at least she didn't want to eliminate that possibility because then we—you—would start to look elsewhere."

"Elsewhere where?" Dan demanded impatiently. "What do you know that I don't?"

"I don't know anything for sure," Arial said, trying to stay close as Shirley passed first the turn-off for Carmel-by-the Sea and then Carmel Valley Road. "But I'm starting to wonder if Frank Cooper is dead."

"Frank Cooper? Didn't you just tell me you were taking care of Monty because Shirley was picking him up at SJC? Frank Cooper isn't dead."

"I think he might be," Arial said, taking one hand off the steering wheel to rub her forehead. "I've been here a month, and he's always in the house working on his crosswords or some project. Or heading off somewhere. I've heard him talking to Shirley and we've called hello to each other. I've seen photographs. But I've never ac—"

"Are you telling me you've never seen the man? That's ludicrous," Dan said.

"I've only been here for a month," Arial said defensively. "And it's Shirley who's my friend. Frank is just kind of . . . there." Or not.

The point hadn't been lost on Dan. "But you heard his voice? How?"

"Maybe recordings? Or AI?" Arial actually did feel ludicrous. But she pressed on. "I walked in on Shirley unannounced this morning and she was supposedly listening to a voice mail from Frank on the phone. But she was sitting in front of the computer and there were tens, maybe hundreds, of sound and video files. Shirley told me she used to record Frank's speeches at conferences."

"You're saying she'd have samples of Frank's voice. To upload for voice cloning, I mean."

At least Dan wasn't going to totally dismiss the possibility. "You don't think I'm crazy?"

Arial could practically hear the smile. "I didn't say that. But with all the deep fakes, it's hard to know what's real."

"Especially if somebody has set out to deceive you in the first place."

"And you think that somebody is Shirley Cooper."

Arial honestly didn't know what she thought. "There's something else. Shirley had an old Sunday *New York Times* crossword puzzle that she said Frank hadn't been able to solve but refused to give up on. It's dated July twentieth of last year."

An intake of breath. "The day or week that he died, maybe? But why would Shirley keep it?"

"I don't know. But I do know that after I mentioned it, she was in such a hurry to pick Frank up that she forgot her phone."

"On her desk. You said. But—"

"But she's not heading north to San Jose. She's going south on Highway One."

"Please tell me you're not following her."

"I was hoping I could catch her before she got too far and let her know she'd forgotten her phone."

"I don't believe that."

OK, so maybe that was just an excuse. But she knew something was seriously wrong with Shirley and, "We just passed Point Lobos."

"Toward Big Sur," Dan said in a low voice. "I'd lecture you for talking on the phone when you're driving right along the cliffs, but you're going to lose cell service any minute now anyway."

"I know." Arial already was white-knuckled, driving as fast as she dared with the shoulder of the narrow two-lane road falling away to the ocean on her right. "I have to catch Shirley before she does something stupid."

"Have you lost your mind?"

It's not like Arial hadn't heard it before. And from Dan. "No. Believe me, I'm not going to do anything stupid. But I don't want her to . . . there must be an explanation for this." As she said it, her voice was cracking.

"It's all right, Arial," Dan said, trying to calm her. "We've got this. I'll get cars out there. Like I said, we'll lose cell signal, but just don't approach her if she stops, OK? We don't know what the situation is."

"Oh . . . kay . . ." Arial was taking in big gulps of air, trying to breathe. "Red . . . Prius."

"Got it." Dan's voice was worried. "Why don't you just pull over when it's safe? We can take it from here."

"I'm fine. Just a little panic attack." She took a couple of long breaths. "Anyway, at first I thought Shirley might be going to Point Lobos. She told me she loves it, but she sailed right by. The other place . . ."

"Arial? Are you still there? What other place?" The connection was breaking up.

"The bridge. I think she's going to the Bixby Bridge."

"Don't panic." Arial was talking to herself and Monty, the cell signal to Dan long lost. Flexing her fingers, she tried to loosen her death grip on the steering wheel. "Maybe Shirley just wants to drive over it. She said it takes her breath away . . . oh, Jesus."

There it was in the distance.

The Bixby Bridge was the gateway to Big Sur and one of the tallest single-span concrete bridges in the world, 714 feet in length and 260 feet high over the steep canyon carved by the Bixby Creek emptying into the Pacific Ocean. At least according to Wikipedia, because Arial had looked it up once after seeing it for the first time on a television show.

In person, the sight was even more stunning.

But the Prius was turning off the road short of the bridge into a viewing area.

"She just wants to calm her nerves," Arial said, her teeth chattering now. "To enjoy the view."

The useless phone was still on her lap, but it didn't matter. For now, Arial was fixated on her friend.

Pulling off the pavement, Shirley seemed to hesitate and then nosed the Prius into a spot parallel to the road, maybe eight feet from the cliff edge. There were no other cars, so Arial parked behind the Prius, her heart pounding.

The wind whipped her hair as she stepped out of the car, her phone slipping to the ground. After a moment's thought, she opened the back door and snapped the leash onto Monty's collar. Maybe if Arial couldn't convince Shirley to come home, her beloved Monty could.

But Shirley was already out of the car and through the white stanchions that separated the parking spots from the viewing area.

As Monty tugged Arial closer, she saw that there was a step up onto a curb and then boulders, two to three feet high and about three feet apart to warn visitors not to venture too close to the edge. A narrow track of sandy soil was on the other side and the emptiness beyond made Arial's stomach twist.

She knew the cliff overlooking the ocean here was a high, steep bank, more sand than rock, dotted with brush and given to landslides. Below the bridge was a beach, but how anybody got down there, Arial didn't know.

And she didn't want to find out.

Seemingly unaware of their presence, Shirley was staring out over the waves breaking below, her jacket flapping in the wind.

"Shirley!" Arial called, her voice barely cutting through the wind.

Her neighbor turned slowly, her face streaked with tears. "You shouldn't have followed me, Arial."

"I had to," Arial said, taking a cautious step toward her. "I'm frightened for you."

"I'm sorry," Shirley said, her voice breaking. "For everything."

Arial tightened her grip on Monty's leash. "Then come back from the edge, and we can talk."

Shirley shook her head and turned back to the ocean. "I don't deserve to come back. I did something unforgivable."

"You can tell me," Arial said gently. "Whatever it is, we can figure it out."

Shirley let out a bitter laugh. "You're kind, but there's no fixing this." She paused, taking a shaky breath. "I killed Frank."

Arial froze. She'd suspected, speculated. But now to hear it—what could she say? Except, "I know."

"I didn't mean to," Shirley said quickly, her voice thick. "He . . . I told you how sick Monty was."

"You said he got into some anti-freeze." Arial glanced down at the dog by her side. "But he's OK now."

"Ethylene glycol," Shirley said, nodding. "Frank was using it in the garage for one of his *projects*." She said it like it was a dirty word to her. "I told you about that day Monty got out. Frank left the garage door open and he had to suspect Monty had gotten into the ethylene glycol, because the bottle was knocked over. Frank didn't even tell me. My puppy . . ." She looked back at Monty, but didn't call him to her. "He almost died, Arial, and Frank couldn't be bothered. He said I was overreacting when I took him to the vet."

"I'm so sorry," Arial whispered. "I didn't know."

"Because I didn't tell anybody. I covered for him, told Chris it was just an accident, that I opened the door and . . ." She shrugged. "But underneath, I was so angry. Such a big man, with his speeches and all. I just wanted Frank to pay attention to us. To feel just one tenth of what poor Monty had."

Arial's stomach churned as the pieces fell into place. "What did you do?"

"I put anti-freeze in his iced tea," Shirley admitted, raising her chin. "It's sweet tasting, you know. I added just a little, enough to make him sick according to what I'd read online. But Frank wasn't a young man anymore and his heart . . . He had a seizure in the garage, and . . . he died."

"Oh my God," Arial whispered. "And his body? You . . ."

"I panicked, I admit," Shirley continued, her voice trembling. "Robbie was gone, or I might have asked him for help. He is a kind, kind man. Simone didn't deserve him."

A shuddering intake of air. "But on my own, I didn't know what to do. Chris was living in the main house then, so I . . . I remembered about the crawl space under the guest house. Frank had helped Robbie relocate a family of possums that had taken residence."

Arial felt the bile rise in her throat. "You moved Frank's body there and you've been living next to it for how long?"

"It was in July. Last July."

"July twentieth is the date on the crossword puzzle," Arial said, moving closer. "Was it Frank's last one? Is that why you kept it?"

Shirley nodded, tears streaming down her face. "Monty would sit by the kitchen table for hours, waiting for him. I didn't realize how sad he'd be, how sad we'd both be. That's why I keep him on a leash all the time, you know. So he won't go looking for him."

"Like the day he got away from me," Arial said.

"Except it was too late," Shirley said. "Frank's body was already gone."

But Monty must have caught the scent of something left behind. Maybe something the removal of the body had stirred up. "And Frank's voice?"

She dipped her head. "We still get the Sunday *New York Times*—you know, because people knew Frank did the crossword puzzles. I don't always read them . . . you saw the stack. But I did see a story about a woman who uploaded audio and video samples of her dead husband to AI to create a clone of his voice. She could type things into a box and hear his voice saying them. Have conversations. It was comforting." She closed her eyes and took a deep breath. "And it was. For me, at least. Monty . . ." She cocked her head. "Well, you knew it wasn't Dad, didn't you?"

Monty, who still had been pulling at the leash, gave a little whine and sat down.

"You used the recordings of Frank's speeches," Arial said. "The ones I saw on the computer this morning."

"Yeah, that was a bad move on my part," Shirley said grimly. "I started to record one last message. Something I could play for you in a couple of hours, when you'd think I had picked him up and was headed back. It would buy me time." She shrugged. "But then you came up behind me and I panicked and left the phone. I thought you might be putting it all together. When I saw you on the road behind me, I was sure."

"Not all," Arial said, wanting to keep her talking. "How did you do it? His voice in the house?"

"The bulldog. You noticed that, too." Shirley almost smiled. "It's a portable blue-tooth speaker, so I would record whatever I wanted clone-Frank to say on my phone and play it through the speaker anywhere in the house or garage."

"As long as you were within range," Arial said. "Like when we stood outside your house and he called to you. And when he," she made air quotes, "'called you' on the phone about the speech?"

"Same. I would have his side of the conversation in Voice Memos on the phone and just start and stop it. Use "speaker" when I especially wanted you to hear something." She'd been looking down at the ground and now she met Arial's eyes. "I know I sound Machiavellian, but this all started because I just wanted to hear his voice again. To tell him I was sorry. But then . . ."

"You realized you could use it to make people think he was still alive. But Shirley—"

"Nobody seemed to suspect a thing," the older woman cut her off, her voice growing steadier. "Guess it shows how disposable we become. They'd hear Frank on the phone or in the house or the garage and convince themselves they'd seen him. All of them except for you."

Arial swallowed hard. "I didn't figure it out until today, which makes me ashamed. I should have seen what you were going through."

"Frank was irritating as hell." Shirley's voice was almost a whisper. "But I did love him."

"I know you did," Arial said. "And I can't imagine how you managed the guilt and grief and still maintained the . . ." she couldn't think of another word for it, ". . . narrative."

A ghost of a laugh. "Believe it or not, playacting for all of you—complaining about Frank and his damn crosswords or the fact he hadn't mowed the lawn—was the most normal I've felt in months. Like the five seconds it took me to stir the anti-freeze into Frank's iced tea had never happened." As she spoke, she was edging between the boulders to the sandy edge.

"Shirley, just stop where you are." Arial was trying to keep her voice even as Monty pulled at the leash. "Come home with us. Monty needs you."

Shirley turned back. "Take care of him for me, Arial. He deserves better than he's had from me this past year."

"Five seconds," Arial reminded her, as tears started down her own cheeks. "You can't undo what happened, but you didn't mean to kill Frank. Let me help you. Let all of your friends help you."

Shirley hesitated, her gaze flickering to Monty, who was barking now and pulling so hard Arial could barely contain him.

"Look at him," Arial pleaded. "He loves you. He needs you."

For a moment, it seemed like Shirley might step back from the edge. But then she shook her head. "He has you now. Goodbye, Arial."

With that, she slipped down the steep bank.

Arial screamed Shirley's name as Monty lunged forward, pulling the leash out of Arial's hand. She made a dive for it, landing hard as she caught it before Monty could go over.

As she lay trying to catch her breath, the dog whined and came back to lick her face.

"I know, sweetie. We'll find Mom, OK?" she said, pushing herself up painfully to hobble carefully to the edge.

But when she got there, there was no sign of Shirley.

No sign of life at all.

TWENTY-FIVE

Arial crouched on the ground by the boulders, fingers tangled in Monty's thick fur, face buried against his. She was vaguely aware of voices around her, asking what had happened, if she was OK.

Then, finally, a familiar one.

"Dan," she cried, jumping up to wrap her arms around him. "Shirley went over the edge."

"I'm so sorry, Arial," Dan said into her hair. "The call dropped, but we got here as soon as we could."

"I know, I know." She pushed back to look into his face as she spoke, her words coming in staccato bursts. "You couldn't have done anything. She wouldn't listen to me. I told her it was an accident. That she couldn't leave us, couldn't leave Monty. She wouldn't listen, she just wouldn't listen."

As she spoke, she'd dropped the leash and was moving toward the spot where she'd last seen her friend. Monty followed her uncertainly for a moment and then stopped. He let out a bark.

"Arial." Dan's hand was on her arm.

Arial turned and saw the dog. "Oh, baby," she said, going back to get the leash. "I'm sorry. I'm not going anyplace."

"I'll have an officer drive you home," Dan told her. "We'll talk later, but can you tell me the gist of what Shirley said?"

Arial glanced at Monty, lowering her voice like he could hear. "She killed Frank. It was an accident. She laced his iced tea with anti-freeze."

"Anti-freeze was an accident?" Dan's voice had come out louder than he'd intended and now he lowered it, probably not so much for the dog, but for the knot of passersby who were gathered by a squad car talking to the uniformed officer.

"Frank, well, I guess he would get caught up in whatever he was working on, and Monty got into some."

"Ethylene glycol," Dan supplied. "It's in anti-freeze, but it's also a solvent and used in plastic production. Frank was an engineer, right?"

"Yes," Arial said. "Monty got sick, but Shirley rushed him to Chris, and he was able to save him."

"But she never forgave Frank."

Arial shook her head. "She said she just put a little in, that she wanted to make him feel sick, so he'd take notice and realize what he'd done."

"But instead he died."

"Yes." Arial looked down at the top of Monty's head. "Shirley said she should have realized Frank wasn't a young man and that he had health issues. He had a seizure and died in the garage workshop."

"So she hid his body under the guest house?"

"It was right next door, and Shirley said she knew that Robbie had moved out. Chris was renting the main house so she'd just have to move the body when he was working or asleep."

"But how did she get it there?"

Arial thought about it. "There's a wheelbarrow next to their garage. Maybe she used that.'

Dan nodded once. "OK, I'm going to get you home. Is anybody there?"

"I . . ." She tried to think. "Chris usually has office hours on Saturday, but maybe—"

"I'll call him and have him meet you at home," Dan said.

"Meet us at home," Arial said, lifting the leash. "Come on, Monty."

Chris was in the kitchen when the officer escorted Arial and Monty through the front door.

He came out to unhook Monty's leash, but when he went to put an arm around Arial, she shrugged him off. "I'm fine. I have to get Monty some water."

As she filled Monty's dish, Arial heard Chris say to the officer in a low voice. "Detective Sotherly filled me in. Is there any sign of her? A body or . . .?"

The officer shook his head. "Not yet, but they know where she went down from Ms. Kingston."

Arial turned. "I know it's very steep down to the water, but it's not like it's a sheer drop. It's dirt and sand and brush, from what I could tell. Chris, you said Shirley is an experienced mountain hiker. The Sierras, I think?"

Chris nodded.

"Is it possible she managed to scramble down?" Arial asked.

The officer was doubtful. "And live? I doubt it, especially at her age."

"But you saw her jump, Arial," Chris said. "Didn't you?"

"Not jump, exactly. More slide over. And then Monty . . ." She could hear the dog still slurping. "He tried to go after her and I fell, trying to grab his leash. Knocked the wind out of myself for a minute. While I was down, she could have—"

"Disappeared?" the officer ventured.

"Maybe climbed sideways," she said, ignoring his tone. "Hid behind some brush? Or even the bridge structure?"

"Why would she do that?" the officer asked incredulously.

Arial and Chris exchanged looks.

If a cop didn't know why a murder suspect would fake her own death and hide, Arial didn't think that murder suspect's friends should tell him. She was pretty sure, though, that Dan wouldn't miss the possibility.

"Thanks for bringing Arial home," Chris said, ushering the officer to the door. "You'll keep us informed?"

"Detective Sotherly asked me to give you his card," the officer said, taking it out of his shirt pocket. "He wasn't sure if you had his number."

"Thanks," Chris said again, shaking his hand before closing the door and turning to her. "Sorry I didn't give you your space. I was only—"

"No, I'm sorry I pushed you away," Arial said, coming up to give him a hug. "I'm kind of numb, but my mind is going a hundred miles an hour." She collapsed onto the couch and held her hand to her lower ribcage. "And I can't seem to take a full breath."

"Maybe you cracked a rib when you landed," Chris said, sitting down next to her. "Or it's stress. Body tenses up, breathing gets shallow."

"More likely that." Arial took in a breath and then let it out slowly. "I feel like I'm trying to protect myself, hold everything in."

Monty, sitting at her feet, whined.

"He saw what happened," Arial said, waving the dog up on the other side of her to pull close. "He wanted to go after her."

Her expression was far off, and then she snapped back. "Do you think I should have let him?"

"Absolutely not."

"But he has four legs; he'd be able to navigate the—"

"You're thinking if Shirley is out there, he'd find her and get help."

"Yes," Arial said. "Isn't that what search dogs do?"

"Trained search dogs. And on that particular stretch, I'm not sure they'd even risk them. More likely they'll put up drones and helicopters first to spot her."

"Oh." In truth, Arial was relieved. She couldn't have faced losing both Shirley and Monty over that edge.

Chris hesitated. "Dan said it apparently wasn't an accident?"

"She said goodbye." Arial's voice broke, and she had to clear her throat in order to continue. "No 'apparently' about it, though Dan is a cop and will have to investigate."

"He said he'll be coming by later to get your formal statement."

Arial nodded. "Did he tell you what she did?"

"Just that she told you she poisoned Frank."

"He's the body under the guest house."

Chris squinted. "But how can that be? We were told that body has been there for close to a year. And you and I saw it was—"

"Nearly skeletonized," Arial supplied.

"But Shirley just took him to the airport a few days ago."

"Think carefully," Arial said, sitting up straighter. "How long has it been since you saw Frank outside cutting the grass? Or bringing Monty to the clinic for an appointment?"

"Shirley always did those things. And since Frank's been retired . . ." He let it drift off.

"So you wouldn't see him go off to work in the morning or come home at night."

"No," Chris said, still puzzled. "But I told you I've heard the two of them talking. I mean, there's only maybe fifteen feet between the wall of the guest house and theirs."

Arial raised her eyebrows. "Could you hear what they said?"

"No, never words. But I heard their voices. Shirley *and* Frank. I can't have imagined that."

"Don't beat yourself up. I should have tipped to something being wrong when I saw Frank's partially done Sunday *Times* crossword puzzle."

Chris wasn't following. "Why's that?"

"The newspaper was yellowed. I noticed that when I was in the kitchen earlier this week, but I assumed it was from the morning sun coming in the window. But most mornings this week have been quite foggy. And if the paper was from just last Sunday . . ." She shrugged again.

"But—"

"Not definitive, I know. But this morning I saw the date. That paper was from July twentieth of last year. Shirley tried to cover, saying it was one he hadn't solved but wouldn't give up on. But that puzzle gives us an approximate time of death. It was the last one Frank started."

"Why would Shirley keep it around?"

"I asked the same thing. When I went into that kitchen the first time, the puzzle was on the kitchen table along with a pencil. I don't think she could bear to part with it."

"Yet she could bear to put him under my floorboards," Chris reminded Arial.

"They weren't your floorboards, because you weren't living in the guest house yet."

"Which explains why nobody smelled the decomposition," Chris admitted.

"Even if someone had noticed when walking past, there's enough wildlife here that they'd assume it was a small animal of some kind."

"Certainly not a human being," Chris agreed. "But if Shirley put the body . . ." he hesitated, ". . . how?"

"She didn't say, but I'm thinking she loaded him into the wheelbarrow in the garage and then wheeled him between the guest house and garage to the crawl space entrance. Then dragged him from there, like we thought."

Chris shook his head. "She had to know Robbie was already gone and not coming back. How?"

"She—" A knock on the door and Aaron Henry stuck his head in. "I just heard. Can I come in?"

Arial waved him in. "And how did you hear?"

"Drones, helicopters, police presence," he said, taking the overstuffed chair opposite her. "Those things don't go unnoticed around here. Everybody will know something bad has happened by now. They just don't know what and who."

"And how do you know what and who?" Chris asked.

"Detective Sotherly," Aaron said.

Arial blinked. "Why would Dan call you about Shirley's death?"

"Because Shirley is the one who gave me the money," Aaron said, leaning forward with his hands on his knees.

"Dan told me," Arial said. "Did she tell you why?"

"She said so I could leave because everybody was hounding me."

"But what connection does Shirley have with you?" Chris asked. "I mean, no offense, but why should she care?"

"I wondered that myself," Aaron said. "My dad was friends with Frank, but that didn't really explain it. Then I realized she didn't want me to do the DNA testing."

Arial nodded. "Because she wanted people to keep thinking the body was your dad."

"She knew very well that it couldn't be," Aaron said.

Arial frowned. "And how did she know that?"

"Because she knew why he left and when."

Chris looked sideways at Arial. "Explains how she knew the house was empty."

"So where is your dad?" Arial asked, turning to Aaron. "Straight answer this time."

He hiked his thumb toward the front window where Monty was now standing guard. "Outside in the car."

TWENTY-SIX

Robbie Henry was a graying version of the sandy-haired man in the crab-boil pictures, but with the same warm smile. Beside him was the taller, dark-haired man who Chris had pointed out in the picture.

"Arial, this is Mark Bennett," Aaron said. "And my dad, of course."

Chris had gotten up when Aaron escorted the two men in, and now he greeted Mark Bennett with a hug. "Long time no see, stranger." He stuck out his hand to Robbie. "Good to see you alive and well."

"Thanks," Robbie said. "I figured it was about time we cleared some things up."

Arial nodded to them both. "Please, come in. Can I get you anything? Coffee? Water?"

"We're fine," Mark said, his tone kind. "But we're so sorry to hear about Shirley."

"And Frank," Robbie added.

They settled into the living room, Monty curling up at Arial's feet as if sensing the gravity of the moment. Aaron perched on the arm of a chair, while Robbie and Mark took seats on the couch.

Robbie glanced at Mark, who gave him a nod. "Mark and I left because we . . . well, we're together."

Arial blinked, processing the admission which suddenly made complete sense. "Together as in . . ."

"We're a couple," Mark said. "And we didn't feel we could stay here and live openly without causing problems for our families."

"And for ourselves," Robbie added. "Emily and Simone decided it was better to say we'd simply left. They didn't want the whole town to know the truth."

Arial leaned back, letting the information sink in. "That's so sad. But it does fit."

Especially given what she knew of Emily and Simone. "And Aaron said Shirley knew, as well?"

Robbie gave a nod. "Frank was a good friend of both of ours. He . . ."

Mark glanced at him. "He seemed to know before we ever admitted it to ourselves."

"I'm not sure he was entirely comfortable with it," Robbie said with a grin. "The three of us were—"

"—Kind of the Three Musketeers," Mark finished for him. "And then things changed. But Frank didn't judge."

This was a different side of Frank from the one Arial had heard about. "So you know for a fact that Frank was alive and well when you left?"

"Absolutely," Robbie said. "We said goodbye in his workshop in the garage and promised to stay in—"

"When was this?" Arial interrupted.

"July first last year," Robbie said. "We'd planned to do it earlier, but . . ."

Mark glanced over at him and took up the narrative. "Simone and Robbie had already separated when we decided to make the move, but I needed more time."

Which must have been why Robbie had rented the guest house for nearly a year after the divorce. Catherine Smythe had been right. He was waiting.

"You have Dickie to think about," Robbie said, patting his hand. "At least Aaron was old enough to understand. Or at least come to understand."

"He certainly kept your secret," Arial said, throwing Aaron a grin. "But back to Frank. You said you stayed in touch?"

"We did," Mark said with a puzzled expression. "We've been emailing with him right along."

Another piece fell into place. Shirley had said Frank was in touch with Mark but hadn't heard from Robbie. Undoubtedly she'd wanted to maintain the fiction that it was Robbie's body found under the guest house. "I think it was Shirley you were emailing with."

"Geez." Robbie shook his head. "Aaron told us Frank died almost a year ago, and Shirley kept it a secret all this time?"

Mark raised an eyebrow. "Well, she did kill him—accident or not—and hide his body. I wish she would have come and talked to me."

Arial had forgotten that Mark was a criminal defense attorney.

"But you were Frank's friend," Arial reminded him.

"She must have been terrified," Robbie said. "And so alone."

Shirley was right, Arial thought. This is a kind man. "She told me she wished you had still been in the house. That maybe she could have told you."

"I wish she had," Robbie said sadly. "She certainly knew where to find us, if she was emailing as Frank."

"I think by that time it had gone too far," Arial said, turning to Aaron. "So you've been in contact with your dad this whole time? No estrangement or . . .?"

"Judgement? Nah." Aaron nodded at Mark and Robbie. "My mom doesn't like it much, but I'd much rather hang out with Mark and my dad than her and Charles."

"And you didn't mind all the secrecy?"

Aaron shrugged. "The way I see it, this is their business, nobody else's—Mark, Emily, my dad and mom. And if keeping my mouth shut makes my mom happy, I'm willing to do that. I love her."

Who knew Aaron Henry would turn out to be the most well-grounded person in the whole situation. "Why did Shirley give you the five thousand dollars? Was it a bribe?"

"I don't know why it would be," Aaron said. "I didn't know anything. But she did say I should go visit my dad in Vancouver."

Canada. Which explained why Dan's search for Robbie hadn't turned up anything. Meanwhile, Emily was telling everybody Mark was living in Florida. Talk about a misdirect.

"That's a lot of money for a plane ticket." Aaron's father was frowning.

"I was going to fly first class."

"Of course you were," Mark said with a grin. "But it never made any sense. If Aaron needed money, he'd just have asked us."

"*Not* for first-class fare," Robbie warned.

Mark grinned, but kept going. "But with the police thinking Robbie was dead and wanting Aaron's DNA and all? The whole thing spiraled out of control."

"All because of keeping up appearances," Arial said softly.

"And living in peace—or at least keeping the peace—with our exes," Robbie said. "Aaron says Dan Sotherby is investigating. We'll fill him in on everything. I promise."

Arial's head was spinning, but she managed a small smile. "Thank you for telling me personally."

Robbie stood, extending a hand. "Thank you for looking out for my son."

"Well, he looked out for me first." She dug in her pocket and came up with the whistle/light.

"You still have those?" Robbie said, grabbing his son around the neck and giving him a noogie. "I bought a dozen of them when he was ten and told him not to go out at night without one."

"Well, he kept his promise," Arial said, walking them to the door. "And made me promise the same."

"So," Arial said, turning to Chris as Robbie, Mark and Aaron drove away. "Is there anything to eat in that kitchen?"

Chris, bless him, had started his famous red sauce.

"It won't be as good," he told her. "It's best after it cooks all day, even better the next."

"I'll take my chances," she said. "And . . . I don't have any idea what time it is. Is it too early for wine?"

"Not today. Chardonnay in the fridge, pinot in the cabinet."

Arial chose the pinot, mostly because it was red. "Reminds me of Emily and her pristine house. Can't serve red wine, can't have a gay husband."

"It's messed up," Chris said. "But she does care about appearances."

"A Karen," Arial said, twisting in the corkscrew. She turned. "You know, Shirley had me calling her that, to her face? I actually thought her name was Karen Bennett." She started to laugh—first softly, then a little wildly, and then it turned into a sob. "Damn, Shirley! How could she do this to us?"

"And to Frank," Chris said, turning to take her into his arms. "And how could we have not known? The man lived next to us, and we didn't know he was missing? *I didn't know he was missing?* What about the voices? Who was Shirley talking to?"

"AI," Arial said into his shoulder.

"What?"

Arial stepped back. "Shirley cloned his voice and played it through a wireless bluetooth speaker. She said she did it at first because she missed him."

"She missed him because she killed him." Chris's sympathy lay more with the victim than the killer, understandably.

Arial didn't argue because there wasn't a point to argue. Shirley had purposely poisoned her husband, whether or not she thought it would kill him. Whether or not she'd gotten bad information off the internet.

But . . .

"Anyway, Shirley uploaded samples of Frank's voice from speeches he'd given. I've read about these companion apps. You can have conversations and they answer you in the person's voice."

"Now *that* is creepy."

"Oh, I don't know. No creepier than stuffing a body under the house, or our not realizing Frank was dead or, for that matter, Simone letting everybody believe her son's father was dead, rather than admit he was gay and left her."

"Agreed," Chris said. "All creepy."

"Not to mention Emily. Mark leaves her for another man and she takes it out on that man's son, accusing him of robbery?" Arial went back to work on opening the wine. "You'd think that she and Simone might have bonded over the situation, but that sure didn't happen."

"It's complicated. But can we go back to the AI thing?"

"Yes, sorry." Arial turned, cork in one hand, bottle in the other. "When we heard Frank's voice, it was the cloned voice saying whatever Shirley wanted—calling the dog, asking about lunch, whatever. She said she used Voice Memos on the phone."

"Entirely possible these days, I guess. She could save

individual audio files—Frank calling Monty, Frank wanting lunch, Frank having sex—"

Arial rolled her eyes.

"—in Voice Memos and call them up to play whenever she wanted." Chris set an oversized pot of water on the stove to bring to a boil.

"How many people are you planning to feed?"

"It's the only pot we have other than that one." He pointed to the bubbling red sauce. "But what I was going to say is what was Shirley's end game? I mean, how long did she think she could keep it up?"

"That's a good question," Arial said, pouring the wine into two glasses and taking a seat at the table. "But she'd seen Mark and Robbie just successfully disappear. Maybe she figured she'd wait a bit and she and Frank would 'break up.'"

"Maybe," Chris said, coming to sit across from her.

They sat silently for a moment before Arial said, "The money she gave Aaron to get him out of town. Like you say, what was the end game there?"

"It would delay testing his DNA. Maybe eliminate the chance of him spilling where his dad and Mark really were."

"So buying time again, even as everything was coming apart. She was making a recording to play for me as she and Frank supposedly drove home. She said that was to buy a couple more hours, too. But for what?"

"Ending her own life?"

"That's done in an instant as I witnessed. Or didn't witness." Arial leaned forward. "What if today at Bixby Bridge was an elaborate escape plan? Maybe Shirley is alive."

Monty, who had been standing next to the stove, nose in the air toward the sauce, came over to sit next to them.

"Sounds surreal, but . . ." Chris reached over to give the dog a scratch. "She pulled off poisoning Frank, hiding the body and then creating an imaginary husband. I'm starting to think Shirley is capable of anything."

"But can you imagine? Living month after month in constant fear of being found out? Shirley admitted that she avoided going to book club, didn't enjoy chatting with the other women. I thought she was just the private type."

"She wasn't always," Chris said, and gestured to the refrigerator where they'd put up the crab-boil photo. "Maybe she stopped socializing, not because she didn't want to see people, but because she was afraid. She couldn't afford to let people in."

"Even to her house," Arial mused. "She let me in, and it may have killed her."

"If she's dead, she killed herself."

Arial took a sip of wine. "I'm not sure I can live with not knowing," she whispered hoarsely.

Chris's expression became a little afraid. "You don't have a choice, Arial. Life is the only choice. Here on the Mayes compound with me and Monty. He's lost everybody; he needs you."

"That's what I told Shirley, but she left anyway."

"She knew he'd have you. She knew she could depend on you, and so could Monty." He looked at her closely. "You're not—"

"Thinking about throwing myself down a cliff? No, I just need to find Shirley, one way or the other. I know we only met a month or so ago, but—"

"You were close," Chris said. "Don't shortchange that friendship."

"With a killer." Arial managed a smirk, if not a smile.

"Accidental killer," Chris reminded her.

The knock on the door startled them. Arial rose, wine glass still in hand, and opened it to find Olivia, Marta, Lucy and Fiona standing there, each holding a Tupperware container and bottles of wine.

"You're not alone tonight," Olivia said firmly, stepping inside. "We're here to help."

Marta nodded. "We thought you might need a distraction. And food."

Arial smiled weakly. "Thank you. That means a lot, but Chris is making pasta. I'm sure there's enough—"

Chris stuck his head out of the kitchen. "Correction. Chris

was going to make pasta, but we don't have any penne. Or angel hair. Or—"

"We get the idea," Arial said. "So we'll keep that sauce bubbling for dinner tomorrow. Now let's see what you all brought."

As the four women unpacked their offerings, Arial edged over to Lucy. "You knew about Mark and Aaron's dad, didn't you? That was why you got so uncomfortable when I was asking questions."

Lucy looked up from the orzo salad she was uncovering, her face flaming. "I'm so sorry. But it wasn't my secret to tell."

"I understand completely," Arial said, putting her hand on the woman's arm.

As the group settled in around the table, food was being reheated, and more wine was being opened and poured. Thankfully, nobody asked Arial to recount what had happened, though she still had to give her formal statement to Dan. The kitchen was filled with the sound of clattering dishes, clinking glasses, and even the occasional laughter, when Arial's phone buzzed on the counter.

She grabbed it, moving away from the table so she could hear. "Dan."

"Arial." Dan's tone sounded weary. "We'll take your formal statement tomorrow, but I wanted to let you know we've arrested one of your exterminators, Harold Wembley, for the burglaries. He rented the car we found abandoned."

Harold. The guy who snickered about the toxic gas killing any living thing in the walls and foundation. Was it a ploy to keep clients away from the house as it was tented so he could do his snooping, or was he just plain cruel?

Right now, Arial didn't much care. "Have you found Shirley?"

"No." A pause. "There's no sign of a body."

Arial closed her eyes, her grip tightening on the phone. "What does that mean?"

"We don't know," Dan admitted. "But we'll start looking again at first light."

Arial hung up, not sure how to feel. Could Shirley be alive and injured somewhere? Had the tide swept her body away?

Or was this another magic trick, orchestrated by a woman she thought she knew?

Sinking back into her chair, the others were watching her, waiting for something—relief, closure, anything—but she had nothing. Outside, the fog was blowing in off the bay.

"She could still be out there," Olivia said softly, as if reading her thoughts.

No one responded. No one knew exactly what to hope for at this point.

Arial looked around the room and took a deep, steadying breath as Monty came to settle his big head on her knee.

She put her hand on his head and raised her glass. "To Shirley, may she rest—"

"Or not rest," Fiona interjected. "You know, depending on whether she really is dead or not."

"—In peace," Marta finished.

"To Shirley and also to Frank," Chris added. "Who didn't deserve to die that way, accident or not."

At the mention of his parents' names, Monty raised his head and let out an anguished whimper.

"Oh, baby," Arial said, pulling him close. "You're going to be OK. We got you, I promise. All of us."

"To all of us," they chorused.